PAPER AND SMOKE

THE CHRONICLES OF WHYNNE

B. A. LOVEJOY

To my mother, to whom I owe this world and several others.

PAPER AND SMOKE

CHAPTER ONE

PEOPLE WERE MOVING.

They crowded the narrow streets, talking to each other and singing of their joy, holding up signs and donning elaborate masks. Parents held their children high on their shoulders, elders walked with their arms linked with one another, and still more people hung around market stalls with various assortments of street food in their hands. All around me, the streets bustled with activity, the small town overflowing as one of the few holidays in Whynne began to swing into action; Sunrise Day. It sent the country into an explosion of life, full of people being unable to hold back their joy as was customary every year on this day for the past century. They were celebrating the expulsion of the Unseelie, and how their queen had once brought back the daylight. They didn't dare to acknowledge the darkness that rolled over Whynne.

The smoke was in the air once more, thick, black clouds mingled with the steam from market stalls, serving to confuse the senses when combined with the loud, mind numbing mixture of sound that the various bands and crowds produced.

The heavy sting of burning wood filled my nostrils yet prompted only a few coughs from other people. They'd grown far too used to it.

It was like they all knew better than to acknowledge it; the measures being taken by the King to hunt down the Unseelie.

The measures being taken by the King to hunt down me.

My back was plastered against the wall of a market stall, and I was hit again by the memory of Adam's plea not to go out that day, to wait until there was a fae available to accompany me rather than walking through the streets alone, my hood drawn tightly around my face and my head down.

But seeing as how Artur had an almost daily claim on every fae in our midst, here I was. Hiding from the royal army yet again. This time at one of the most outrageous celebrations of the year. It'd been a month since we'd left the mountain side, and I'd only left the estate three times.

I swallowed as a group of young men walked by carrying a scarecrow with long, pointed ears and matching pointed teeth balancing on top of a pole with a group of rowdy children following closely behind. Children who, as soon as it was placed down in the square, would begin to beat the scarecrow with sticks and other hard objects, aiming to be the one to split its head down the middle and collect the single silver coin that sat inside in place of a real Unseelie.

They'd had no luck catching one this year, towns often had no luck catching any. Especially not with the smoke in the air forcing the Unseelie deeper and deeper into the forest.

Sunrise Day was far more brutal in the rural parts of Whynne; I often forgot that. When I was a child, it was simply my mother taking Winry and I to the market, the two of us getting small pastries and hoping that we would be lucky girls and receive one that had a small porcelain princess in it. Supposedly if you got one, that meant good luck.

Here there were no porcelain princesses. Here there were no scarf dancers or fae singers. Here there were only brutal traditions and guards, so many guards that it was hard to keep hiding from them all.

And I'd caught the eye of one of them.

I held my breath, veering around the corner of the market stall, hoping that he would have gone away. Nope, he only drew closer, his face even more determined. Just my luck.

"Miss," he began to call. "Miss, I just want to speak to you."

"Oh for the love of—" I began, practically swinging myself around the corner of the stall to take off once again.

All it took was one soldier and one second, then they'd know.

The worst thing was that I couldn't go home with him trailing behind me. It'd be disastrous for news to spread that the old, abandoned Kinsley estate that sat on the edge of town was bustling with life once more.

"Oh Wren, I will take your silver and buy you a fine cape," I muttered in imitation of the lazy old monk who no doubt sat counting his cards. "It'll be black as night, and thick and heavy. Nothing like the military uniforms. You'll wear it and no one will know who you are." I sprinted across another clearing of people, spitting, "don't mind if I pocket the rest of the cash!" There was no way that this cloak was worth seventeen silver. He probably lost the rest while gambling.

Artur was an awful gambler, and it seemed like once a week Adam had to set out and win back everything he'd lost. Why we continued to humor the old man was beyond me—aside from his many business ties and almost astonishing ability to convince people of a forgery's authenticity.

"Oh Wren, we can stay in one place," I muttered, mimicking the voice of Kristin Kinsley. "I'm sure no one will notice an abundance of forgeries turning up near the old Kinsley Estate.

You don't mind if your window is broken and leaks a lot, do you? Don't ask too many questions about the estate, it's a sensitive topic."

The guard appeared once more and I zigzagged again, landing in an alleyway in a more established part of town and throwing my head back against the wall in irritation.

Droplets of rain greeted me.

"Oh Wren, we cannot leave now; I have a garden to tend to," I complained, imitating my sister's voice. I looked to the side of me, eager for a way out.

No such luck.

Leave it to me to pick a dead end.

"I am afraid that I am not a good teacher Wren, but I'm sure you know enough of the basics," I put on my lowest, most charming voice for Adam, as I looked at my hands in exhaustion. Nothing. I'd worn myself out running, magic took a certain amount of energy. Energy that it was very apparent from my panting I did not have.

Oh, this was not going to end well.

"I think that if you run into any trouble, you should just kill it," I said, pretending to be Lindy. And, just as I informed her in that moment, I repeated, "because I am surely capable of that, and no one will notice the dead bodies piling up." Not good, this was definitely not good. I could hear the soldier's footsteps, they seemed so much louder than everyone else's.

"Miss?" The voice rang out again. I clenched my eyes shut.

And with my final imitation, I muttered, "you always had a way of getting into trouble, Wren." And for a moment, the voice didn't even sound like mine.

I opened my eyes, but it was not him. No.

It was the soldier standing in front of me, a small patch indicating his humanity. He was young and bright eyed.

Callum, the small, embroidered tag read on his breast, whether that was his first or last name I did not know.

I swallowed as my hand fell to my side, my fingers spreading, the random, sharp pain slowly starting to rise to my skin. He knew me, I knew he did. He knew who I was.

"There you are, I was almost sure that it was you, I've seen pictures—" He prattled, and I wondered if the King was so cruel as to not tell the officers of his army how dangerous I could truly be. But then he continued, "when the Captain looked at the photo in his wallet, I couldn't help but remember it. He looked at it so intensely. You're his girl, aren't you? His lady. Leave it to him to find a way to be stationed here—"

I suppose I should have been grateful that he assumed me to be his Captain's lover.

"That's—" I began, struggling to speak. "I'm not—" No doubt he really thought I was, not many women donned short hair in the countryside, not unless they were young—it wasn't in style. Not many women had a splotch of black on their left hands, the stain of ink that the newspaper's descriptions warned to look for.

Even to an untrained eye, I was distinctive.

And then, like a beacon of hope, a voice spoke from the end of the alley, just a simple statement, "I've finally found you." A stranger's face spoke it, but the voice was familiar. I would know it with any face, his or whatever stranger he sought to replicate via his minor illusions.

The soldier blinked just as I did, his face clouded with confusion as he took the other young man in. Luka strolled down the alleyway, his hand immediately reaching for mine, tugging me into his side without a second thought.

"I'm sorry, but this is..." the soldier began.

"My fiancé," I supplemented quickly, the lie rolling off my

tongue all too naturally. "This is my fiancé, I have no idea who the man you are talking about is. We were just trying to enjoy the festivities." I honestly wished that we could have.

The man beside me stiffened, and I was sure the soldier's eyes moved to him at the same time as mine did, likely taking his rising shoulders as being that of concern, since a soldier had just chased down his fiancée.

I knew them to be because I had lied, and he had no way of helping me. Because his pointed ears screamed that he was a fae, and any false words from his mouth would bring about awful pain. The soldier would know that too.

I wrapped my hands around Luka's arm, pressing the back of my head against his chest as I stood beside him, silently begging with him to find a clever way to play along. He had heard enough, hadn't he?

And it wasn't a lie, not entirely. Because Luka and I were lovers, just not engaged; just not marked in any way.

"I swear, I saw a photo of a girl who looks just like you in the captain's things—" He began. It was likely a wanted poster.

"That's not possible," I said, my fingers digging into Luka's arm. He was supposed to be smart, he was supposed to find a way around this sort of thing. "We've been together for quite some time, I wouldn't be with anyone else."

Easy statements, ones he could say yes to. And just like that, Luka knew to play along. "We have," he said easily. "You must be mistaken, I do not know of anyone else who would put up with her."

He definitely deserved my fingers sinking deeper into his arm.

"Ah..." said the soldier, looking between us. I wondered what we looked like to him; likely a young woman irritated with her lover for leaving her alone in the market. I suppose that was a close enough of an approximation to what we really were. "I must have made a mistake," he said doubtfully. "I'm sorry about that, sometimes I get overeager."

"It's the smoke," Luka provided. "It makes it hard to see." It did a lot more than that, especially when my eyes traveled over Luka's jawline, taking in how tense it was along with how pallid and clammy his skin appeared. The smoke made me feel sick too, it was a reminder of what I'd almost done, of how Adam and I had almost burned the Unseelie tree.

"Well, I'm sorry for bothering your fiancée, sir," the soldier said, his eyebrows knitting together as he looked between us. It appeared that he would only address Luka at that moment, most of the soldiers did. Most of the soldiers were equally as irritating. "I do not like to think that I've scared a young woman."

"It's fine," Luka said gravely, his hand wrapping around to rest at the small of my back. "There are far more terrifying things out there for a young woman like her to be worried about." The soldier could not know the true depth of those words.

The soldier nodded hesitantly, taking one last glance between the two of us before turning away.

We still stood together as he walked away, my hand wrapped around Luka's arm and his fingers flexing on the edge of my cloak. We waited like that for a few seconds, and then the illusion Luka wore flickered, his true face appearing.

"Fiancé," Luka said after a minute, still looking to the street. "Interesting."

"Do not ask, it seemed far more official," I said, pulling my hand off of his arm, letting my breath go as danger finally left. "I've learned that men often don't listen unless you give them another man to refer to."

"I'm not upset," Luka said, the strain in his voice betraying him as he turned to look at me. "I was trying to find you anyway, though I had no idea how I would explain it once I did, since you are currently supposed to be at home, holed up in your room copying yet another manuscript." Eventually Kristin and Adam would have discovered my lie.

I frowned, cocking my head in question at the idea of him needing anything from me at the moment.

"Artur is at the tavern begging for you." A common occurrence, but people did not often give in to him.

"So you left him there alone?"

"I am fairly certain he cannot walk," Luka said, stepping towards me and pulling the strings of my cloak loose. He gathered the edges of the cloak and pulled them closer together, beginning to re-knot the ties so that less of me showed.

"Artur is a conman," I said as he secured my cape, pulling the hood a little bit further over my eyes. "You should not trust him, not with money and most certainly not to stay out of trouble." I was probably the only person who could trust him, and that was only because he found me useful.

"He's almost soiled himself twice today," Luka informed me, "and it is not even noon. He's convinced that he has a large contract for you, and that the man he's spent hours speaking to is rich. I tried to argue against bringing you, but then he started yelling out for his girl—It caused a scene. I figured that we don't need scenes today of all days."

I frowned, pulling my hood back to look Luka in the eyes. The unspoken question of why we even indulged the old man in his habits passed between us. I almost opened my mouth to ask, but then Luka pulled up the hood of my cape again, turning on his heel and beginning to walk—obviously expecting me to follow him.

I huffed, reaching up once more to adjust it. I would not walk blind.

"Don't," Luka warned, throwing a look back at me as he held out his hand, obviously knowing that was the best way to keep me close. "The market is teeming with guards."

"I'm already aware of that," I sighed, stomping up to him and putting my hand in his. I almost thought to ask him why he wasn't wearing a hood, but then the familiar tingle of magic hit the air and I remembered perfectly.

His face changed into that of someone else, earning a shiver from me. My prior experiences had not made me fond of Unseelie magic, and I wished he could have kept his real face. Luckily, I knew Luka's appearance to be only an illusion, one that could not hold up at closer distances when tried... Unlike the Gancanagh. Still.

"I'm not fond of this one," I lied, tearing my eyes away from him. He did not move to use his magic on me. He had not used Unseelie magic to disguise me since we left the mountain.

"Should I change it?" He asked, and I felt the magic lingering in the air.

"No," I said tightly, quickly adding a joke to cover my distress, "I'd rather you be ugly."

He snorted, his thumb running across my knuckles. I was sure he could see through me, but he didn't care to inform me of that. "Would you prefer I drop the glamor? Perhaps if they capture me, you won't need to complain about me hogging the bed anymore."

"I know that you are doing it to con me into lying in your arms, Kinsley," I said, wrinkling my nose. "You're not too clever for me."

"Such a crime, how dare I wish to hold you," he mused, simply rolling his eyes. As if to emphasize his point, he tugged me a little closer, my thigh bumping into his. In a small, quick motion, he leaned down and pressed his lips to my hair in a short kiss. "Let's move quickly, I don't think you need another run in with the guards and I don't know about you but, I'm not very fond of this holiday."

I shook my head, following along closely as he moved into the square, careful to keep my hood down. Of course Luka wouldn't be fond of it, it could have very easily been him on the pole I saw, instead of the scarecrow.

Still, it was a novelty to hold his hand and be allowed to walk through the market stalls with him during a festival.

Even if he was wearing another face.

I took in this one, the squat nose and the far too large eyes. A part of me wondered if Luka had seen the man in the tavern before while watching Artur, since it had a sort of off look to it. God knows Artur was not known for having good taste when it came to drinking establishments. I think it was because Artur knew he'd get kicked out of any of the more reputable ones.

Then again, we couldn't exactly march into places that weren't considered shady. At least at the Salted Fish, the King's army knew that they weren't welcome. A more than favorable feature, seeing as how the market was filled with soldiers today.

Every day, another squad of soldiers arrived in another town, searching for the faces printed on the posters they all carried. Desperate to find who the King was looking for. Some more so than others, as fae felt the consequences of the forest burning while the King was working out his grand solution; forcing the hands of a young man who he once held in his thrall, and a young woman who he convinced himself was of equal value.

And now that the Unseelie of the forest seemed to be looking for me as well, I could not say that his thoughts were completely unfounded. If we were found, they would stop sectioning off portions of the forest and burning them to ward off the Unseelie. I think even the Seelie recognized that as important, because their magic weakened with every flame burning on the forest floor.

Feeling the eyes of one of the soldiers travel over me, I moved closer to Luka, briefly hearing the pounding of his heart as my ear brushed his chest.

Luka would never say that he was scared, but I was certain the celebration around us verged on horrifying for him.

"Sunrise Day," Luka repeated. "I can't tell whether they made it larger this year to rally the troops, or if it was always this obnoxious in the smaller towns of Whynne."

"They're closer to the forest," I reminded him, my eyes traveling across the plaza, not able to see the trees but knowing where they were. Everyone knew where they were now, you just followed the smell of smoke.

"Artur thought to buy a newspaper," Luka replied simply. "Largely because he wanted to check the odds of a tournament and see whether or not he'd won his bets, but there was still useful information in there."

I raised my head slightly to ask him about it, catching a glimpse of another guard before quickly deciding otherwise.

"The King is finally admitting that there is a war," Luka said, knowing what I wanted to ask. "He's also elaborating on your story, he's saying that you were abducted by a jilted lover."

"Jilted?" I scoffed. "Is that what you are?" I would say that of all of the people in my life, Kinsley was the furthest from a jilted lover. Considering the fact that I had traded everything to be beside him. But whatever helped the King sleep at night. I didn't care to think about it too much, but I knew that he would tell whatever story ensured I was brought back to him.

"Yes, did you know that you broke my heart and drove me to madness?" Luka asked. "I could have forgotten if they did not inform me. It's hard to remember all of the details when I'm so busy kidnapping you and bending you to my will."

I risked looking back and tossing him a smile, the laugh escaping me. I could hear the smallest chuckle escape him too, and I knew the face beside me was also looking down, smiling at the ground. It was moments like these, the smallest ones, that made life feel a little more bearable.

Because, if we were still in that cabin, or at the camp, or God forbid in our estates—We would not be walking together like this, and he would not have been laughing.

But just as soon as that joy found me, it left, my eyes trailing up and seeing a man with a familiar face, looking out from the sidelines at me. The soldier from earlier.

He did not look any less suspicious. I pulled my cloak closer, covering my face entirely.

"We should hurry," I said, picking up the pace. The tavern was a familiar walk, one that I usually got to make when the guards weren't all over. We weren't far from it.

"I'm moving as fast as I can," Luka responded, his leg was still not completely healed from being shot a month prior. I didn't know why he was healing so slowly, a normal fae would have found themselves fully healed in less than a week. A month was concerning when it came to the healing powers of a fae.

In the distance, I heard trumpets blaring, a clear announcement that more soldiers were arriving, this time ones with status. They were flocking in from their stations in the woods, unable to go home but still wanting to celebrate. Not a good sign, but...

A good distraction.

People began to move, all turning in interest as the trumpets grew louder. No doubt the soldiers in the square had to pay their respects to the higher-ranking officers. This was it, our chance.

"I hope this does not hurt you too much, Kinsley," I said simply, gripping his hand and casting him a look over my shoulder. He responded with a questioning expression, then sighed, bracing himself for the oncoming hustle. We had to make it back to the tavern before the crowds became too thick.

CHAPTER TWO

Luka practically toppled over when I slammed the door behind him, the pain as evident on his face as his irritation with me for dragging him along, his hand still around my wrist and his breathing heavy. It was not a short run, nor an easy one; a part of me felt bad. He was gasping for air.

I didn't know what good that did him, since the air was smokier in the tavern than out on the street, a feat I would have previously thought impossible. But I suppose it was a different type of smoke, not the smell of the forests of Whynne burning but instead the unpalatable stench of cigars dangling from the mouths of several of the patrons.

There were no soldiers or guards in the tavern, just as usual. That felt like more of a relief than ever, occasionally I would have been glad to see them if only to stop Artur from being robbed blind, but now? Now I could do without seeing another one for a great while.

Luka finally caught his breath as I looked around, squinting through the smoke to see if I could spot Artur. It was crowded, people were squashed shoulder to shoulder at the bar; that should have made it easier to find Artur.

There were so many young faces, too many bearing scars on their features. Defectors from the army, no wonder they were sitting in the bar as the soldiers filled the plaza. There'd be hell to pay if another soldier looked upon them and realized them for what they were.

I hadn't been to the bar in a while, at least a week or two. It seemed like their number had grown since then. You could always tell what they were from their ages and the marks left on them—gouges from skirmishes with Unseelie, but not wounds severe enough to gain discharge from the army. The King was becoming more adamant about keeping soldiers in his employ, and he had also been drafting in larger numbers. Most folks didn't take well to that.

"The Unseelie in the forest have been growing more unwieldy," Luka informed me. "Or so the gossip says." That was explanation enough for what was going on, there'd seemed to be more violent attacks since the forest had begun to burn, and I wondered what percentage were provoked by the burning or staged for the papers... and what the consequences of invading Unseelie territory was.

It was hard to tear myself away from looking at the former soldiers at the bar. Their battle worn faces were distracting, almost making me forget to look for the short, round monk. Artur was normally easy to find, but there was no sign of him, not in the main bar.

"He's not here," Luka informed me, his hand loosening around my wrist. "They paid for a private room."

"A private room?" I asked, raising an eyebrow as he began to move around me. I trailed closely behind him. "Artur doesn't like to play in private rooms, he says less money exchanges hands there." One of the many lessons he taught me as my tutor.

"I am well aware," Luka stated, frowning. Artur was not skilled at gambling.

Kristin, Adam, and Luka had been careful not to mention how much money Artur had lost. They'd come to the conclusion that the benefits largely outweighed the heavy cost of keeping the monk. Either that or they didn't trust him not to turn us in if we were to try to be rid of him at this point—Which was fair. I knew Artur the best, and I wouldn't trust him as far as his weak little legs could carry him.

"He made these friends just an hour ago, and therefore he trusts them with his life," Luka said somewhat ironically. "Or wants them to believe that he does." That sounded about right.

"Who are they?" I asked, wondering why it was such a pressing manner.

"Seafarers," Luka said, as if that was not a strange fact in itself.

"Whynne only has a few yards of coastline, and we are far from the coast," I said, narrowing my eyes. I scrutinized all the people that we walked by, trying to figure out if they were capable of being trusted or not. This wasn't exactly the best place to be in town, and with new visitors crowding the square to celebrate Sunrise Day, I could guess that there were more than a few characters in the bar. Thus, why Luka kept his glamor on for a while longer, I supposed.

One did not want to be found as an Unseelie on such a day.

"I will not disappear," Luka called out my tightened grip on his cuff—I hadn't realized I'd reached to grab him again, or that his hand had left mine. It was just far too instinctual to hold onto Luka.

"I seem to remember this holiday being a lot more fun in

Greenable," I said under my breath. "I wish we could have experienced it at home, things were much tamer there."

"I don't like it either way," Luka said. "I have never celebrated Sunrise Day, even in Greenable."

I guess he wouldn't, I guess that seeing crude drawings of creatures like himself wasn't exactly his cup of tea, even if he didn't have to watch the children beat effigies of them with sticks. I let my shoulder bump against his, gaining his attention again for the briefest second, "why did you agree to come out today?"

"Because you were going," he said simply, walking behind the bar and pulling a curtain on the far wall aside for me.

"You do not need to go wherever I go," I informed him, brushing through the curtain and into the backroom.

He followed behind me, his face turning back to normal as he stepped through the fabric, the expression on his face more familiar than the features. A look that stated that his answer would be so obvious that he shouldn't have to state it. "I just had to save you from a soldier. If I were you, I would not say that you do not need my help so shortly after I rescued you."

"He thought me to be his captain's lover," I murmured as the back of the booth came into view. "He would not dare harm me."

"And what would you do if he took you to see his captain?" Luka responded.

Probably be recognized and arrested immediately, but I didn't tell him that, he would only respond with a shake of his head. Instead, I focused ahead, taking in the faces of the men crowded in the booth. Artur had not just made one new friend, but many it seemed. Six of them. Six men in far better shape that Artur had ever been.

Two of them were wiry, a redheaded man and a tall one with slicked black hair and a prominent Adam's apple. One was rather large and muscular, he was squeezed in tightly. Another one had tattoos. All looked to be unsavory characters, they all scanned the room every so often like they were waiting for something awful to happen.

I could tell which person Artur was by his balding head, but just in case I couldn't, Artur reeked of booze so strongly that it carried on the air around him.

I was fairly certain that if Artur ever stopped drinking, he would be unrecognizable. The alcohol that oozed from his pores had shaped too much of him. He was oily and bloated, a short man with small hands but a big mouth. In front of him and all along the sides of the table, tall stacks of gold coins stood, cards thrown down in front of them.

"There she is," he said, catching sight of me in the doorway. "My little Birdie, I told you that her husband is very in tune with her, that he would find her in an instant."

I'm pretty sure Luka murmured something along the lines of, 'another promotion,' behind me.

"You were just saying that you found her husband to be grating," the smallest of the men said, a redhead about a foot shorter than me. I shot Artur a look, but he did not falter.

"You must have misheard me," he said plainly, gesturing to me once more. "There she is, the steadiest hand in all of Whynne, here for your every need. The finest replicator. My dearest daughter." I was definitely not his daughter, that much was certain.

"She is a woman," another man spoke, the one covered in tattoos and with features sharper than any knife. "More than that, she is a married woman. Not many countries will allow you to do business with a married woman."

"She's only married if you would prefer her to be," Artur said easily. "If you wish her not to be, then I can assure you that she's not."

The man ignored the statement, thankfully. "She's not Haldian," the same man spoke again, narrowing his eyes in my direction. I was not sure the look I gave Artur could get any worse, but it turns out it could.

"That is my other daughter," Artur said.

"You have a Haldian daughter and a daughter from Whynne?" The man asked, incredulously.

Artur was not a handsome man. "I assure you, I'm very charming, I've had several lovers—" Luka cleared his throat, stopping the man's lies. "It will be two for the price of one," Artur said quickly, ever the one to bargain. But about what remained to be seen.

The tattooed man, obviously the leader, only nodded and his companions started to pull papers out of their bags. They formed tall, unordered stacks, ones that threatened to blow apart with the slightest motion. The papers I could see were covered with intricate illustrations, ones with art that looked distinctly foreign. Ones that the red-haired man thought to throw his arm over when he noticed me staring at them.

"I'm sorry, but what exactly am I doing?" I interrupted.

"You are copying images and translating a manuscript for me," the man said, digging into his own bag. "In exchange for safe passage from Whynne to Haldia before a fortnight has passed, just as the old man bartered for. Believe me, that is more than a fair price. People are dying to get out of here and go somewhere safer—at least the smart ones are."

"Haldia?" I asked. Why on earth would Artur wish to go to Haldia of all places?

"It was his idea," Artur interrupted, casting away the blame. "Speak to your lover."

My eyes landed on Luka, my jaw tensing.

Immediately Luka's hand snapped onto the corner of the table, holding something down; a newspaper. I looked at him again, my head tilting. I thought back to how he had mentioned the newspaper before, he was holding something back. "It was Adam's idea," Luka said icily, glaring at Artur, "he merely told me to ask you."

"Is this not a good time?" The seafarer with the red hair asked, unaware as to what he had walked into. It was far from a good time; it had not been a good time for a while. "Is there a problem between the fae and his wife?"

"It's hard to get passage to Haldia, it's a popular route, and going on it without being reported is an even more difficult feat. I've already agreed to take you per your father's request so, if you would..." The tattooed man gestured to all of the papers behind him. "I'd like to get started."

"I'm afraid I have no interest in Haldia," I responded in a clipped voice.

"She's lying," Luka replied. I shot him a glare.

"Can we hurry this along," Artur insisted, his words slurred. "The streets are teeming with danger, so let's get something written down."

"I agree," the tattooed one said—

"No," I stated, "because I need to inform *my husband* of a few things."

But it was like the world knew that I wanted to speak. Because right when I began to open my mouth, a voice rose up in an astonished gasp from the main area of the bar.

I didn't even need to hear the words to know what it was by all of the frantic scrambling around me and the sound of people diving for a small door that led to an alley at the back of the bar. The six men in the room dove for their papers, shoveling them back into their bags. In the front of the tavern, I could hear an even greater commotion as people tried to leave while the soldiers entered, a series of loud shots paralyzed me.

For a moment, I forgot that this was a frequent event. Our

companions didn't even seem to realize, so busy trying to collect their papers before the guards burst in.

"Nikko," a voice said from behind me, and I caught the red-haired man hauling off the tattooed one, a single piece of paper falling out of his hand. He almost seemed to hiss at the loss, but he didn't know enough to stay. People from other countries had not exactly heard gleaming reviews of Whynne and their military.

And then there was only Artur, Luka, and I. My eyes did not leave the door, incapable of looking away. I wasn't afraid, not at first, but I quickly became it.

A vibration hit the air and I felt a sharp pain in my ears, my body tumbled to the ground and another body quickly moved to cover it as Artur scrambled in the background, hooking coins off the table with a sweep of his arm and ducking beneath the table. Each coin fell on the ground with a loud clink, no doubt alerting the guards to the fact that there were people in the back room.

Leave it to him to choose money over our immediate safety.

Luka's body laid over mine as he supported himself on his forearms, his eyes closed in concentration as he struggled to cover as much of us as possible. It was easier to turn one thing invisible.

Another gunshot rang out and he rolled me over him, my cape falling to cover the two of us, his lips so close to mine that the slightest motion made us touch.

I could not see his face in the darkness of my cape, but moments later it turned transparent, invisible to all but us. In the background, I heard Artur whimper... but it was not as believable when followed by the jingle of coins.

"You're still going to yell at me about Haldia, aren't you?" Luka whispered, his black eyes meeting mine. He was not worried in the slightest, and I suppose I shouldn't have been either. But old habits die hard, and old fears die harder. I could not help but think of the last time I heard bullets fly.

I could only stare at him, flinching as another gunshot rang out.

"Now, now, now. There's no need to panic, if you do not draw weapons, there will be no need for bloodshed," an authoritative voice spoke from the bar. "You all know how this goes."

Another sweep. That's what it was, one on a holiday, one when people wouldn't expect it. Nothing was going to happen to us, even if my brain screamed otherwise.

I closed my eyes, letting my head fall over Luka's shoulder. It was almost a relief to realize it was only a sweep. Far worse things had happened in the past month. A sweep was hardly even a close call. This was normal.

"We are looking for the Unseelie and the unsavory," the soldier ran through his normal script, justifying what they were doing as crashes and thumps could be heard from the main room. No doubt they'd soon move to the backroom as well. "This is just another one of the many ways that your King keeps you safe."

Adam once said that they only reimplemented the sweeps for show, they didn't expect to find anything. This was how they got people to justify the war and the burning of the forest. If they were constantly aware that something might be amongst them, then they thought it all to be justified. Not to mention, it helped to remind the defectors that returning to the army should be one of their main concerns.

"Should we stay, or should we go?" I asked, not moving at all. So long as I spoke, I did not need to think. "They've not yet come back here, they're being thorough for once. We have time."

"Do you think he will part with his coins?" Luka

responded. "We could disappear with the crowd if we are lucky enough. The streets are full today."

My eyes slid to Artur, taking in his quivering form located underneath the table, his lip bobbing up and down. "He will not easily be separated," I said. "But I would rather not risk it on today of all days."

Luka grunted his agreement, looking to the other man with tired eyes. We had to leave.

CHAPTER THREE

"A THOUSAND GOLD COINS," ARTUR SLURRED, "I HAD A thousand gold coins and you made them disappear."

"You did not have a thousand gold coins," Luka hissed, struggling to carry nearly the entire weight of the man on his shoulder as Artur limped along the path between us, swaying from side to side with his feet not even touching the ground. "You hardly had two to rub together to begin with, and anything beyond that was not truly yours."

Ahead the overgrown lawn of the Kinsley Estate, the western most one, sat—barely visible through the dense vegetation that the Kinsleys had long since allowed to run wild following their father's death. We'd been there for about two and a half weeks, and Luka and Kristin still did not care to tell me the story behind the mansion, stating only that the King knew it, and that was why he would never suspect them to be there.

But what I would have given for them to have at least hired a gardener for the place, it seemed like nearly every time we went out I almost twisted my ankle in one of the many divots in the ground and carrying Artur did not prove to be an exception. I was all too tempted to flop him out on the lawn and let him dry himself out like a sheet on laundry day.

"You're rotten," Artur declared. "A thousand gold and you would not let me collect it. He is a rotten man, Wren. We should have left him at the bar."

"It was not a thousand gold," I corrected, rolling my eyes. "And you should be thanking Luka for caring enough to take you out of the tavern, we very well could have left *you* there."

In the distance, the old Kinsley mansion grew closer. The one that Luka had apparently spent most of his time in as a child. It was a tall, sprawling thing, one composed of pale rock cut with jagged edges facing outwards. Unlike the other Kinsley estate, it had no glistening windows or spiraling towers. It was closed off, every source of light in the building coming from narrow, slanted windows, and all the doors seemingly built purposely to be tall and imposing. The mansion seemed to loom over you, daring you to enter.

I think I might have hated it as much as the Kinsleys did.

"A hundred gold then," Artur carried on, unwilling to stop complaining.

"Likely that," Luka admitted, "but you'd be lucky to carry ten pieces of that, you've been drunk for so long that you can hardly keep your pants on, I cannot imagine you making it back with all of that gold scooped into your pockets."

"I would have done it," Artur announced, "I would have been able to, had you not grabbed me so forcibly nor given me any time." Leaning conspiratorially towards me in a way that only an exceedingly drunk person considered secretive, Artur whispered, "you should have left him, we could have found you a much better one. Much richer, far more fit. There is still time, you know."

Luka gritted his teeth in irritation, merely swinging Artur

forward and onto the ground as we reached the only bit of uncracked pavement leading up to the main entrance. "Oh, will you look at that, we've reached the steps. Surely you can get up them yourself, can't you Artur?" Luka hissed, shooting a look my way in case I did not hear the annoyance dripping off of him.

I rolled my eyes, the slightest grin pulling at the side of my lips as Artur struggled to sit up in the dirt, a few loose coins flopping out of his robes and driving him into a mad scramble to retrieve them.

"Welcome home, Artur," I said. "And congratulations on alerting the whole estate." No doubt everyone heard. I could hear movement from behind the too tall front doors of the building, a creaking of hinges as a pair of brown eyes peeked out.

No need to guess who it was.

"We've collected the smelly one, Lindy," I said as she opened the door, stepping away from Artur and closer to Luka. Lindy never bothered to learn Artur's name. "Are Adam and Kristin here?"

"Yes," Lindy said, opening the door further so that we could see her, the Haldian girl was dressed down in an old pair of clothes that Kristin must have worn when he was about eight. Artur reached a hand out to her for a moment, then realized who it was and recoiled, falling down onto his back in disappointment. Lindy was not one to spare pity.

"Where is Winry, dear sweet Winry," Artur bumbled, gasping her name like a fish out of water. Likely because she was the only one who would pity him.

"In the yard with her notebooks," Lindy said, pulling the door further open for Luka and I. "Making note of things that will never be of any use to anyone; as is the Whynne way." The younger girl was still not too impressed with our country.

Not that anyone could blame her with the introduction she had received.

"Upstairs and to the left," she said as we walked inside. "I will handle the oaf."

The dusty, cracked staircase stood in front of us, crafted from white marble like the rest of the house. No sooner had Lindy closed the door behind us, stepping out to no doubt drag the monk up the stairs by his collar, then we heard voices coming from upstairs.

"They're arguing," Luka acknowledged, pulling something out of his pocket. I watched closely, squinting at it. "Surprise. It seems like every day there's another squabble here."

"You are still in trouble, I'll have you know," I informed him, watching as he began to unfold the thick paper square. "You should not be conspiring against me."

"Amazing, everyone really does love a house full of arguments," Luka said sarcastically, the paper he had shoved in his pocket earlier quickly coming into view. The newspaper. The one he'd tried to keep me from seeing. "For Adam," he said, "not you."

"I should see it first," I insisted, trying to swipe it from him as we walked up the stairs, he only snorted, holding it high above his head. I raised an eyebrow at that. "I could easily stomp on your foot or trip you," I informed him impatiently, taking his arm with a scoff as we ascended the stairs. He merely shook his head.

The estate was nowhere near as magnificent as the Kinsley estate in Greenable, being more of a vacation home than anything else. That was a relief, however, because even though the staircase was as wide and garish as all noble house staircases were, it was shorter, and the rooms were closer together. Which made it easier to know what was going on in the house, primarily that unwelcome guests had entered. We would have been able to hear them, even if they entered one of the many sealed rooms.

I much preferred the Greenable estate; the library was much grander, and there was more privacy. In the estate we were currently in, it seemed like almost all of the walls were paper thin, made only worse by the brothers barring a significant number of the rooms from visitors.

Still, I could see that it was once beautiful and once useful. There were decorations still on the wall, coated in thick layers of dust and knocked off balance. There were elements of luxury like intricate tile floors and crystal doorknobs around the estate, and the clothing left in the closets was far finer than that of the average family. It was nicer than the Laurents' vacation home, even if on the ground floor weeds had begun to spring through the floorboards.

I had always wanted to ask how long they'd left it for and why, but thought better of it. Luka would tell me if he wanted me to know; I had learned he could be silent when it came to discussing more difficult situations, especially when it came to his family.

"You've given up?" Luka asked me, taking my silence as a sign of surrender.

"I figure there is no point," I admitted. "Soon we will be in the study anyway, and then I will know." I was slowly learning to be more patient... when I knew that the payoff would be immediate.

"Mhm," Luka agreed, the leftmost door to the study grew closer and closer. "I would like to see what Adam makes of this first before you and I revisit old arguments."

"You mean before we jump the gun and run to Haldia?" I asked, shooting him a look out of the corner of my eye. He averted his gaze from mine. "How long did you think we would last? Did that newspaper make you think that a few days would be worth it?" His averted eyes said everything.

I was right, whatever was in that newspaper had inspired him to ask Artur to find passage, not Adam's requests. It was frustrating and I almost thought to tell him that. But today was not the day.

A flash of the scarecrow from earlier played in the back of my mind, prompting my hand to close tighter around his arm.

Perhaps that was why he tried such a daring move in our reoccurring argument today of all days. I'd thought he'd given up on Haldia a few days prior, but maybe Sunrise Day inspired him to try again.

The worst part about starting to like him, then inevitably falling down the awful rabbit hole of love, was that I could not fault him as much anymore. He had somehow steeled me against being fully annoyed with him, especially at moments like this. Because when he looked at me out of the corner of his eyes, there was a softness.

A softness I was sure my gaze echoed.

"Enter," called Adam on the other side of the door in response to Luka's knocking. I hadn't even realized he'd started to knock, instead I'd been trying to squint at the newspaper to get a hint of what it was about. Adam continued, "if it's you Lindy, we've been over this, I will not discuss for the hundredth time the many reasons why you will not be allowed to hunt in the woods."

Nice to hear that Lindy was keeping herself busy annoying Adam.

"Ah," said Adam the second the door opened. "It's you two." There was a different exasperation in that, one that was well met by both Luka's and mine when a large figure dashed by me, scooping Luka up and forcing my hand from his arm.

"There you are," Kristin said frantically, lifting his younger brother up in the air. He had always been burlier than Luka. "I did not even realize the day, I could not believe I made such a mistake, and then Adam went looking for Wren..." Kristin turned in my direction, as if realizing that I was there for the first time and scooping me up as well, my feet dangling an inch or so off the ground as he lifted me in his other arm. "You did not run into any trouble, did you? When Adam told me, I felt awful."

"And only worse upon the realization that Wren was gone as well," Adam said from behind him, leaning against the large desk in the study and looking rather unimpressed with me. "Should I remind you that the King is looking for you, and you have no business walking around that town without anyone knowing."

"Luka knew," I said defensively, allowed to touch the ground once more as Kristin released me and threw an arm around Luka, casting me a moderately scolding look.

Adam glanced over at Luka, a silent question passing between them. "I have the utmost faith that Wren can take care of herself for the most part," Luka said. "They'd be unlucky to catch her, especially in a festival of all places. Wren knows how to kick up a fuss." *Love at its finest.*

"You two are too dangerous together for your own good," Adam informed us, tapping his foot against the ground as he looked between us, silently exasperated.

In the time since he'd met me, it seemed that Adam had been forced to grow up a lot quicker than he had before, largely because of Luka and I—and living on the run did not suit him either. The beginnings of a beard sat on his face, taking away his once boyish handsomeness and crafting it into something new. It only barely hid his newest scar, a line across his lips from a deal made with Kristin. I struggled to remember the Adam before this, the one that my sister and I had spent three long years mooning over at balls.

Kristin only echoed Adam's appearance, a sort of wildness growing on his features over time. Luka had been rather vocal about how annoying he found the scruff Kristin insisted on sprouting.

"Well, do you two have anything to say for yourselves?" Adam demanded, sounding every bit like he was talking to Lindy. He definitely knew what day it was.

He was definitely aware that Luka and I knew the significance of the day as well.

"Go easy on them," Kristin began. "They probably wanted to go to the festival together—"

"A festival in which all of Whynne celebrates the destruction of Unseelie—and to add to that, they decided to take with the constantly drunk monk?" Adam pressed. Yep, Artur didn't exactly spell out romance. Not while he was likely vomiting on the front lawn.

I doubted Luka and I could have carved out a single moment for ourselves.

Luka stretched out his hand, giving Adam the paper he was holding earlier as if in explanation. The newsprint sat folded small in Adam's hand, and Luka gave him the slightest nod to encourage him to open it. Kristin stood by Adam's side, his brow furrowing.

Adam unfolded the newspaper and I found myself crossing the room to stand beside him, desperate to get a peek at it. The image of a familiar woman with a full frame, a sharply cut bob, and narrowed green eyes stared back at us.

Camden. Suddenly I wished I'd not seen the paper at all.

Adam's eyes were traveling up to Luka's before I could even

read the first word. It was hard not to look at him, not to stare at the squaring of his shoulders and the heavy swallow he made. "Nice to see she's keeping herself busy, there's no better way to speed up a wedding than to spread rumors about yourself and how soon it will be coming," his mouth was set firmly downward, his thumb moving and blocking out the face of the blond-haired man who stood beside her, Theo. "But you likely already suspected that, didn't you, Luka?"

"Of course she is," I muttered. "She wants that crown on her head."

"I don't care much about her wedding," Luka said. "Only that she's looking to completely shut down all borders."

"I care about her wedding," I informed Luka with a glare. "Considering the fact that we live here."

It seemed like nearly every man averted their eyes from mine at that assertion.

"King Theo made it very clear that he's interested in Haldia," I informed them. "So your plan would only work for so long."

"Excuse me if I don't feel like storming up to the castle and socking the King in the jaw, Wren," Adam said.

How did he know that was one of my many ideas? "Seeing as how the soldiers edge closer every single day, I'm confident that you three can talk about moving all you want, but we're still not going to get out of this country."

"When did you become so pessimistic?" Luka replied, and I could have laughed at that. When? The moment he came back from Audon and I got involved in this whole mess.

I rolled my eyes, dismissing his claim and trying to act as confident as possible... up until Adam flipped over the paper and another photo of Camden appeared.

"We can discuss this later," Luka began as my eyes took her in, the smug look on her face and the way that she possessively held onto the King's arm. His hand slid into mine, dragging me back to reality. "Wren and I have things to attend to today."

Things? My eyes slipped to his, silently begging the question. I got no response.

"Show up to dinner today," Kristin demanded in the background, no doubt we'd rehash the same conversation there as well. "You're looking thin, Luka."

"Mother hen," Luka murmured, raising his hand in dismissal. "I'll be fine."

"We're not going to Haldia," I said the moment we entered the library, not even waiting until his body was completely through the door.

"Yes, you've made your position on that relatively clear," Luka dismissed, moving past me and into the library. "If you have a country you'd prefer, please do tell. Adam seems rather determined that it should be that one."

"I prefer this one," I snapped, storming in after him as he began to thumb through the books of the small library, his fingers leaving prints on the dust covered spines. "I thought that that was the point of all of this, I thought that we agreed that we were going to do something to save Whynne. That's why we went out of our way to get Artur."

"We have Artur for a variety of reasons," Luka muttered. "Mainly monetary, not at all for companionship."

"We're not leaving Whynne," I said, glaring at his back. The library was tiny, it was only one room and no bigger than a storage closet, he did not have anywhere else to go.

"We are seven people, Wren," Luka informed me, pulling a book from a shelf. "They have an army, and to add to that, you have Unseelie showing interest in you as well. I'm just beginning to come to terms with reality. I've read the papers, I've looked at how many soldiers are walking about, and I've come to my own conclusions."

"This is not reality—"

"Wren, you can't even look at a photo of Camden," Luka said, finally turning away from the shelves to look at me. I deflated immediately. "I kept the newspaper away from you because I knew that you couldn't, I know that you're scared of her."

But he couldn't know that. No one could. I didn't tell anyone... except, it was probably quite obvious considering my expression every time I so much as heard her name.

"I hear the sounds at night, Wren. I know why you started sleeping in the same bed as me, even though you complain," he said. "You have nightmares about her and you have nightmares about the Unseelie, the woods, everything."

"—That doesn't mean that I can't be here," I said plainly, because I was not the type to give in to such things.

Luka cast me a look, shaking his head and moving around me. There was only one seat in the whole library, a single armchair, and he chose to take it, leaving me floundering about and staring at him. For a moment, I thought that that was it.

He eyed the novel in his hands, moving it between his fingers, seeming to consider it for a while longer, and I could only wait for him to crack open the spine. He didn't so much as look at me. But then he set his book aside, his face frowning and his body slumping forward.

"Please Wren, I told Adam I would think about it," he said. "I am begging you to just consider it. Be rational."

"Perhaps you should be irrational for a bit," I countered haughtily, only earning me a sigh, his hand reaching for my wrist.

I let him take it, but only after offering him a scowl in return, then sinking onto his lap with a warning glare.

"Kristin and Adam will be going back to town tomorrow," he said. "Maybe I am wrong and things will begin to die down since Sunrise Day will have passed, but I have an awful feeling that they will not."

"You're the pessimist," I informed him. "Not me."

CHAPTER FOUR

"You need to stop moping," Winry said as the boys crossed the lawn, hardly looking up to watch them walk away, even if their adventure would likely be the most interesting thing of the day.

"I'm not moping," I said, I most definitely was. Adam and Kristin had decided that they would be going back to the village the next day, and though I had asked to go as well, I was still in trouble for being out during Sunrise Day.

Even though Luka had known where I was and I was more than capable.

More than that, they got to go out without Artur, an enviable feat. The poor monk was still drunk, but his hangover was coming quick, leading Winry out into the yard to grab some herbs that would settle his stomach. Traveling anywhere with a thoroughly drunk Artur was a recipe for disaster.

"They even took Lindy," I complained, kneeling beside my sister as she dug in the yard, ignoring the small laugh that she provided at my irritation. "No doubt she'll sell them even more on the idea of Haldia and eventually you and I's opinions won't matter." It didn't matter that they'd only gone to see if the army presence had decreased.

"She won't sell them on going to Haldia," Winry claimed, digging out the roots of a particularly large plant and pulling her gardening knife from her hip. "Besides, if she does, you and I just won't go."

"If I don't go, then Luka won't go," I said simply.

"Exactly," Winry said. "And if Luka won't go, then Kristin won't go. It's a nonstarter if anyone disagrees... Save for Artur, who I would most gladly leave behind," she grimaced. My sister had been nice to the monk for the most part, but when he left the room she voiced her complaints; he'd been playing on her nerves. She didn't quite understand the value of a man who could find a way to make money wherever he went and then lose it just as quickly.

I did. "He's a family friend."

"He's not a family friend. He's someone who my family hired to teach you a trade, one who stole from us the whole time and that we could barely trust to begin with," Winry said. "The fact that's he's not turned you in for a bounty is only because he thinks he can make more money off you otherwise."

She likely had a point there. "Luka's said the same thing more than once or twice," I agreed.

"Where is Luka?" She countered, cutting off a hardier, stockier root and covering the rest with soil. "He's not gone with the other boys, and normally he's right beside you. I thought that he would be interested in checking that the village was empty, he's been so concerned as of late."

"Another squabble," I said simply, prompting her to shake her head. "I'm still mad at him for conspiring with Adam and Artur to set up passage to Haldia. I'm fairly certain that he's doing it because he feels that if he shows me they have a plan, then I'll inevitably agree to it. Little does he know I'm far more stubborn than that."

"No," Winry said, moving onto the plant beside her and taking out her shears to remove a few leaves. "I think Luka is well aware of how stubborn you are."

I huffed, giving up on kneeling beside her and simply letting myself fall back to sit on the grass. I was no help to her, of course. I'd never been of use in the garden, save for picking up rocks when I was younger. "Why are they so obsessed with Haldia anyway?"

"Because it has a wall," Winry pointed out. "Walls seem fairly appealing when you're dealing with our king and have seen firsthand what the Unseelie are capable of."

"Walls can be scaled," I said. "Walls will be knocked down if Camden becomes queen," I pointed out. "I don't believe in momentary solutions."

"Adam mentioned Camden in his long-winded explanation for why I should change my mind and agree to go to Haldia yesterday," Winry said, shoving her leaves in the bag at her hip before turning around to face me. "I told him that I would agree to moving within the country, but never out of it."

"Artur's been trying to get passports made for the past few months," I informed her, prompting her to make a sour expression. "I'm just waiting for him to try to convince us as well—Actually, I'm just waiting to do anything. All of this standing around and hiding from the guards doesn't suit me."

"You'd think they'd want to stay and fight, isn't that what men typically concern themselves with? I've met Camden before and I don't think she's that frightening," Winry said.

"You've met Camden before?" I asked as she dusted off her skirt and made to stand. We'd never discussed Camden before, aside from the first night that we'd left, and even then it had been the briefest acknowledgement of who she was. Not this.

"When I was about ten, she's five years older than us," She shook her head. "Unlike the prince, who is in his forties at the very youngest. She was nice. Nothing amazing, but pleasant to me. I suppose it helps that I'm fae."

Normally the thought of Camden churned my stomach, but the descriptor of her as nice was surprising enough to make me nod my head at Winry, encouraging her to go on.

"I don't know what you're expecting, she was different than she was now. She's not from a noble background to begin with, much like my family. Her father is a general or was a general, I guess he's long since passed now. I just remember her being really nice to me when the other girls weren't, on account of the fact that we were kind of in the same situation. We were outsiders," she seemed to dwell on that a lot, and I moved to follow her as she walked towards one of the side doors of the estate. She yanked it open, and I trailed her as she struggled to juggle her tools and the roots that she'd gathered.

"I would never compare you to Camden," I said. "Nor would I imagine her to be an outsider in any sort of way. She's the type of person who puts her claws into people to gain enough leverage to pull herself up."

"She didn't have the fanciest clothes or anything, and she didn't look half as good as she does now. I guess she kind of learned the same thing that everyone like us does; that marriage is capital for young women, and as women who weren't born into a noble upbringing— we have to either buy or earn our way up, and a good marriage can really help."

"I can't imagine her as any sort of outsider," I admitted.

"You'll have to if you want to know who she really is," Winry informed me impatiently. "I know the older girls used to say she had dwarf blood in her lineage, and that her outfits were ugly and she was plain. She must have taken that to heart, now they all probably regret it."

"If any of them are still alive," I said, pulling open the door for her as she fiddled with the gardening tools secured around her waist. The belt she wore was loose, far looser than any we had at home. It was left over from the Kinsley's old gardener, left amongst the objects thrown about the place as if the gardener might have come back at any moment.

The abandonment of the estate seemed to have been a sudden one, one that happened the moment the head of the Kinsley family had passed.

"I wouldn't put it past Camden, she has the status now," Winry said. "That's a fun thing that you never got to learn, the fact that who you marry counts for everything."

"Because you were signing me off," I joked.

"It turned out for the best," Winry finally acknowledged, though it didn't seem like she agreed. I'd come to a recent conclusion that she liked it better when Luka and I were separate, because then we were each individually hers.

"It could have been worse," I said, "I could have followed in Artur's footsteps instead."

"And how would you bring about the end of the country that way," a voice said from behind us, I didn't have to turn to know it was Luka.

"Shouldn't you be in the library or something?" I asked, not so much as turning around. Beside me Winry was not shy in showing her exasperation.

She definitely did not like to share.

"Perhaps I want to make sure that you're not poisoning Artur."

"Mint for his stomach, rosemary to help wake him up, and fennel to help him actually digest his food," Winry said, listing the three ingredients on her fingers without looking back at him, the slightest gleam in her eyes at the opportunity to use her skills. "If we wanted to poison him, we would just pour him another cup of ale."

"Mhm," said Luka, falling into step behind me. He didn't sound like he fully believed us. But then, as if sensing my bad mood, he noted, "there was no smoke today, did you realize?"

I froze entirely.

Winry stopped just a few steps ahead, casting a curious look in my direction as I wracked my brain, trying to remember the slightest hint of smoke in the air. There was none.

Why had they stopped?

"I just noticed that looking out the library window, I tried to squint and see it, then moved to the other side of the house to look as well. Nothing." That didn't mean much, or shouldn't have meant much, but the smoke carried far.

"What do you think it means?" I asked quickly, my eyes snapping up to meet his as my voice took on a grave tone. My sister was all but forgotten.

"It means that they're finally tired of playing games," Winry tsked, surging forward to grab my wrist with an impatient expression. "Honestly, it probably means nothing. You two get so worked up over these things." Probably, but...

I looked to Luka as she pulled me away, a great, heavy weight settled in my stomach. I didn't trust it, and from the look of him, neither did he.

"Perhaps I should go back to making more copies," I said quickly, the idea of silver far more enticing than watching the creation of a hangover cure. Maybe it was a good idea to earn as much as I could before we had to leave.

My hands were covered in dark indigo ink by the time that Kristin and Adam returned. I sat on the floor of the main floor's sitting room, another sheet of paper laying in front of me as I took advantage of the uneven texture of the worn grain beneath me to make the words look more weathered. To my side the project, a small atlas that Artur had snatched from a library years ago and always had good returns from, sat barely open. Behind me, Luka made notations in his book while lounging in one of the wingback chairs, his eyes occasionally flickering up in annoyance to look at the man at the center of the room; Artur, who was quickly sobering up.

Artur was all moans and groans, insisting that he would have fared better if given another pint of ale instead of the hangover concoction. He did not cease his whining when the two broad shouldered men's frames appeared in the door.

"I just do not understand how you can sit there and watch me suffer, boy," Artur groaned, the small chunks of hair he had remained plastered to his head and his body practically toppled off the couch with the slightest motion. He raised his hands in the air while he spoke, his voice clipped; he was in far from a good mood, "you have two perfectly good legs, and I'm sure that Wren and Winry will not die in the time it takes to walk back."

"Nice to hear that people are getting along well," Adam interrupted, earning yet another groan from Artur as he did not so much as turn to look at the visitors. "I'm sure no one cares to hear about your hangover, Artur, considering the fact that you brought it upon yourself." He chuckled, leaning against the doorway as Kristin only grinned, only halfway amused by Artur's predicament.

"Oh it is so fun to kick me when I'm down," Artur complained.

"There's no other time to kick you, considering the fact that you are always down," Adam laughed, he was in high spirits tonight, no doubt the weathered piece of paper in his hand was to thank for that.

I sat up a little bit straighter when I saw it, wondering what on earth he could have found of interest. It had to be something good, Kristin was smiling as well. I think Luka realized that they had something at the same time I did.

"You two seem to be in a good mood," Luka acknowledged, nodding towards the piece of paper in Adam's hand. "News that the King has fallen? A sale on razors to shave off that ridiculous scruff you both are growing? Or something else."

"You wound us," Kristin grinned, stroking his facial hair thoughtfully. "Something interesting is brewing in the village. We've found flyers announcing it."

"And what exactly is brewing?" Luka pressed.

Kristin's grin faltered. "You know I haven't got the slightest idea, but the King's men have filed out and that in itself is almost cause for celebration in my eyes. It's been days since the village was empty of soldiers..."

"And the smoke was gone from the air," Luka acknowledged.

"You sound like Wren," Adam said. "Smoke this, smoke that—" It had been a concern of mine for the past few weeks. I knew how important those trees were to Whynne, and Adam did too, but he didn't see anything too concerning about the smoke, stating that only a few feet of the forest were burned a day.

"It is a pressing concern," I interrupted. "They're burning the forest, there has to be consequences to that."

"There are," Adam admitted. "But none that we should worry about now. Besides that, I heard that they're replanting every so often, putting down rowan trees here and there along with ash; perhaps Theo is just being frivolous and trying to redecorate the country as a whole." Adam knew Theo better than anyone...

But still. I wrinkled my nose at the thought, no one would

be so absurd—save for Theo and Camden. But my thoughts were soon interrupted by a small gurgle...

"Will there be booze at this party?" Artur asked, processing the concept of a celebration at last.

"Not for you," I said quickly. "You are done drinking. Someone will have to stay behind with you."

"I'm not a child," Artur complained, ignoring the fact that ever since we'd grabbed him, we'd been taking care of him. The money Adam gave him regularly was far too much, it let him buy whatever he liked. But Adam insisted that if he did not indulge Artur, he might very well run, and that Artur escaping proved to be more dangerous than anything else.

"Of course you're not," I agreed, reaching behind myself to pat Artur's lower leg. "You're merely a drunk."

I could tell that he wanted to reply, his sour face stated it. Unfortunately, his drowned brain could not come up with a proper retort.

"Will you go, Luka?" I asked, turning to him instead. "Maybe it will be nice," I said, but I meant so much more. What I really meant to say was, 'maybe we can find out what's going on, and why, even though the smoke has dissipated for the time being, there is still a terrifying silence clinging to the air.'

Luka's eyes connected with mine, understanding immediately.

CHAPTER FIVE

It was dark by the time we left. I could not remember the last time I went out in the dark. It must have been when we were home, our real home, the one where there weren't monsters creeping about or guards watching over us in a camp and waiting for us to die at the hands of the Unseelie. The one where civilization seemed like a realistic concept. But there we were, out in the night, and all around me no one seemed to be worried.

The masks were gone, as were the crude posters. All that walked about were 'normal' people, their faces completely visible and their bodies still darting between the market stalls that should have been long gone. It was closer to the way that I remembered things, the way I knew holidays should be celebrated. In the center of the village sat a raised platform, one like the one Greenable had for storytelling on holidays, one like the one I had crowded around as a child. I still didn't feel settled, not completely, I hadn't for months now, but this felt safer, like for a moment I could forget.

And standing there with Luka's hand in mine once more was a normalcy that I tried not to crave.

"You only charmed your ears today," I noted, taking them in. He'd only removed the scars, no other modifications. It was strange how wholly Seelie that one detail made him look, I knew that even the most educated in the village would not know what he was.

But still, it was strange to be out together, and to see his real face. I could look over and know that it was him then pretend that we were allowed to do such a thing all the time.

"I thought it would be a nice change," he said. I blinked at that, my hands adjusting around his. Maybe he was nervous, though that was unlike him. He looked a little pale.

"Do you suppose Adam's mad that he has to look after Lindy?" I asked, watching Adam and Kristin walk ahead, the Haldian girl darting between them and looking at everything around her in fascination.

"Of course not," Luka dismissed. "My brother thinks her to be a novelty, I'm sure the sentiment is similar with Adam as well. Kristin always wanted a little sister."

"Mhm," I agreed, my hand tightening around his and my head resting on his shoulder. The others kept moving far ahead of us, but it was nice to stand beside Luka, looking at all of the paper and glass lanterns alight around us. My own lantern was tucked into the front of my dress, not allowed to be viewed for fear of identifying me, but I could still feel it sitting heavily against my chest.

Luka's thumb ran across the back of my hand, his head slumping slightly to the side to rest on top of mine. I wondered if he felt the strangeness as well, how odd it was for the two of us to truly be out together. He had said that we would have had to remain secret even in Greenable, but... I wondered if he thought about things like this too.

"If you were quiet and we were very quick," he said almost inaudibly. "We could steal away entirely. Perhaps then we would have better luck finding out what's going on. As much as I enjoy my brother's company, his head is only concerned with finding out just enough to survive and move on. I'm curious about what's really going on with the forest."

I nodded imperceptibly, eyeing the two men in front of us. "I can see your point." We needed to know, and word of mouth was likely our only chance. But, so far we'd neither heard nor read anything about the smoke that had begun to move through the skies of Whynne.

"Then we'll leave," he said softly. "The first chance we get."

"Agreed," my eyes fell on the men in front of me, knowing that they would be upset but also knowing that they wouldn't realize we were gone until it was too late. We just had to wait for the right moment.

Luka's hand held mine firmly, not willing to be parted.

Kristin turned to laugh at something Adam said, his eyes closing in mirth, and suddenly I was pulled to the side, off the pathway and behind one of the market stalls. Both of us disappeared out of view.

All that was in front of me was Luka, the two of us left staring at each other.

It'd been a long time since I'd gotten to look at him like that. I opened my mouth, almost about to ask him what to do next, then closed it. He stood still, watching me.

"Well, we're alone," I said. "We should get going, before they realize that we're gone."

"You're right," he said, near breathlessly. "We should," his voice implied that he wished to do anything but that at the moment.

And then his hands were in my hair, almost knocking off

the hood that covered it, and his lips were pressed against mine; hungry, devouring.

It was such a strange, bold move to make in public, I couldn't help but look at him with wide eyes as he pulled away, my hands rising to cover his as they cupped my face. This was not something that people like us did.

His black eyes were on mine, something unspoken and barely understood resided in them. I reached up once more, my lips barely touching his, my breath coming out in a rush.

And quietly, his lips pressed against my forehead. Moments later, he admitted, "it was not entirely to ask about the smoke. I like to think that I have a strong will, but sometimes you test it." He cleared his throat at my confusion, "I liked the way that you looked at me just then. Don't force me to admit anything more."

I was caught in between laughing and leaning in once more, his embarrassment being almost endearing. "You've already admitted far more damning things than that to me."

"And you continue to use them against me," he replied.

My hand moved from his, touching his cheek and feeling the warmth under his skin as if wondering if he was really real. At times, it didn't feel like it. "I'm trying to think of the smoke and how the world is falling apart, and you push me aside for this," I bit my bottom lip, trying to shake my amusement.

"Maybe I like to see you smile every once in a while," he admitted. "Maybe I find myself to be very fond of you."

"Maybe you should be quiet," I mused, my thumb slipping over his lips, and maybe you should just enjoy things."

He hummed in agreement, leaning forward once more, his mouth pressing against my thumb in a soft kiss as he looked at me with a searing gaze.

"What has gotten into you," I whispered in amusement. A part of me, a selfish one, imagined a world in which it was just the two of us. In which we left everyone else behind. But then the laughter of Adam and Kristin far away in the background brought me back to reality along with the bustle of the market-place that we stood in, and the people around us taking glances in our direction with slight amusement.

"Excuse me. I felt, at least for a moment, thankful," he said, borderline sarcastically. "And just a little bit afraid," those words came out serious, far too serious.

"We should see if anyone is talking about the smoke," I mused, he only hummed in agreement, finally pulling away.

"I can still smell it," he said. "It's awful enough that it should be easy to find out more, people like to complain."

But the problem was, it wasn't. Or at least, no one wanted to talk about it, not with us. We could not find a single person willing to spare a detail, most pretending it wasn't even there as if it didn't hang in the air like some sort of curse.

"There's never been any smoke," one man told us, as if his age somehow disguised the fact that he was lying. As if the smell hadn't grown stronger. He scurried away quickly, as if our questions had made him uncomfortable.

They all scurried away.

It was as if they were waiting for something, some great event to take place that we hadn't been informed of. Obviously they were, the flyers in Adam and Kristin's hands said as much, though they gave no information as to what it was. It was as if everyone was already aware of what to wait for, save for Luka and I.

And as the night carried on, it became more and more difficult to pretend that wasn't what was going on. Lanterns were running low, and people seemed to be waiting for something. The night was becoming darker, soon Winry would wonder where we were.

Luka and I sat at the edge of the town when it happened, at

an assortment of tables nearest the trees, ones where communal dinners would take place during holidays. Orange and yellow balls appeared amongst the branches, the low hum of a beat beginning, and for a moment, it seemed like we were the only ones who heard.

But then slowly heads turned.

Luka sunk against the seat that he sat in, his hand in my lap, his skin damp with sweat. Kristin and Adam were nowhere in sight as the drums grew louder.

And the smell of smoke grew stronger.

And then it was as if the trees parted, the sound coming at full force. A familiar face appeared, holding a torch by the edge of the trees. He'd bothered me just the other day, the soldier named Callum.

He looked young but authoritative as he led the way through the throngs of people, crusted blood forming a line across his eyebrow and his mouth set in a grim line. Behind him, other soldiers walked, moving tightly, keeping something just out of view but not out of hearing.

There were at least twenty soldiers, some marked in the same way he was, some looking far too proud. They walked in a tight line, their heads high and their eyes facing forward. Suddenly everyone was looking at them.

I heard a single cheer rise as people began to move, edging closer to the soldiers, looking eagerly. This was the spectacle. This was what they were waiting for. The guards parted just a little in the other direction to entertain the curiosity of a few children, making the crowd go silent with awe.

There were groans. Loud, pained sounds of agony hit the air. Someone was there amongst them... or something. For a moment, I thought it was a lost civilian, some unfortunate soul who had walked into the woods and been attacked by the Unseelie.

But then the soldiers got closer, rounding the crowd and stepping onto the small, raised platform in front of them, the one that Luka and I had not seen earlier. That's when it became apparent, something bad was happening. Something awful.

I looked to Luka as the soldiers approached, his jaw was tight and his face was growing paler and clammier. And then I realized something, something that I had not experienced for the past few hours.

There was smoke in the air once more, and it was heavier than before. I gripped Luka so tightly that it hurt.

In the distance, I could see orange and red flames dancing through the trees.

"Ladies and Gentlemen," a voice spoke, and my head turned so fast to face it I almost felt dizzy with the action. "We have a show for you tonight." A show?

And then I saw what they were holding up between them, and it hit me that this was not a show. This was far from it.

There were only three of them, but there had to be at least twenty guards and a hundred spectators; and those people, the beings they held up by their shoulders with harsh hands, who were barely breathing?

They were Unseelie.

The King's soldiers hadn't found them in time for Sunrise Day, but they had them now. They would make a spectacle now. This, according to the king, was the proper way to ring in the return of the sun to Whynne.

My eyes tore away to Luka, taking in the way that he swallowed but did not look away. Why did he not look away? Didn't he understand? My hand pulled at his, his fingers were loose.

I couldn't see Kristin or Adam; I couldn't hear Lindy. I couldn't find a way out, and Luka grew more and more pale.

He knew. He knew exactly what was going on, but he couldn't bring himself to move.

"Look upon them," said one of the soldiers. "They hid so well for Sunrise Day. They retreated so far into those cursed woods, but now look at them. Look where they are. In front of us, paying for their sins, as they should be."

A small, knobby Unseelie with stringy blonde hair, likely a hobgoblin, stood within the guards' reach. He wrenched up her chin, showing her to the crowd, making us look at the pain on her pointed features. Then, just as suddenly as he grabbed her, he moved on. A short man, hardly a head high, was held by a kneeling guard. It was a red cap, vicious things, but noble warriors all the same. Not that I would call that a noble warrior... He was old now, so old that he could barely stand on his own. And then lastly, the guard shoved forward another Unseelie, one nearly human, one with long ears that reminded me of Luka and weathered skin long since dried out.

"A Nokken," Luka said. "They're meant to live in the water." There was something unsaid about that, the fact that it must have been driven from its home.

All of them must have been driven from their homes by the smoke, and now they stood before us, or tried to. That was the entertainment. This was the show. People lobbing insults and throwing things at them. You could see it begin to happen, watch the splatter of tomato against the Nokken's face as a woman pelted the creature. This was what they were all waiting for.

And it wasn't over yet.

"We'll have them face the forest as we do this," a familiar voice spoke, its owner rising from the shadows. A man I recognized far more than anyone. One with gills on his neck and delicate scales that gleamed in the moonlight and accented his handsome face along with the gentle cascade of red hair tumbling over his forehead. "So that they may look at their home and know that the days of hiding in the woods and stealing children are over, that they will never hurt another human or Seelie. We'll let them say goodbye to their home." Nikolas was a captain now, the leader of a squad.

He was my worst mistake.

Was it possible to regret saving someone? To wake up every day and wish that you had done It differently? I would learn, I suppose. I would look back at my mistake and wish otherwise. Because Nikolas Harding was still alive, and he stood ahead of the pack. A captain.

He'd been rewarded for his treachery.

And in the hand of the soldier I had seen just days prior, the one who had chased me down, was a pistol. A familiar pistol. One loaded with engraved bullets. One that, just a month prior, had been pointed at me. It sat against the Nokken's temple.

I felt the shot in my very core. I felt it in the loosening of Luka's hand, in the hooding of his eyes. I felt it in my heart that still beat rapidly from a memory... And I felt it in the way it all slipped away just as suddenly as Luka did.

"Luka," his name left my lips and I realized that he was not there.

He had slipped through my hands as the trees behind the platform began to burn white, as the smoke filled the air and came over us like a wave. But he had not left me. No. Because it would have been too kind for him not to have seen that shot, nor have seen the next one when, in a foreign tongue, the redcap began to pray.

I flinched with the next shot, my feet moving backward of their own volition. "Luka," I repeated his name, not caring who heard it, just needing to know where he was, that he was okay. No response came.

I tore my eyes away as the final shot rang out, practically spinning on my heel. "Luka—" My voice caught in my throat as the smoke grew heavier, cloaking all around me, I fell down onto my knees, my hands desperately clawing.

"Luka," I called his name, but it did not gain me a response. "Luka, Luka, Luka," my hands clawed, searching the ground for him. I was desperate to hear him, desperate to feel him, to feel anything. Why was he not responding? Where had he gone? I knew he was there; I didn't know how but I did.

I could barely make out his closed eyes as my hands shoved their way under his shirt, pressing against the skin, feeling for that small, persistent beat.

"Luka," I cried once more as the crowd burst out again, moving forward to scream in agreement with something that was said, my hands grabbed his collar and pulled him up, away from the danger of blind footsteps. Only then did I feel it, only when my eyes closed and the scream caught in my throat; A heartbeat, the faintest heartbeat.

CHAPTER SIX

I STARED AT HIM, NOT KNOWING WHAT TO DO, NOT knowing what to say, as the people around us moved, pushing closer to the stage through the smoke, struggling to see what was going on. Behind me, I heard the voices continue. Another long speech, another dedication to the King. I couldn't care less about that.

But Luka...?

"Miss," someone noticed us and my hands immediately snapped downward, covering the tips of his ears, listening as the softest exhale escaped him. "Miss, wait here, I'll get help—" I didn't even look up.

I couldn't speak.

Tell them no, a voice said in the back of my head. But they wouldn't listen. As people began to move forward, more saw him. My hands stayed clasped over his ears, my own ears ringing. "Luka," I tried once more, "Luka, you need to wake up. This is not a good time for this."

Nothing. Those loud, stupid drums began again in the background, and Kinsley was still out. Unconscious and not responding. Someone tried to reach around me, attempting to touch him, I slapped their hand away, my breath ragged.

"Lindy!" My voice rose above the crowd, uncaring who heard. "Adam, Kristin! Someone!" Anyone but the people around me, anyone but the people who had cheered when the Unseelie fell.

I could practically hear him chiding me in the back of my head, telling me to be rational when I ripped my cloak off of my shoulders and tucked it under his head in the guise of cushioning him, but really to hide what they shouldn't see. Because, though this town had never seen such scars before, someone would come to their own conclusion if I was unlucky.

And I already knew myself to be unlucky. I could hear the soldiers' footsteps beginning to move off the stage. They would try to come and help, they would see me without my cape on and him, Luka Kinsley, and they would take us.

Fine, I thought in exasperation, *do it, so long as someone did something to help him.*

Luka coughed, just the slightest sputter, and I saw a small trail of black dribble from the side of his mouth. Rationality declared it to be ash, but my mind was leaping ahead, it read it as blood.

"Kinsley," I muttered. "Kinsley, please. Wake up."

"Miss, we're going to take care of him, we're going to—" Another person, another attempt, I practically threw myself on Luka, desperate not to have him taken away and then, another voice, a different voice.

"The tall man is sick."

I had never turned so fast in my life.

And there she was, standing there with her tightly plaited hair, donning boys' clothes and looking at us with her round eyes. Her accent thick, her mannerisms rude as always.

"Lindy," I choked out.

"What has happened to him," she replied. "Why is he sleeping here?"

"Get Kristin and Adam," I said quickly. "Now. Please." Her face glimmered with understanding. One look at me, one look at him, and she was off, disappearing into the crowd.

And Luka and I were still there. Gaining unwelcome attention. Unable to move.

I yanked his head onto my lap, taking one last look before pulling the cloak over his face. His heavy eyelashes were down, casting shadows on his cheeks as he breathed softly, his sharp eyes and sarcastic smile gone. But it was not a peaceful slumber. It was fitful, pained.

"He's fine," I insisted to another man who leaned down, his words not even processing as I covered Luka's face. "It was the excitement." I could see the doubt. My fingers tightened on Luka's clothing.

How long would it take? I closed my eyes, counting the seconds as they passed by while voices still tried to talk to me and persuade me. None of them mattered.

The hurried footsteps around me only served to quicken my heartrate. I did not dare to open my eyes.

"Wren," a voice spoke my name again, and for a single second I forgot that it was no longer a cursed sound, that the person who spoke it was no longer to be feared. My eyes opened slowly to look at him.

"—Luka," Another voice interrupted, and suddenly someone was kneeling down in front of me, the crowds beginning to part as he did so. "Luka," he tried again, his hands reaching for Luka's shoulders. I let out a strangled sound as Luka was wrestled away from me, I was unwilling to give him up. My body shook when he was pulled from my arms, my eyes unable to leave him even as he was gathered into the arms of another.

"Wren, you need to snap out of this," a voice spoke beside me, trying to get me to focus. "You need to listen to me. You need to tell us what happened."

My head was pounding. I felt the slightest prickle at the edge of my skin, the hint of blue raging to life in my palms—

A dark-skinned hand grabbed my wrist, stopping all magic. My eyes shot up to the owner, my mind finally processing who was speaking.

"Wren, we're going to get Luka home but you need to tell us what happened," Adam said.

And there was only one answer, "the smoke."

I COULD NOT FOCUS ON MUCH ELSE. NOT DURING THE walk there, not as he bounced over their shoulders, thrown like a bag of flour and frequently passed between them. Even the oddity of Lindy's small hand in mine did little to distract me. All I could think of was Luka, his half open mouth, his empty eyes.

That and the smoke. We could still smell it at the Kinsley estate, still see it burning from the front lawn. It was close to us. There were bits of the forest butted right up against the wall, soon it would be even closer. But what did the King's men care about an empty estate?

"They stopped the fires to collect the Unseelie for their little exhibition," Adam said, as if I could still care. All that mattered was that Luka was hurt.

I could think of little else, even as Winry pressed a teacup in my hands.

Luka was alone upstairs. We left him alone upstairs. Why did we leave him alone?

All of us sat downstairs in the sitting room, perched on an assortment of chairs grabbed from around the house, and Luka laid alone upstairs. Kristin seemed to realize this as well, occasionally looking around and shifting in his seat, but I doubt it compared to the worry I felt. One second Luka had been okay, not amazing, but still present. The next...

"Wren, you need to focus," Adam's voice filled my ear once more as I looked around anxiously, tempted to tear out of there anyway and tell them to debate amongst themselves. "We need to talk about what happened."

"Nikolas is a captain, and Luka is upstairs, choking on smoke in a house that I don't think he wants to be in," I said quickly. "I made a mistake," I added, not bothering to clarify what it was.

Only Lindy nodded in agreement, knowing. She would have left Nikolas to die.

"We need to move again," Adam spoke once more, his voice commanding. "I don't care about your little garden, Winry, we need to move." I couldn't even see my sister's response to that, my eyes were on the stairs.

Winry prattled off something, I didn't care. I was waiting for Luka. *Wake up.* I could feel Kristin's eyes on me, knowing exactly what I was thinking. *Just shut up and come to a conclusion, he's upstairs.* Luka could die for all of their squabbling.

"That's not something for you to decide," a voice chimed in. Why was it that when matters were the most pressing, everyone wanted to take their sweet time discussing them?

"—Wren can stay with me," Artur cut, and I almost rolled my eyes. I didn't have the faintest idea what was going on. "Her and I know each other more than anyone. I'm practically her father."

I'd kill Camden. I already decided that, as I sat staring at the staircase. I would kill Camden. I would blame her for this, and I would be the one to end her. The idea was almost consuming.

"Wren," again Adam's voice demanded, his fingers snapping in front of my face to get my attention. "I need you to respond to me."

"I don't care," I said quickly because I didn't. Whatever they wanted to decide, it didn't matter.

"She's lying," Winry said beside me. "She does care, she's on my side." Winry was always the one to rope me in.

"Then she's unreasonable," Lindy said dryly, leaning forward in her chair. "Wren is not so stubborn as to stand by your side."

My eyes finally returned to them, flickering up in interest.

"Stay or go," Kristin reiterated. "And where." He had more patience with me, he understood my distraction.

"Go," I said, because at the moment it seemed more appealing. The fires were growing closer, the soldiers coming with them. Evidently, this was, however, not the right answer. Winry looked irritated. "And if I go anywhere, it's in Whynne," I said. I needed to be there. Camden would soon know why.

"We shouldn't leave," Winry began. "It's been peaceful here—"

I whirled around to face her; my voice sharp, still murderous with what had just happened. "We watched three Unseelie get executed and Luka fall unconscious from the smoke in the past hour. This is not peace; this has been us biding our time waiting for something good to finally happen. Now something awful has begun and you don't want to admit it."

"Then Haldia—"

"I don't want to go there," I informed Adam, irritated. Beside me, Lindy tsked in disagreement, but then I added, "I have scores to settle here." If there was anything the Haldian could understand, it was that.

"Wren," he tried once more, his voice patient, far too patient.

"Stop," I demanded. "Stop now, because I will not say yes to leaving, especially not now. Luka is upstairs and he is half alive in my eyes, the smoke did something to him. Camden did this. Camden has been doing all of this, she's trying to drive us out. And how do you plan to respond? You want to run. Adam, I can't—"

"Do you think Luka can survive your revenge fantasies?" Adam shot back. "Do you think Luka would be okay with this? He passed out, he fell unconscious in the middle of a festival to celebrate the end of the Unseelie. Now you're talking about insane things, about finding a way to the princess, when you know that it's not possible. You need to—"

"Don't tell me what I need to do," I snapped. "Might I remind you, up until a few weeks ago, you were the King's dog. No one else has forgotten. Now you're eager to run away once he's kicked you, but not all of us are so inclined to follow you. Not all of us are afraid or wishing that they traded us in when it was most convenient. You would place your head at the king's feet for just a crumb of affection, Harlow."

Adam's face shuddered, falling almost entirely.

"You don't mean that, Wren," Kristin said, not to me but to Adam. "She doesn't mean that, Adam. Wren's just stressed."

I didn't, not when I saw Adam's response. The guilt I felt was immense, he was honestly hurt. "I'm tired of this," I said softly. "I was not made to run, and now this has happened. Luka is," I paused, unable to find the words, "he's mine," I settled, "and I do not want anything bad to happen to him. I also do not want the other Unseelie to suffer as well because of Camden and the King."

"What if it's something to draw us out," Adam countered. "Camden is no fool."

"Then it's successful," I said, rising from my chair, finally making a choice. "Congratulations to King Theo for finally having a plan that worked, I hope the god forsaken man celebrates it with champagne and pastries. Meanwhile, I will sit beside Luka and wait for him to wake up, hoping that he is alright." I shook my head, "I will consent to move, but I will not leave this country. I have too much unfinished business here."

CHAPTER SEVEN

The smoke was thick outside. Even in the daylight, it was like we hadn't really been freed from the promise of endless night. Those dark, thick clouds hung overhead, back with a vengeance, and every time I looked away, every time I dared to peer out the narrow window, I saw them.

Even as rain trickled down the cracked glass, the smoke continued, unhindered. The droplets fell, stained black with soot, and in the distance the faintest crackling sound of the flames licking the trees could be heard. They were burning right outside the village.

I tore my eyes away from the window, looking back at Luka, practically hearing his voice in my ears telling me that staring would do very little, both about the fires burning outside and him lying there, unconscious. Still alive, but...

My hand reached out to his face, brushing an imagined speck of dust away from him, relishing in the irritated huff that sounded in response as he turned to the side away from my hand. In fairytales, it would be one kiss and he would be awake.

But in the book of fairytales he had grown up with, there

were far more simple solutions; ones that I was tempted to try, like pinching his nose or blowing air in his ears. His nanny did not care for fantasy when he was a child, and she only allowed the smallest hints of magic to remain in the stories when it suited her best as an aid to correct his behavior. She was far different to my mother, but then again, she was a human woman entrusted with a half Unseelie child, one who eventually grew into a half Unseelie man and became my problem. One who I desperately needed to wake up.

My hand lingered above his head, tempted to turn it once more to make him look at me, if only so I could reassure myself that he was still there. Another cough escaped him, however, and my hand fell to his back, gripping his shoulders as cough after cough followed, creating another array of grey specks across the sheets. There was already a fair amount on the other side. The ash had filled his lungs, affecting him more than I, or anyone else due to his mixed heritage.

"You are lucky that Lindy managed to find us, and that Kristin and Adam were capable of picking you up," I whispered, and then I corrected myself. "I am lucky." Because I was. Because he was still there, because the crowds were consumed with trying to see through the smoke to view the execution, because Nikolas did not spot us, because Lindy was nimble, because—Because—

His name echoed in my mind, my throat still hoarse from calling it, from begging him. I could see the faint lines of pink on his skin where I had dug at him, desperate to find his heartbeat. They cascaded over his shoulders, nearing his neck.

I felt sick at the sight of them.

Only a few months ago, I had tried to kill him. Not once, but twice. Now those stupid lines bothered me, barely there tracks from my fingernails that would fade in a day's time.

"Winry will find you the right herbs, and then you will feel better," I reassured. "We'll wake you up, and then you'll be alright. We'll leave here and move to another part of Whynne, and you'll be fine." My hand tightened on him, "you will not die," I said desperately, my fingers moving over the lines I'd left.

A world without him. This world without him. It was unimaginable, it felt like a joke. Even though everyone had reassured me, including the monk, that he would eventually awaken. I still felt sick.

But then he moved under my hands, and I felt my whole body tense.

"Not so long as you watch me, no," he said, and I jerked my hand back as if I'd been burnt, surprised to find him looking back at me, wide awake.

Alive, despite the voice that screamed in my head.

"I am far from death," Luka mumbled, still tired, but turning under my hands, his whole body moving to face me. His face was painted with tired annoyance, the edge of his mouth dotted with the same grey as his bedspread. "Wishful thinking on your part. Try again."

I could only blink at him as his black eyes bored into mine, threatening to close again at any moment.

"Staring at me will not make me better," he said, as if he knew what I'd been doing, that I hadn't so much as slept a wink as I watched him. His eyes began to shut again and despite myself, I clapped a hand against his cheek, still as wide eyed as before, still as amazed. "Wren?" he asked, raising his head up off the pillow and grasping at my hand, his eyes meeting mine.

"I should get Kristin," I decided immediately, rising from my chair. He would want to know; he would want to be the first one to talk to him. But Luka's hand was on my wrist before I could move, his eyes connecting with mine, his voice commanding.

"Stay."

I stared at him, bewildered as to why he would ask for that, even with our relationship. Kristin was waiting, he was worried. His brother was beside himself.

"For all intents and purposes, pretend that I am still asleep," he said, and I could only gawk. "Wren," he said, begging, and suddenly my arms were upon him, his hand and my wrist thrown over his shoulder and I tried and failed to gather him up in my arms, overwhelmed by the need to hold him and be close to him.

Still there. It echoed in my mind; he was still there. It felt impossible.

Luka's hand rose slowly to the back of my head as I plastered myself against him, a sob escaping me. "Wren," he said, his hand stroking the back of my head. "Wren, it's okay."

It was not okay. It was not okay in the slightest. "You are not allowed to die," I commanded, shoving him away furiously, glaring into his eyes as I sat on the bed beside him, my fingers bunching in his shirt. "And you are not allowed to do that again, not to me. You are never allowed to do that again."

"Wren," he repeated my name once more and the urge to strangle him broke through. "I could not help it." I wanted to demand to know if he knew what would happen, if he knew what the burning of the woods would do to him. I wanted to ask if he knew that Nikolas had been promoted to captain, if he only charmed his ears because he was feeling weak. I wanted to demand a thousand answers.

"You do not do that to me," I demanded, my fingers bunching further into his shirt, balling so tightly that it hurt. "You do not faint, you do not disappear, you do not leave me." I shook my head furiously, "that is not how this works, Kinsley."

"Okay," he responded, surprised but still gentle. Definitely more awake. "Okay," he repeated, his hands moving to mine. "Wren, I understand."

"No, you do not," I spat, looking at him. "You do not understand at all, Kinsley."

And he could have argued, I think, but he didn't. Instead, he moved slowly, his hands working mine off of him. "I will not do it again," he promised. "If that is what calms you, Wren. I will not do it again." Though I knew that he had truly done nothing at all.

A promise would have calmed me, but I knew better than to look for that from him. "I'm going to get Kristin," I said, my hands finally releasing him, his head falling back against the pillow with the motion. "I'm going to get Kristin and tell him that you are awake." I couldn't help but be irritated, both at my own uselessness in the situation and at the way that he behaved so calmly.

"Wren," he said once more, and I turned to him with the most furious glare, sobs threatening to escape me again. "Wren, stay."

Stay? I stared at him, straightening from the bed. Kristin would be waiting to see him.

"Please."

He looked desperate. "Did you know?" I asked, because it burned at me, what if he went and knew? What if he had an idea what was happening to him? What if he was keeping that secret from me?

What was happening to him?

"No," he said, swallowing thickly, and I waited for more coughing to begin. I waited for him to scratch at his throat, begging for release, because it seemed like something he would know, something Luka would have been able to predict. Since he was fae, he couldn't lie.

But nothing came. Even though ash coated the back of his throat, no further coughing came.

"Please," he repeated. "Wren, I do not think I can stand up to chase after you. I'm tired. Don't be difficult."

"Of course you can't," I said softly, reaching once more for him, desperate to feel him. "Luka," his name felt heavy on my tongue. "Luka, what happened to you?"

"Smoke from the elder trees," he replied, and that was that. Everything I already knew. "Please come here so I can see you," he said, and I could not stop myself from doing so.

I fell against the bed, his arms immediately wrapping around me, pulling me close to him. My chest pressed against his, my head thrown over his shoulder in the tightness of our embrace, and my breathing moving in tune with his. Suddenly, everything around me was Luka. Everything was the smell of him, the warmth of his body, the desperate way he clutched me closer, exhaling with the same strain that I did.

I could have cried. My arms slipped around his torso, my forehead resting against his shoulder. "I hate you," I said simply.

And because he could not lie, he could only respond. "I hate this house."

The smallest laugh escaped me as I finally pulled away, placing my forehead against his, all tears forgotten. His eyes met mine, but he was not affected by our distance. A small part of me realized that he was used to it, that he had been thoroughly indulged. He did not smile or blush at my proximity, merely treated it as a fact of life.

"I do, I hate this house, and I'm beginning to hate Whynne too," he said, and I couldn't help but laugh again. "Things like this would not happen in this house."

"Things like what?" I asked, my eyes closing slowly as he continued to speak. A part of my mind knew that I should have stopped him, that he should return to sleep. But he was awake now, and he was talking. For the past few hours, he had not been.

"You, lying in my arms, laughing with me and not basking in the fact that the smoke outside is slowly killing me; that should not happen here," His eyes closed at the statement. "I would lie here and think about you, from the moment I met you until my father died, but that love could not happen. Not here. You would never do anything more than stick your tongue out at me when you thought I wasn't looking.."

"Because you were Luka Kinsley," I summarized, "and I was Wren Nettles, a maid."

"Because nothing good happens here," he corrected. "And nothing good happens in Whynne. I've come to that conclusion recently. You are the only thing of worth here."

"And you teased me about being pessimistic," I said. "Think of the fact that you woke up today. Some might think that to be good."

"There is no other way for me to be in Whynne," he repeated, shifting closer. "If I do die," he whispered, "lie in my arms before I go, then I'll be happy."

I pulled away, wrinkling my nose at him. "Awfully morose."

"If I tell you something," he said quietly, "then you must not tell anyone else. Otherwise I promise you that I will let myself die out of sheer spite." I raised my eyebrows, knowing that half of this was for my entertainment. "When I was younger, I mused that once I touched you, I would never be able to stop. And now I am here, and I love holding you," taking in my amusement, he added, "it's a huge embarrassment to have such great interest in a girl who leaves ink prints wherever she goes."

I hit his chest teasingly, snorting at the statement. "Tell me something useful."

"I think it hurts because I'm both Unseelie and Seelie," he

said, moving on from my disgust, earning him a snort. "My mother did not fare well when my father decided to engage in landscaping to punish her. More than that, I think it's built up over time. I shouldn't have gone to the village again so soon."

"Your mother was an Unseelie," I pointed out. "You are still half Seelie."

"Which is why I feel sick," he said simply, "and Kristin does as well, but he does not wish to alarm Adam." I tilted my head in interest. "You know that the fae are tied to the forest," he dismissed.

"But you said Unseelie respond differently," I said, settling closer to him. It did not feel as imperative to grab Kristin anymore, or even to wait for Winry. If anything, I could have done without them. "You don't talk about your mother often," I pointed out, and he only blinked in response.

"Are you interested?" As if I ever wasn't.

"No," I lied, and he saw through it plain as day.

I saw his eyes go over my shoulder, looking at the black drops on the windowpane no doubt, and he seemed to consider them for a moment. I could tell that he was mentally debating with himself, having an argument about telling me something, and then, suddenly, he said. "My mother lived here as well."

Ah. "You and Kristin boarded up her rooms then."

"She did not have rooms," he said, and I couldn't hold back my interest.

He was quiet for a moment, not looking at me but still looking out the window. A part of me wanted to turn to look too, wondering if something great had changed to get his interest.

"Seelie can be cruel," he said simply. Because in his experience, that had been true. "She did not have rooms, but he kept her here."

I shifted closer to him, not pressing more, not wanting

more. Instead, I felt his heartbeat beneath me and listened to his breathing. "We'll move again tomorrow, you'll be fine by tomorrow," I said with a sort of finality. "We'll make it to the other side of Whynne, then we'll know what to do."

He nodded almost imperceptibly at the statement, his hand raising to my hair and pushing it back, tucking it behind my ear. His thumb lingered there, just behind my ear, tapping the skin lightly and considering me.

"Luka?"

"Thinking," he said, and I waited for a sarcastic quip to follow it. But none came. Finally, he decided to speak again. "Mainly about you, if I have to admit."

"Luka, you should go back to sleep," I whispered, settling against him. "Might I remind you, you almost died today."

"You keep saying that, but I'm reassuring you that I did not," he said. He was chatty now. "We'll leave as soon as possible," he agreed. "I want to leave." He held me tightly, too tightly, like I was the only thing keeping him from sinking under water. "Even if it is to just another corner of this hellish country."

CHAPTER EIGHT

He was not better the next day, he was still tired, not even waking up when I did, nor commenting on it when I stared out the window. The charred skeletons of the trees from the night before remained, and they crawled closer to the Kinsley estate, visible through the thinning leaves of the forest. It would be only a matter of days before they were outside our door.

Artur was wary but justified. We had no place in mind, just the idea of leaving settled. Even Artur, who lived as a bachelor and spent much of his life on the run, tended to have some sort of clue where he was going. But I don't think he'd ever gotten into half as much trouble as us.

And so, with Kristin refusing to leave Luka's bedside and Luka obviously out of commission, it fell on Adam and I to take Artur to the tavern to calm him, and even Lindy did not envy us. Especially since a sort of awkward unease had settled between the two of us.

"How many more drinks do you think it will take before he is ready to leave," I asked, eyeing Artur at the end of the bar as he swallowed down yet another cup. I fingered the edge of my cloak as I watched him, the hood drawn over my head doing little to counter the fact that every so often Artur would slip up and call me by my name.

"I am tempted to cut him off," Adam said. "Kristin is an awful drunk too, but nowhere near as bad as Artur. This monk could drink us out of house and home." He sighed while tracing the edge of his beer glass as he watched Artur wearily, unlike the Kinsley brothers, Adam was not feeling patient enough to allow Artur to gamble that day, earning him a few drunken ramblings about how inconsiderate Luka was for falling ill.

"He's had eight glasses," I noted. "Most people would be done by now."

"And yet the bartender continues to serve," sighed Adam. He did not have the same patience for the seedy locations Artur chose to drink at, nor the seedy bartenders. A part of me assumed that he secretly missed his previous life, one where things were far more upscale and everyone who served you made sure to do it well, not letting you go past excess. But he didn't say that, in fact, he did not say much at all.

He merely looked down at the paper in front of him whenever he thought I wasn't paying attention, his half-hooded eyes taking in a familiar face.

Why he bothered to still look at pictures of the King I did not know.

Why he wanted to leave Whynne so badly, I did not know. If anyone should have wanted to stay and confront Camden and Theo, it should have been him. But a newly minted scar sat on his lips, and with that came a feeling of responsibility, I guessed. Maybe he wanted to go back. Maybe he was only humoring us because he was bound to Kristin now.

"Has anyone ever told you that you think extremely loudly?" Adam asked. "I'm not mourning my relationship with Theo, if that's what you're wondering."

Wow, he'd caught me. "I'm not," I lied.

"Right," Adam said, "and Artur is perfectly sober. Theo tried to kill me; I do not harbor positive feelings towards him. I want to end things as badly as you do, but I understand that we need to set the board before we can play; it's all about strategy. If we were to survive as we are against the King of our country, the King of one of the largest, most sophisticated countries in our part of the world, it would be by sheer dumb luck alone, and I don't consider myself a fan of that plan."

Right, I almost caught myself saying, echoing his words. "Dumb luck has served me well before," I said. "Believe it or not, it kept a man from singeing off my eyebrows once."

Adam laughed lightly, looking down at the paper in front of him once more. "I wish we knew more of our situation, these things do me no good, there's no truth in them, it's all propaganda. Theo's second cousin runs half of them, and she's a real treat. Relying on Artur's social skills is not serving me well either, which won't do good for voyaging. I wish that we could just go up to the soldiers and ask them."

My eyes slipped over to him, brows raised.

At the end of the bar, Artur was cackling, his voice so loud that almost everyone looked. He almost fell off his chair with laughter. But Adam's eyes slid to mine, and immediately he understood.

"I think he's had enough," I began.

"This is incredibly stupid," Adam started.

"Artur will surely get alcohol poisoning if we hang around much longer... But perhaps we could find a kind soldier to help us carry our friend to the outskirts of town."

"We are the two with the most recognizable faces in town and have no ability to shield them—"

"I don't know about you, but I am feeling much too tired to carry my dear old dad," I insisted. "But surely some brave, strapping young lad..."

"How do either of the Kinsleys stand you?" Adam retorted, rolling his eyes as he pushed away from the bar.

It wasn't a no. I looked at him closely to see what his definite answer was, watching as he placed his hand on Artur's shoulder.

"Come on, old man," Adam said, his eyes connecting with mine. It was a go then. My, what stupid ideas are bred between humans.

ARTUR STUMBLED BETWEEN US, HIS SHAKY, FRAIL LEGS hardly able to hold up his body as the effects of liquor set in. The main key to thoroughly incapacitating him was just standing aside rather than actually helping him. With that small action and Adam and I trailing behind him, Artur went flying everywhere.

"It's a shame," I said, almost saddened by the sight of him. "He can be quite clever, and he is talented." Alcohol took that away from him and, wanting to keep his mouth shut, we had given it to him. Even though it turned his skin yellow and made his breath smell so vile that it was almost like he was rotting from the inside out. "Believe it or not, Artur can be a fairly good friend."

He kept asking and, because his hangovers were cruel and his tongue could be sharp, we let him go to the taverns. It was easier than having him berate us.

"Does he have any outstanding warrants?" Adam asked.

"Not that I am aware of," I said. "But it is likely."

"Hopefully, he does not provide his name," Adam mused. I could have told him that Artur almost never provided his real name, but I thought that much was already implied. Anyone who had spent five minutes with the man could have guessed that.

Ahead of us, Artur tripped, landing on his face for a moment then quickly scrambling up. He was not let in on the plan, but he did understand that he wanted to go home, and he wanted to go now. If he knew which direction that was in, I did not know.

If any soldier could have turned up, that would have suited me just fine.

But none were interested in helping a drunken old man, not so long as he wasn't causing any trouble. All Artur was doing was knocking a few things down, not making it more inconvenient for others or attacking. The soldiers only passed him by. But then, finally, he did something of use.

An awful sound hit the air as Artur fell again. Not a crack or a pop, but a choke. A gag. Adam slowed at my side as it hit once more, the man quickly becoming sick in the middle of the walkway.

And because people were not too fond of vomit flooding their dirt paths, a soldier finally moved forward, pulling Artur off to the side and sitting him in the grass. Game set, begin.

Adam jogged up and I trailed behind him, trying to look every bit the concerned daughter, but willing to let Adam speak. It was better he talk than I did, after all, save for a few new inches of my hair, I looked almost completely the same.

But Adam? With his face now covered in thick facial hair and the scar dancing across his lips? I doubted most people would have recognized him.

"I'm so sorry, sir," Adam said in that smooth, charming voice of his that he had previously saved for chatting amongst nobility. "Is there a problem? You've found my father; I thank you kindly. My sister and I have been so worried about him." Adam was far too good at playing the part of the concerned son.

"Oh," the soldier pulled back as the broad shouldered, bald man looked at Adam with slight irritation, as if accusing him of failing his duties. Which I guess, since his father was supposedly wandering around drunk, was a fair assumption. "I just found him; he was dirtying the paths with his bile."

"Was he?" Adam said as Artur blinked up blearily in his direction, giving the slightest shiver as the guard lifted him back to his feet by the scruff of his collar. "I must apologize, my younger sister and I struggle to get him home when he is like this, it has been many a hard night for our father since our mother passed away last fall." How did Adam do that? How did he know exactly the right words to say to win someone over?

"Has she?" The soldier looked to Artur with something, it was almost akin to pity, as I finally caught up to Adam's side, keeping my eyes down as if in shame.

"Yes," Artur agreed. "My poor wife, she was beautiful, wasn't she?" Even drunk, he knew how to play along. Though he definitely did not look pleased about it. A conman like Artur knew that every interaction with the law was a risk taken.

"A great loss to our family," I added, my voice far higher and lighter than usual. "He has been wallowing for many a day now."

"If you could be kind enough," Adam continued, "perhaps you could help us take him to the edge of the village, surely we can find our way to our farm from there, it's just so hard to transport him in this state."

"What do you mean by *that*?" Artur half-slurred, but the guard only nodded.

I widened my eyes at Artur, hoping that he would take the hint and let the man walk him instead of being overly offended.

Artur only glared back, sobering up quick with a soured expression.

"Well, we must hurry," Adam said quickly, deflecting the soldier's attention from Artur. "My sister is young, everyone knows how dangerous nighttime is in Whynne. I would hate for something to happen."

"That is not a worry you shall have for long," the soldier grunted, but grabbed Artur all the same. I think he was a little pleased with himself, easily supporting most of Artur's weight while Adam, a burly man in his own right, claimed to be unable to manage.

"Why should we not be made to worry," I asked, rushing to his side as Adam pointed him in a direction and claimed that was where the farmhouse we lived in was. Unfortunately, it was the very opposite direction to the mansion in which we lived.

"Well, with the fires the Unseelie are less of a problem," the soldier said, training his eyes forward as he began the trek. "Little girls like you do not have to worry as much, so long as the fires are high around these parts. Of course, the King doesn't like it mentioned, but I think they're helpful. You must feel glad at the very least."

I could easily defend myself and was worried more about the King and his men than the Unseelie, but sure, I was glad. Glad he was talking.

"They've been working hard to keep us safe lately," Adam said, reaching for my shoulder as if reassuring me. "My sister has an awful fear of the Unseelie," he said. If he were a fae, he'd be choking by now.

"Don't we all," the soldier said, and I thought to look away before he could not so subtly look back at me. "No fear, the King has been hard at work taking care of that."

"I'm sure he has," Adam said, agreeing with such enthusiasm that it was almost obnoxious. "I'm sure he's been busy taking care of everything these past few weeks, and with a wedding on the horizon. There is far too much to address as of late, it would send my poor head spinning."

"Mine too," I agreed with a nod.

"You both make my head spin," Artur said poisonously at the soldier's side.

"No worries, it may seem overwhelming, but soon we will gain a little peace," the soldier continued, adjusting his hold on Artur to allow for the way the man tried to duck out of his reach. "We will be closing the borders soon, so that our efforts to take care of the Unseelie problem do not lead to it leaking out elsewhere, nor will we need to revisit it." Once again, he turned in my direction and I turned away. "No more worrying for girls like you, I know my younger sister is relieved."

"Forgive my sister, she's shy," Adam said, and I could feel his eyes on me. Perhaps I should have tried to be more subtle. "Closing the borders? That's quite a lot of work, but I suppose it ensures that no one leaves. However will you manage it, though? I've heard of so many defectors."

"We have double the number of new recruits coming in tomorrow alone," he grunted, and I felt a chill in my veins.

"Double?" Adam asked. "Double seems a bit much just to run the borders?" His voice was careful, still complimentary, but tense. Even Artur grew visibly strained at the assertion that there would be more soldiers.

"It's necessary," the soldier said. "We wouldn't be able to start checking travelers as they leave in and out of the country otherwise. We'll barely have enough to begin with—"

"Checking travelers," Adam said with a clipped voice. "Starting tomorrow."

The man nodded, not realizing what exactly he had divulged, or who he had divulged it to. "It's a hard job, but I am glad, I can keep my family in better conditions working these longer hours, and my captain is kind—"

"Your captain is Nikolas Harding," I said, hating the name. The soldier turned to face me and for once I did not think to look away. Surprisingly, he did not recognize me.

"The best captain one could have, the greatest tracker in the military," he informed me. "He's the one they sent to find that missing girl, the human one. Apparently he's got skin in the game, and they don't think anyone else would be capable of finding her. Like she was so average that most of us would not know her if we saw her," he scoffed. "I would recognize a proper lady anywhere." Somehow, I doubted that.

"Well," said Adam, not even caring that we were nowhere near the edge of the village yet, practically shaking with the knowledge that he had gained and the urge to tell others. "I must thank you so kindly for settling my sister today, but I believe we can take our father the rest of the way home."

"Really?" Asked the soldier. "It is no trouble, I could take him to your door if you'd like—"

"Oh no," I said quickly, wracking my brain for a proper reason why. "You mustn't, he has traps all over," we were in the countryside, after all, "incase those dreadful Unseelie come back. It's hard for us to navigate around them, let alone strangers."

"Ah," said the soldier, considering the man he was supporting, "well then." He released Artur, who tumbled to the ground in a regrettable heap that made the soldier grimace. The young man reached down, trying to help Artur once more, but I butt in.

"It's fine," I said. "He normally crawls home."

CHAPTER NINE

We took the soldier on his word since he did not seem to have much to lie about. We had to leave that night, the sooner the better. That much was clear, nearly everyone was in agreement about that.

Nearly.

Artur had kicked up a fuss, insisting that we should stay a while longer. He had bets going, and he didn't want to lose them. Kristin had hesitated, stating that Luka was not healthy yet and that our bags were not packed, but Adam shut that down immediately. Which meant that Artur was in a foul mood, talking about how we'd all swindled him.

If we stayed, we would have awoken to the army on the Kinsleys' front lawn, but Artur didn't seem to care about that.

But still, even knowing of that fact, not all were convinced. Not when hearing that we would need to move in the darkness, through the one area of Whynne where it was anything but safe.

"You need to talk to him," Winry said, having already decided that we were going no matter what. Winry didn't want to leave the plants she'd cultivated, but she also didn't want to watch them burn. She had a sort of rationality to her, knowing that she could not stop the army that was approaching even if she tried, and that she had halfway won... since there was no way to make it out of Whynne in time.

How long it would remain locked down was anyone's guess, likely until Camden found us, but that was not a pressing concern at that moment.

The fact that Luka refused to leave during nightfall was. Even though we all knew why, that there would be only one way out once the night took over, through the forest. The woods that we had nearly died in just a month prior.

He refused. Still sick and still bed bound when I left that morning, he refused to even discuss the idea.

Which set Winry off.

Watching her stir the tea she'd brewed; I couldn't help but wonder if she'd regretted coming along. She could have been happily settled with Eli, the man who had tried to court her so long ago, had she not come to visit me, and she truly gained nothing aside from my company in being here. But there she was. There we all were.

Worried about being found. Scurrying once again like rats, because there was no answer when one asked how to bring down a king. This was it.

"You're going to give him this," Winry said. "You'll tell him it's from you and it'll put him in a better mood." Never mind the fact that Luka had never indicated a liking for tea. But Winry had known him longer than I did. "He'll take it if you give it to him."

My sister placed the cup and saucer in my hand, warmth emanating from the plate, and the tea a dark brown color that was nearly black. I wondered if she had found the tea in the cupboard and added a little something of her own to it to aide in relaxing him.

Not even Kristin had been able to get him to agree to leave, but Winry believed in me. She believed that I could convince him to get out of there and I wanted to believe the same.

He had stated that he hated the estate anyway, and we could not stay. I failed to understand how he could argue against leaving.

Still, looking down at the tea made me swallow hard, not knowing what was coming was difficult. I took a sniff of it, an earthy scent typical of tea filled my lungs, and then I looked once more to the door that stood in front of me, Luka's door.

I knew he would not answer it. I knew he could still not walk far, and that his brother was hoping for a miraculous recovery. A part of me wondered if I should knock at all, but then I thought better of it, knowing that if he thought it to be anyone else, he might have been insulted by a lack of knocking —but then, who else would visit him? Lindy did, I suppose, in short spurts when Adam came, she followed the young man like a shadow. But Adam would come with Kristin as well, who was not prone to knocking—

I was stalling.

Stalling because I didn't want to argue, not while he was sick. Not while the soldiers hunting the Unseelie drew closer outside. I just wanted him to agree.

I closed my eyes, raising my hand and stepping forward. I didn't even get to rap on the door before it opened in front of me, Luka's face appearing, blinking down at me as if he wasn't expecting me. I took the slightest step back, not anticipating him to be walking again so soon.

"Wren."

"Luka," I replied, raising the cup of tea up to him, more to act like a barrier between the two of us. He looked down at it, surprised that I, of all people, would be bringing him tea.

"I thought that you had more copies to make, and that you couldn't come until later. Not that I don't find receiving your company earlier to be a pleasant surprise."

"I've been sent to convince you," I replied and then, realizing how meek the statement sounded, I added, "I tried to convince Kristin to simply strap you to the roof of the automobile instead."

Luka gave a small laugh, the corner of his mouth twitching as he stood aside, allowing me into his room. He looked better, more fully colored, more mobile. It was a relief.

"You've made quite the improvement since I left this morning," I acknowledged, not having expected it. Kristin had claimed his bedside for most of the day, so I had tried to do my best to stay busy, going off with Artur and Adam when asked. But I was not ready for how quickly a fae could heal.

"I'm not completely better," he replied, and I could feel his eyes following me as I moved around the room, watching as I carefully set the tea for him on his bedside table and sat atop the large mattress that we often shared. "My magic is still not fully returned, thus why I'm hesitant to go into the woods, or rather, to let you go into the woods knowing what's out there."

I nodded in understanding, averting my eyes as he walked around me, picking up the cup from the table and inhaling the scent. His body was in sight, but his face was not, which was good, I didn't know how I could convince him if I looked him in the eye. Lord knows what he would say.

"You made this?" He questioned. "For me?" Did people not often do that for him?

"Yes," I lied, keeping my eyes low. "I did." I could hear the cup clatter against the saucer once more, its contents untouched. "Do you not like it?" I asked, raising my head to look at him. His eyes flicked over to mine, a strange look upon his face.

"No," he said, and that was that. Winry was wrong that it would calm him. "Wren, do you want to go that badly?" He asked, his thumb brushing the edge of the cup as if contemplating the liquid inside.

I scoffed, looking at him in astonishment. "They are hunting Unseelie here, you are an Unseelie—"

"Do you really want to go through the forest in the dead of the night," he asked, his voice still even. "The Gancanagh is still out there."

"It's not about what I want," I said. "It's the only option that we have left." Not the right thing to say, in hindsight. At least, not by his reaction.

He sighed, finally sinking onto the bed beside me, his thigh pressing against mine. "There are times where you should choose your opponent wisely," he began. "This would be one of them. It would do you well to remember the last time."

"I am choosing the Unseelie over the maniacs burning the forest," I informed him. "I would hardly say that that is a bad choice, knowing that the last time I was there, most Unseelie would not touch me—"

"Because you were practically claimed by one," he retorted, his eyes narrowing at me. "Do not forget that, I haven't. Neither has he, I'm sure."

I turned to look at him head on, a glare spreading across my features. "I handled it."

"You got pulled out of the forest by Adam the first time, then collected by me the second."

"I can take care of myself," I retorted. "I handled myself before you arrived." With a little help but, it would do him well to remember that I disarmed a powerful Unseelie with a very strong burst of electricity once. I was not helpless.

"You lack control when it comes to your powers, we're lucky that you haven't electrocuted yourself," he informed me, causing me to swerve around, gaping at him. I could not fully contest the accuracy of the statement, but— "Wren."

"I am not waiting—"

"Then I will stay here—"

"I will haul you into that automobile myself," I snapped, my face stopping just inches from his, gasps of my breath hitting the air as complete and utter outrage filled me. "Do not threaten to stay here now when you were planning to flee to Haldia just a few days ago, you are coming with and you are staying beside me. You are not staying a moment longer in this stupid house!" I jerked him down by the collar, pulling him even closer as I informed him, "you are ill, and there are men hunting people like you. I would rather die—"

"I am trying to help you," he argued. "Put your ego aside for five minutes and admit that this is something you do not want to do. Admit that you do not want to walk through that forest in the middle of the night. More than that, admit that it is dangerous."

I could have laughed. "Make no mistake, Kinsley, I am the one who is saving you from your own complete and utter stupidity here, not the other way around. I can hold my own—"

"I am not arguing that you cannot hold your own," he said. "Although, I will say that you are untrained and have yet to master your powers, but I do not think you incapable with them—"

"Then you are afraid because I am a human," I snarled.

"I am not afraid because you are a human."

"Then a woman—"

"Not that either," he proclaimed, looking at me incredulously. "Wren, it is dangerous any way you go about it, and is it so hard to believe that I would not want that for you when I cannot even lift a hand to help you? Because to watch you fight on your own would make me feel useless—"

"Then be useless for a matter of hours," I proclaimed. "So long as you come with, be anything you like. I do not care."

He scowled at me, his hands raising to where mine knotted in his collar, attempting to peel them off.

"Luka," I insisted.

"Wren," he replied. My fingers tightened on him. Threatening to stay here? Wanting to stay another day knowing that he was in danger? He was trying me. "You're being infuriating."

The nerve.

My shoulders rose in irritation, every bit of air I inhaled not feeling like enough. He took it all in, the way that I looked just about ready to murder him.

And his eyes softened.

His face fell, concern coating his features, but he looked at me all the same, his voice soft and uncertain. "This is what you want?" He asked, as if such a thing were not obvious.

"Luka, we don't have any other choices."

I don't know why, but he looked sad about that. I think for a moment, he was going to remind me that I could wait, but then his hands were on mine again, untangling them from his collar.

"This is really what you want," he repeated, sounding miserable, and I didn't see how he could fail to realize it. "Wren, I want to be able to protect you—"

"I'm not asking you to," I argued.

"I want to," he proclaimed.

"Drink the tea," I insisted. "I worked hard on it, it'll calm you."

"Winry made it," he summarized with a scoff, and I realized how transparent I was in my desperation.

I folded my hands in my lap, sighing. I knew I had lost

already. He took one look at me and leaned over, his fingers on my chin forcing me to look in his direction.

"I'm sorry," he said softly.

"Another day is everything, Luka. Another day means more of the forest burning and more smoke, more dead Unseelie," I began before his thumb pressed against my bottom lip, silencing me.

"I know," he said, exhaustion showing on his face at the thought and only doubling when his eyes drifted from mine, looking over to where the cup of tea sat. He regarded it, shaking his head before turning back to me. "I don't need to relax, Wren. I don't think I could."

"You're sick," I said, my brow furrowing. "You need to. You'll only make things worse this way. You need to relax."

"Need and want are very different things," he explained rather obviously. And then, as if he heard his own words, his face flickered, his hands lowering from my cheeks. "Another day and I will be fine," he insisted, but even he seemed to realize the problem with that statement.

I would have reminded him we did not have another day if he didn't know that already.

"This is the consequence of running, I suppose," he said. "We've put all of this off, and now it's caught up to us at the worst possible moment. I should have argued against Adam, but I did not wish to side with you either," he said, and I pulled away, sticking my tongue out at him. "Careful, I'm tempted to bite it," he joked.

I quickly pulled it back.

"Come here," he said, holding out his arms.

"Not until you agree—"

"You've already won, Wren," he admitted, spreading his arms out further. "No lavender tea or mint leaves required." Is that what was in there? Vile.

Deciding not to wait any longer for me to contemplate the awfulness of tea, he wrapped his arms around me, pulling me down onto the bed with him as he laid on his side, his lips pressing to my forehead.

"I will not sit in the vehicle that Kristin will no doubt insist that we bring, nor will I stay with Artur like a useless lump," he declared, ignoring my huff of protest. "I will not let anything happen to you," he said in argument. "Whether you can take care of yourself or not does not matter, I know that you're capable. It's just..."

My lips pressed against his, stopping him before he could come to the right word.

"I love you," he said once I finally pulled back, he cradled my face, looking at me in a way that made me feel like it was too much. I was too seen, too known, too wanted. "Wren, when all of this is done, we are not coming back to this house. Nor the mountain. We are never coming back. We will go wherever you want, so long as it is not here."

"Greenable," I said, because that was the only place I wanted to be. "We'll make it back to Greenable together."

"Greenable," he agreed. "We'll steal the estate from my brother. He can stay somewhere else."

"And this place?" I asked quietly.

"We'll sell it, or leave it to rot," he said. "This house is a monstrosity, and if it catches fire from all of this, that's all the better. I do not care, so long as I have you and you are where you want to be, I could not care about anything else."

"Then you should get ready to walk," I said.

CHAPTER TEN

The sun sat low on the horizon, sinking further and further out of sight, the moon not destined to rise on that night as darkness had painted the sky. In front of us, trees stood, their white and grey trunks jutting from the ground; thin, knobby structures, the leaves from their branches having fallen, leaving them barren. They looked like the bones of some great beast, one long since slayed. Nothing moved amongst them, and not a sound was heard, save for the whipping of the wind through the gaps in the forest.

Below our feet, stifling even the heaviest of noise, sat piles of white ashes, carried onward by the wind. They blew across the landscape like sand in a desert, sometimes lingering in the air. It was like a fine snow, one that had fallen to the ground and drowned out even the hardiest of plant life, clinging to anything it could find. Unlike snow, it did not reflect the light, it merely swallowed it whole.

It was dark, not full darkness, but bound to become it at any moment, and in my sister's hand, around my neck, and at the front of the car sat the only sources of light there would be, lanterns. Adam was not daring enough to spare a spark of fire when so many trees around us had been burned already. We couldn't risk any more than those lanterns, not while we travelled along the edge of the forest. There was too much of a risk that a guard would see us and report back to his troop about what he had seen. The orange light of fire was a suspicious thing, and though it burned at the military's hands, they knew when it wasn't from them.

So we would travel in near darkness through the woods, the most dangerous forest in the world. All we could do was hope beyond reason that we'd make it out alive.

"You'll be safe," Adam insisted for the umpteenth time, holding Artur's arm. "There's a small, narrow road, and you'll be riding in the car. I assure you; Kristin is an excellent driver." From my previous experiences with Kristin, I knew that statement to be a lie.

Artur stumbled while trying to argue with Adam, "yes, but don't you think it's wiser to stay here? A nice house where we have a roof and no expenses, a pleasant little village nearby. Don't you think that is preferable to this? To walking to our own deaths?" He wrung his hands together nervously, looking back to the Kinsley estate with a sort of wistfulness as the two neared the car, not even being allowed the time to pack a bag.

"The Unseelie are far more scared of you than you are of them," Adam insisted, pushing him forward a little more. Artur had never been in the forest, he'd avoided it for almost all of his life. Now he was forced to face it, and he reacted accordingly, like a cat being thrown into the ocean. To Adam's other side, Lindy huffed, unafraid.

"I do not wish to ride," she repeated for the umpteenth time, not caring for the conversation that took place next to her. "Only cowards would ride. My age should not force me to be beside this one." Under her breath, she added, "he smells."

"Now, now, Lindy," Kristin said, leaning against the automobile with a smile. "Don't say that in front of Artur. I'm sure that, if given the chance, he could be very brave." He was still in good spirits, glad that Luka had agreed to the plan. Even if Luka and I insisted on staying close to each other, the two of us scanning the tree line over and over again, it meant that Luka was there. Better walking through the forest than waiting for the guards to arrive.

Still, Kristin shivered and I guessed it was at how empty the woods seemed.

"It'll be fine," Winry insisted from beside us, annoyed that this was our largest concern. "What's the worst that could happen? We made it out once before, what can stop us now?"

"That is not the question to ask in our situation," Luka muttered, taking another quick glance behind him. The smoke had parted, and aside from the darkness, one could see straight through the woods, but that meant very little when it came to the Unseelie. "There is no guarantee that you will exit these woods a second time."

"Everyone needs to stay calm," Adam said. "If anyone gets nervous," he not so subtly looked to my sister, "there is always a seat up front. This includes you Wren, no need to show off today. If you're tired, you go in."

"No thank you," I chimed in bluntly, squinting at the car. "I've seen Kristin's driving." I barely wanted to ride with him on a street, much less a poorly maintained trail through the forest. And if there was only one seat, then I already made up my mind on who would be the one to take it. Even partially recovered, Luka still looked weak.

Thin, long white bark peeled from the trees outside of the Kinsley Estate, exposing the reddish-brown core of the trees. Birch, they had been planted long ago by the old Kinsley gardener, then they'd been swallowed by the forest, bleeding into an eclectic mix of trees, making up the backyard of the Kinsley estate. Their bark peeled off in the cold, sections of it waving like paper in the strong gusts of wind that blew through the all-but deserted forest.

It did not make the woods seem inviting. I don't think anything could have.

"Just a reminder, I will be in front of the car. Wren and Winry will walk on the sides, Luka will be on the back. You go inside if you start to feel tired, Luka," Adam said.

"I will not," Luka informed him curtly. "I will continue to walk in spite of it." Thankfully, Adam was used to being argued with at this point.

"Great," he replied sarcastically. "Well, then," he turned, facing the woods, his teeth gritted as the mouth of the forest seemed to stare back at all of us. "Here goes everything," and indeed, there it went.

CHAPTER ELEVEN

It was a slow journey. I suppose every venture into the woods was like that, regardless of who you were or what you were capable of. The Unseelie were far too dangerous for you to travel through the woods without taking due caution.

And our lanterns were far too dim too feel safe.

The pathway leading out of the forest seemed to disappear the second the car had rolled past the first tree, all the trunks standing just close enough to each other to feel restricting. It was supposed to be a path, a back entrance cut long ago by the Kinsley's patriarch before his passing. But it felt very little like a road, and very much like a trap. Even Luka struggled to keep his breathing even as we pushed further into the woods, the air leaving him in audible breaths.

We did not truly know where we were going, just that so long as we cut through the woods, it would be very hard for the guards and soldiers to find us, which was ideal. The road had to lead somewhere, and wherever it went, that would hopefully be where we set up camp. It was almost as if we were putting our trust in the woods, but I suppose we had had to trust in a lot more unsavory things as of late.

"Do you remember when we were younger," Winry spoke, barely audible as she stood on the other side of the vehicle, her lantern visible through the closed windows. "And your mother used to tell that story about the girl in the woods, the one who followed the trail of clover to get there?" It was a distraction, a small one to prevent the fear from growing in her. There was more rustling in the woods, more sounds as we walked further from the village and the estate. I knew from the reflection in the glass that the streetlights were quickly disappearing. "I wish I had asked her to sing the song that went with it more than once, I can barely remember it," Winry continued.

"I wish I remembered it too," I said, trying and failing to keep my eyes forward, the air beginning to feel almost as if it was tightening around me. "She said it was from her village."

"I want to go there some day," Winry said, and I knew that her tan skin was turning white at the knuckles around the handle of her lantern. A loud pop sounded from behind us, Luka moved to grab my wrist and I stayed firmly attached to his cuff. "I want to see where she was from," she said tensely.

I heard the cracking of a twig coming not from behind me, but close to my side, and I flinched. "It is not much," I admitted, my voice catching. "But she missed it greatly. She always wanted to go back, but there was never a chance."

Adam cast a look back, and I knew that he wanted us to be quiet but could not bring himself to ask. I could hear the tension in Winry's voice, the bravado leaving her as the evening sun dipped lower and lower, now but a sliver that was barely visible in the woods. It was coming, darkness was coming.

"Keep moving forward," a voice urged, and I looked back to catch Luka beside me. Him. I knew it was him, no one else, not the

Gancanagh returning. Still, I reached back, my hands tightening on his cuff, not caring where he was meant to stand or that he had fallen out of line, just that he was there and I did not lose him.

And then, the sun fell. And there was darkness.

My eyes clenched shut, even as the lantern in front of me blazed. I heard the softest whimper on the other side of the carriage and the shuffling of feet in the trees. We were there, we were in the woods, and the Unseelie were awake.

I could see them moving amongst the trees as we pushed forward. Their fur rubbing against them, their yellowed eyes staring out at us. I saw a few thin creatures that looked to be young women who stopped when they crossed our paths—their eyes lingering too long on the human members of our party. I could hear the bark crack beneath the fingernails of other curious fae. Out of the corner of my eye, I saw a large, black cat-looking creature, one with hungry lips that seemed braced to pounce but did not move. I had forgotten what it was like moving through the forest.

It felt like every shadow was watching us.

"Do you remember when we were children," Luka spoke again, because they knew we were there and there was nothing we could do to stop that. Across the way, Winry was no doubt faltering. "Do you remember when you would pick pine needles for me, Winry, and you would make your nanny boil them so that there was this awful tea?"

A small murmur of agreement sounded across the way, and I saw the other lantern start moving slower out of the corner of my eye.

"I still hate that vile drink so much, and all thanks to you," Luka said, his eyes no doubt tracking Winry at the same time as mine did. "But you made me drink it every time I saw you, you said it was my medicine. Every single day, when you weren't watching, I would go to the kitchen and beg for a pitcher of water to wash my mouth out. My brother thought that you were trying to drown me, since he picked me up soaked once or twice."

A small laugh, not a real one, responded. Winry was scared.

"Winry," Luka said tightly. "You have to keep walking. We can put you in the car, but you have to keep walking to get to it. We can't stop moving."

"But I can't see in the car," she said, "there are eyes looking at me." I saw Adam's shoulders square at that.

"Keep walking, Winry," I said, because I knew what she did, but so long as they stayed on the sides alongside the trail, we were alright. "You need to keep walking."

I heard the lantern clatter, but I did not see it fall. She was still there, she was still walking beside the car.

"Put your hand on the doorhandle, Winry," Adam requested. "If you hold on to it, then you won't fall behind. So long as we stay together and no one slips behind, we will be alright. I swear, Winry."

"Why are they looking at me like that," Winry asked, her light still far from the car.

"Because you are Seelie," an unfamiliar voice responded, and I heard Winry's lantern clatter, Adam disappeared from in front of us just as quickly. I could not breathe, I could not even begin to think—

"It's alright, Winry," Adam said as the car slowed to a stop beside us, Adam kneeling beside Winry just a few feet behind it.

Her face was whiter than any sheet.

"They do that to scare you," he said, slowly helping her to her feet. "They can carry their voices, it's no worry. They just like to play with you... They love playing with Seelie." Winry did not look as if she wanted to play, and Luka and I looked on in terror, waiting for something to come. Thankfully, it didn't, but... "Shhh, it's alright," Adam soothed, practically carrying her as she stumbled upon standing up. "You're fine." He was well versed in calming the ladies of the court.

"Luka was right," Winry said, her voice so quick that the words almost smashed together. "We're going to die."

"We're not going to die," Adam soothed, patting the back of her hands. "You're going to go in the car..."

"I'm not going in that car," she spat, looking at it with terror in her eyes. "They will break in there and they will kill me."

"They're not going to kill you, Winry," Adam said.

"How do you know that," Winry whimpered, nearly dropping her lantern, Adam quickly lunged for it, catching it before it hit the ground as Luka tensed beside me.

We needed to start moving, and quickly.

"Winry," Adam warned as Winry tried to pull away, no doubt wanting to scramble out of the woods the way that we came, not knowing how disorientating they could be. "Winry, you need to listen to me."

The driver's side door of the car opened behind Luka and I, and Kristin's head popped out as he no doubt wondered what had removed Adam from our path.

Winry was in tears when I looked back, bubbling over with fear. I wanted to go back and comfort her, but Luka's hand remained on me, his eyes casting a warning look in my direction. Behind us, we heard a moan.

And then more noise. More and more sounds growing in the woods, coming closer to see what the commotion was, and to address the smell of humans in the air. Not good. Not a good time for Winry to seize up.

The car behind us groaned when Kristin stepped out as Adam struggled to calm her, the girl practically fighting in his arms. I didn't even see Kristin walk by us, but then, there he was. He took one look at her, her sobbing face and desperate claws, and he let out a sigh of exasperation.

Then, without so much as a word from Kristin, he reached over and flung her over his shoulders, prompting her to scream. Not that he cared much about that, he simply walked on by, Winry wailing in fear in his arms, and jerked open the car door, practically tossing her in there. I think he offered her a single pat of assurance, but that was all.

"It's nice to see that such great patience runs in the Kinsley line," I whispered before Kristin rounded the vehicle behind us, getting into the driver's side and slamming the door.

Luka did not respond to my jab, instead he kept his eyes on the trees with startling intensity. I thought back to what he said about protecting me, and my hand rose to rest on his shoulder.

If the Unseelie did not know that we were there before, they most certainly knew it now. Adam seemed to realize that, lifting his hand momentarily by his head, seeming to consider it for a moment before ultimately lowering his hand once more, not flicking his wrist or calling flames to life. The lack of fire spoke volumes about what he was really afraid of.

"We need to move," Adam murmured, pushing past Luka and I. "You two can stay together, I don't care. Just start moving and don't look back."

We nodded, tearing our eyes away as the car began to rumble, the engine turning over. Once, twice, three times Kristin turned the key, the engine whirred, but the vehicle did not spring into motion. Around us, the woods echoed. My hand jumped from Luka's cuff to his fingers at the sound of a twig snapping nearby, all eyes on the car as Kristin tried to get it moving.

A long, weary sigh was the only response that Luka could provide.

"What's the hold up," Adam called the moment that the car

window was wound down, as if we didn't already know. It was almost as if the world around us was mocking us. The moment Adam asked, the car let out a pop, smoke pouring out from under the hood.

"Magic," Luka said, and my fingers tightened around his, willing my eyes to stay forward as he not so subtly glanced back, pulling me in closer.

"The whole forest knows we're here," I summarized, eyeing my reflection in the car window, unsure as to whether I'd rather be in it or out. "They will not let us move."

"Don't say that," Adam barked, hearing my statement and turning away from Kristin, almost looking half crazed as he approached me. "Do not say anything along those lines, Wren. When you say things like that, you're willing them into existence."

"But why not say it," said a voice that was neither mine nor Luka's, "if it is true?" The voice carried on the wind, seeming to wind through the trees.

In an instance, Adam's hand was up, the flames roaring into existence within it. In my empty hand, I felt the sting of my own magic, my eyes wide with concern as I looked for the source of the voice.

There was nothing, just the trees, which were hardly trustworthy to begin with.

I felt my back touch the side of the vehicle, I hadn't realized that I had been backing up until that moment. I struggled to swallow my breath as it sat like a lead weight in my throat. My hand rose, the blue sparks climbing higher as I looked around me warily.

"Do not worry," spoke the wind. "I will not be the one to hurt you." Definitely not reassuring in the slightest.

"Hello?" I called out, and in a half second Adam's hand was on my mouth.

"Wren, for god's sake—" Adam began.

"Hello," the forest echoed back to me, my voice distorted and drawn out, the sound seeming to dance in the air. The fingers clasped over my mouth seemed to press even harder at that. I felt Luka stiffen beside me.

Still, there was no hint of where it came from. I could tell that both men were mentally flipping through their glossaries of fae, trying to find an answer. But this? This did not feel like a singular entity, nor a traceable one. This felt like the forest itself.

And for some reason that was more horrifying than anything I could have imagined.

"Get her in the car, Luka," Adam commanded through gritted teeth, but Luka made no move to hide me. "Luka, get her in the vehicle."

"She doesn't want to go," Luka spat quickly, and I didn't. Not in the slightest. But we all stood there, plastered against the side of the vehicle, waiting because there was no other choice.

The moment seemed to drag for hours, even if it was only just a matter of seconds. The three of us stood, waiting for more words to come, for that strange voice to wrap around the trees once more. But we did not talk to it, we did not dare to make a sound. And so, it did not speak back to us.

We were left in silence, the creatures of the night undoubtedly still moving around us, and the car behind us still stalled. The harsh darkness made the trees seem whiter, they almost seemed to glow. A cold wind, one that roughened the skin and made hair stand on end, blew through, lingering around us.

I could feel it brush through my hair in the briefest of moments, lifting the strands even as I stood surrounded on nearly all sides, forcing my eyes to shut in fear that I would open them and see some other being standing there in front of me. Instead, it was just the wind.

Crack! It was loud and sounded akin to a gunshot, almost making me sink to the ground, but the car sprung back to life after a matter of moments behind us, the engine puttered loudly as the dull sound of Kristin's head hitting the steering wheel in relief complimented it. Adam peeled his hand from my mouth, first turning slowly to the woods, then back to the car.

I had no doubt in my mind that he was thinking to himself that he wished it was him in the car. We had a long night ahead of us but, I did not feel as if anything would touch us anymore. Whatever had happened, whatever brief contact had been made, it kept the other Unseelie at bay; a fact that made me shiver with dread.

CHAPTER TWELVE

"The trees keep shifting," Adam said. "They're growing restless."

The sun had long since begun to climb high in the sky and pale blue light leaked into the forest through gaps in the dense branches. Yet even with the sunlight, there was no release. We were supposed to have found our way out hours prior, but we still wandered without an end in sight, moving through the night for the sheer matter of fact that there was no stopping in the woods of Whynne. And while those in the automobile were capable of sleeping safe and sound; Adam, Luka, and I were faced with the frightening realization that we were no closer to leaving the woods than hours before, and our bones were growing weary.

"Maybe if we're lucky, they'll put down roots," I said sarcastically, earning me no amusement from anyone else.

"We should stop," Luka said for the umpteenth time, no doubt eyeing how I stumbled and feeling disorientated himself. "This is not doing us any good." We were both beyond exhausted, that much was clear, and even Adam's shoulders had begun to slouch. I wasn't even sure that Luka had recovered enough to use his powers yet, since traveling had no doubt affected him.

I knew it did me, I could feel blisters forming on my blisters, the shoes I wore somehow burning through their soles over the course of the night. All of that walking, and we had not gotten anywhere. I was tempted to scream.

Maybe if I did, I would get lucky and the Unseelie would do me the favor of putting me out of my misery.

"We cannot stop along the tree line," Adam insisted, looking down once more at the old compass that Kristin had pulled from the vehicle's glove compartment for him, refusing to give up. I think he felt like he had to guide us and do it well, because if he didn't, we might question his loyalty.

As if anyone had the mental ability to question anything at that moment.

Mentally, I fought the urge to just throw myself on the car and sleep on the hood somehow, letting everyone else continue on. I was never made for late nights or early mornings, I was solely a creature of the afternoon. Moving through the night had all but killed me, and when that sun first rose, I felt a greater fatigue than I had ever felt before. I'm pretty sure Luka was waiting for me to collapse.

That assumption, along with the pure spite that ran through my veins, was what kept me up and walking.

"Every time I turn around," I muttered under my breath in irritation, "those trees have moved again, and I understand why the King thought it so imperative to burn them." They certainly were trying me. "Does the compass even work?" I said, squinting at Adam, "I thought that compasses and other magnetic devices didn't work in these woods. There might not be any point in staring at it."

Adam did not respond, prompting Luka to murmur in my

ear, "Wren, I do not think that is a question he wants to answer. The forest might be playing with him a bit."

"If it is, he is most certainly not a willing playmate," I responded, eyeing Adam as he sat his hand down on the automobile that moved at a slow saunter beside him, cursing under his breath as he looked down to the compass once more. "I don't know why you bother, Adam," I called. "I thought we were supposed to be moving in a straight line! That seems like a difficult thing to mess up."

Yep, definitely not a good topic to bring up. Adam grumbled, shooting me a look that was far more malicious than any I'd ever received before, and then turning his attention to the skyline once more.

Beside me, I heard the door of the automobile open, despite the fact that it was most definitely in motion. The motion allowed a small set of feet to step out, an overly irritated look painted across the owner's face as she ignored the requests that she get back in the vehicle.

"The monk is telling stories," Lindy spat, moving to walk beside us. "And not a single one of them is true."

"You would actually be surprised how truly depraved his life really is," I said in response, glancing over at the girl as Luka not so subtly glanced over at the vehicle, no doubt processing the fact there was now an empty seat. "Artur has done many horrible things, the more disgusting the story, the more you should be inclined to believe him."

Of course, Luka didn't move to fill the seat, even if he was still weak.

"If I were a coward with a gambling problem, I would not be so proud," Lindy declared, wrinkling her nose. "It is unbearable in there between him and the one that jumps at every little noise. Then the big blonde one keeps talking. I wanted something to show up so then they would be quiet."

"Kristin can be overly talkative," Luka agreed, sliding his hands into his pockets as he walked behind the two of us. We'd pretty much abandoned Adam's idea of flanking the car. "Most people find him quite charming, actually. He's a very genuine person."

"It is not that I don't like him," Lindy said, squinting at the statement. "He is the most favorable amongst them, but at every silence he talks. I cannot stomach it, and the monk snores, so I cannot try to sleep through it."

"Perhaps we should take a break?" Luka's voice raised hopefully, prompting a response from Adam.

"We are coming up on something soon," Adam replied, his voice clipped and his pace quickening. He was far too confident in himself to stop at this point. That would be admitting defeat.

I groaned, throwing my head back in irritation. No one so much as acknowledged me. What I would have given to rip that compass out of Adam's hands and throw it into the trees at that point.

"I have seen a great many Unseelie this trip," Lindy noted as I whined. "Yet not a single one has approached us. It is disappointing. I heard these tales of how they are great and powerful beasts, yet they cower before a pair of headlights."

"They have other things to be scared of, Lindy," I said.

"The woods are rather fond of Wren, they would only send her their absolute best," Luka added dryly, and I couldn't tell if it was sarcasm or a bitter admission. "The only things that will come out to bother us will be the most horrifying beasts of the lot."

"Like the Gancanagh," I said with a shiver, my eyes drifting down to the ground rather than staying upwards. I didn't know if I would ever recover from him.

"I wish to meet him again—" Lindy began, earning her a

foul look from Luka. "He is interesting," she said bluntly. "I like things that are interesting."

"I should think that no one would like to meet him again, Lindy, considering the fact that he very well almost killed us all."

"He is not the only thing to try to kill us though," Lindy said, dismissing Luka's concern. "Nor will he be the last," she sounded fairly sure of that, which, considering our situation, was reasonable of her. Lindy was ever realistic.

And Adam was ever optimistic. "Do not speak of us dying," Adam commanded from ahead. "Not while we're in these woods. It's not a good idea, Lindy." Lindy only huffed in response.

I shook my head at her, the slightest smile pulling at the corner of my lips as I turned to look at Adam once more, taking in the way that the scenery around us changed. The trees overhead seemed to have more of a curve, their barren branches forming arches above our heads as the leaves that undoubtedly once covered them laid in a thick layer on the ground beneath our feet, wet and therefore silent.

I had an odd feeling that I had been there before. But my memories were still occasionally hazy, and I couldn't completely trust them, still... It felt like we had traveled far further into the woods than intended.

"We would know if we were back on the mountain," I said suddenly to Luka, unable to shake that feeling. "I would be able to tell, right?"

"Hopefully?" He looked at me with concern, not for our situation but likely for me. "It is a bit of an incline, Wren. We would realize if we began it."

"Right," I said, looking away from him and back towards the front once again, still unable to escape from that feeling. "I suppose you're right, mountains are rather obvious, aren't they?"

"If you're of sound mind," Luka stated. I rolled my eyes at the implication.

Still, I let my head fall back as we walked below the canopy, unable to stop thinking to myself that if the leaves were still there, it would look all too familiar. Much like where I had been a month earlier, where the cobwebs darted between thick leaves and fluttered in the wind like rags.

"This is not incidental," I muttered, because it couldn't be. Someone had once told me that there were no coincidences in Whynne. "It's too familiar, Luka."

There was no way that we were not approaching that clearing. I'd had the nightmares too many times now, I could recognize it anywhere and anytime, even in the dead of winter. My eyes lifted to the branches over me and the way that they guided us further. I heard the breath catch in Lindy's throat, looking down to see the severe expression painted across the younger girl's face.

But the trees themselves, once teeming with life in that area, were silent.

"Adam," Luka warned, even Kristin had stopped driving, realizing where we were. But Adam? Adam kept walking, almost as if in a trance. He did not even try to stop, perhaps knowing that we would follow.

Or perhaps, whatever was forcing him onward knew that we would follow.

"Adam!" I didn't have the patience for him to turn around, nor did I believe he would. I snapped out of Luka's grasp and away from the others, running after Adam and catching his arm in my hand, jerking him back to face me.

His hazel eyes were dazed. He tried to pull away from me—Something had taken him. Perhaps the woods itself.

"Adam!" My hand snapped across his face, spinning his head with its force.

A gurgled breath responded to me, his hand lifting to his cheek as he looked at me, shocked. But then, he seemingly realized what he had been looking at just a split second before due to the force of my blow, he turned back in that direction, a strangled sound escaping him.

I felt my blood go cold in my veins. My hand still hung in the air from slapping him, the sting of his rough skin meeting mine echoed across my flesh.

I had a feeling that I did not want to look.

"Wren," Adam said my name at the same time it was called in the distance, the rest of the group speeding up to catch up to us. I just stared at him, the thick black curls that had begun to cloud his dark skin, the roundness of his hazel eyes as his mouth fell open...

And then his hand rose to my chin, jerking it to look in the same direction as him as Luka and the others caught up, the sight rendering me breathless.

Because they should not have been there. Out of all of the people in the world, they should not have been there. Not in that clearing, not where the trees parted in the woods.

And more pressingly, we should not have been there. By then, we should have been halfway across Whynne, well past the woods, and approaching a new town already.

But as the trees twisted and shuffled, they guided us there. They lured us closer and closer, masking the terrain, and now we could see what they wanted us to. Our greatest fears. They were leading us there, begging us for help as something far worse than fires and deforestation awaited on the horizon.

Rows and rows of tents were set up in the clearing under which the Unseelie tree's roots laid. Thick, red, weatherproofed tents in red crowded the space, nearly filling the whole clearing. Soldiers, not trainees or humans conscripted for war but actual trained men, sat around their fires in the middle of the forest, waiting for orders. Waiting to do what? We could only guess, but if prior experience had served me well, I knew that they meant to destroy what laid beneath their feet however they could.

They sat polishing their pistols, engraving their bullets, and readying for whatever might come. This was the King's great war, the one advertised in the papers. A bunch of men sitting in the forest, fighting that which could not fight back and calling it justice, murdering the innocent for a little slice of fame and glory. Just like Nikolas, those men had probably grown up dreaming of being heroes.

And this was their great heroics? Dragging old, weakened Unseelie into town squares for executions. Digging at the earth in the center of the forest, knowing that nothing would stop them, that nothing could fight them as they reached for the roots of the Unseelie tree.

"No," Luka's voice was light and barely there in my ear, so ripe with disbelief that I could hardly recognize it. He kept talking, but I could not understand him. Not as I stared, scanning the tents in front of me.

My eyes searched for one so large and ostentatious that it spat in the face of others. The only kindness being that it was not there. The King had not deigned to sit and watch. Instead, he sat in his castle, far from the Unseelie and far from the men who camped out in the forest, ready to do his bidding.

But he knew. I knew that he knew. I knew that he had ordered them to be there. I knew that he was aware that the Unseelie would not put up much of a fight.

I thought of that night so long ago, when he had dragged Adam and I out here, was that the last stand?

"This is where running gets you," I said, my face growing

pale with the sight before me. "This is what a month of avoidance, of planning, of trying to be smarter and better does." I tore my eyes away from it, an almost strangled feeling resting in the back of my throat. "I hope you're happy," I said, moving back to the car. "We need to find somewhere very good to hide, and quick." Because that was all we ever did, wasn't it? We ran and we hid and we wished that we were strong enough to do something else.

CHAPTER THIRTEEN

Soldiers moved below us, different than the guards I had known. Far more deadly.

Each one no doubt looking to carve their own tale of heroism, each one no doubt knowing nothing other than a hatred for the Unseelie. Humans and Seelie alike, each wearing the dark burgundy uniforms that had become so important in the past month, their youthful faces still filled with life and hope unlike their fallen compatriots who sat in taverns with deep scars marring their skin. A few of them, however, were injured yet undeterred, likely only more determined to ruin the Unseelie just as the Unseelie had wounded them, their bodies supported on canes and their limbs wrapped in heavy gauze. They had recently come from fights.

I wondered if they even knew what they were doing. I wondered if they knew that below their feet sat an essential part of Whynne, that soon they would be the ones to destroy it, ending the Unseelie entirely. I don't think anyone had dared to dream of such a thing in a hundred years or so.

One of them smiled, big and bright, his eyes twinkling as he laughed at something someone else said. He reminded me of the Nikolas I used to know, before Luka and before the war. When he only dreamed of following his family's legacy.

The last time I saw Nikolas, his eyes were dead, and his pistol was in the hands of another. He watched without emotion as his men shot the Unseelie, as if he was there but not really there. Distant. Broken. Would these men end up like Nikolas?

"I do not see the point of sitting here and watching," Lindy complained, slumping over herself as she sat on the stump directly across from mine, looking down at the soldiers gathered in the valley below us. She was not weighed down by the sight.

"We're making sure that they don't get near us," I said. "Because there are roughly two hundred of them, and seven of us."

"Equal odds," Lindy huffed, leaning back. Behind us, the others rushed to make camp, afraid of what was going on below, but not willing to pass up a moment of sunlight in the woods. It was better to rest soon, while the sun was still high in the sky and the worst of the creatures had subsided, than regret it later, when we would have to hunt once more for an exit from the woods.

Kristin had offered to let Lindy watch him repair the vehicle or sit and figure out the location we were at with Adam; but Lindy had chosen to perch beside me, watching the men below go about their day and hoping they would not look up and see us.

Her eyes were narrowed, as they always were, in constant defiance as she watched the soldiers, no doubt thinking hundreds of things about how ill prepared they were and about what sort of country Whynne was. Her hands moved over the intricate braids she wore, her once sleek black hair having become frizzy and untamed but still mostly braided, as she continued to watch. Though she would never admit it, I thought it might have been a nervous tick.

Which would make sense, because after knowing her for a month or so, I could not imagine her being more than fourteen. And now she was embroiled in the conflict of another country.

But for some reason, that didn't faze her. Even as it terrified me, even as Adam paced back and forth, thinking of a thousand different things we should do. She did not seem to worry in the slightest.

In fact, Lindy looked down on the groups of men, and she almost smiled. She had a look to her that spoke of conquering. Losing was not an option.

I could not imagine being so bloodthirsty, and at only fourteen. Then again, I knew nothing of where she came from, and she knew very little of Whynne.

"I wish I could say that it's not always been like this," I said to her as she watched the men below move, her eyes followed them like they were ants running around their hill and she was the god watching over them, kindly for the moment, but willing to destroy them at any second. "But I suppose we are so used to Whynne being this utterly awful, disastrous country that it doesn't strike us."

"This country has been fighting itself for a very long time," she agreed, I didn't know how much history she knew, but that was a pretty accurate statement.

"Seelie vs. Unseelie," I said, "for hundreds of years now. The funny thing is, there's not that much difference to them if you ask me, aside from point of origin, I guess. There are Seelie that eat children just the same as Unseelie, they just have the added benefit of walking around in the daylight."

"You'll find that it does not take much for wars to start," Lindy replied, shifting in her seat. "Everywhere you go, people fight over these small things, and then they make them disastrous. This is just a place where the fighting seems to go on and on."

"That's a good way of putting it," I agreed with a nod, my eyes drifting up to the palace above it all, wondering if Theo could watch the soldiers from his balcony. Almost as if to reassure myself, I looked down to my hands, spreading them and watching the electricity move across them. I had gotten much better control recently.

"We could just roll a boulder over them and be done," Lindy scoffed, ignoring the fact that there were no boulders to push and that we would still be far from done, especially now that the King had found the area again.

I hid my smile, "and what will that do, Lindy?"

"It'll cause us more trouble than it's worth," said a voice gruffly from behind me, as Adam moved around me to crouch down with us, looking out at the scene before us. "It's hard to realize how absolutely fucked you are until you're staring down the other end of a cannon," Adam noted, shaking his head at the scene. "We've royally pissed him off."

"Watch your language, there's a child," I began, grinning when he looked over at me with an expression that could have bitten my head off. "I seem to remember it being a brilliant plan to keep running, one that would never backfire in anyway. I mean, what was the worst that the King could do, gather reinforcements? Oh... wait."

"Keep quiet, I'm already hearing enough of it from Luka," Adam said. "He's pretending that he hasn't agreed with me on more than one occasion."

"I think he just wants to point out the wide assortment of soldiers made available to kill us," I said, shaking my head. "King Theo really does miss us. Of course, I would have settled for an invitation to the wedding instead of this."

Adam rolled his eyes, turning away from me and back to

the scene. "He's really going to do it, isn't he? All of these years that I've known him, and I didn't think he had such a thing in him, but he's going to do it."

"Camden—" I began.

"It's just as much his fault as it is hers," Adam said. "She may whisper in his ear, but he's the one that listens. This is Theo's beast, just as it is hers. They've already married themselves to each other in so many ways, they should both go down together, regardless of whichever one is directly responsible."

"Your king should not be allowed his crown," Lindy said. "He cannot wear it after all of this is done, he won't have the head to do it. I can promise you that."

Adam swallowed, every bit aware of what she was saying, but likely not wanting to agree. There were very few ways to take a king off the throne and keep him off it. "Who would be king if not him?" Adam asked warily, and that was the question that had consumed me as well.

But Lindy did not so much as think about it. "You," she said, not bothering to even look at the man. "You should be king."

"That is not—"

"You're a good person," Lindy said, as if that was the only pre-requisite for ruling a country. "Winry has said that you come from a good family too, one that is experienced in politics and change, though she also speaks of dowries and large houses most of the time when it comes to you."

Adam scoffed, "I will not marry Winry."

"No, you will become king," Lindy said as if it was as simple as that, her fingers drumming against the stump in a constant beat. "You are human, you befriend the Unseelie, you are kind to me, and you even show empathy for the tall one. Out of all of the people I have met, I would like it to be you."

"I think I would too," I said, and at the moment I knew I

meant it. It seemed so overwhelmingly stupid and optimistic to talk about such a thing, but I did anyway, "if we're supposed to be these great heroes rather than just a bunch of misfit kids dealing in magic, then I think that we should get a say in who gets the crown. I'm saying you. You're the lesser evil, I'd rather not leave it up to bloodlines and hearsay."

"Why not you?" He asked in amusement.

I shot him a look, a single eyebrow raising as I grinned at him. He already knew why not. I was not made for leadership, I was far too impulsive. "Because once this is all done, Luka and I will be going back to Greenable. We've already decided that, and I know that we will do so." It was the most optimistic thing I had said in a long time, but the others played along with my impossible future.

"What will you do there?" Adam asked, a smile tugging at the corner of his lips.

"Sit in the library and read every single book, make Luka get on his hands and knees and scrub the floor like I once did. Have peace and quiet, and never have to listen to your voice again," I said. "It sounds heavenly, doesn't it?"

"Ah, but I will be king," Adam teased. "You will have to listen to me."

"And we'll ignore every summons that you send," I informed him. "Just as I ignored all of the letters you sent me before. Luka and I will pretend that you do not even exist, staying alone in our little house until the end of time."

"And where will Kristin be?" Adam asked.

"At the capital, of course," Lindy scoffed as if it were obvious. I didn't know how much of this was pretend to her, and how much she considered to be an official future. "And I will visit you, once you make me ambassador to Haldia."

"Ambassador," Adam marveled at the girl. "You, dealing with other people?"

"I deserve some sort of pay for all of the trouble you've caused me since the day you picked me up from the docks," Lindy dismissed. "I will settle for such a title."

"And Winry will have her garden and Artur will have mountains of booze, we'll even build him a little cabin in the backyard to keep him comfortable," I summarized. "And whatever goes wrong next in Whynne, it will not be the crown's fault. And it most certainly won't concern the Unseelie."

"A beautiful future, Wren," said a voice from behind me, and I grinned as I looked back and saw Luka standing there, Winry nearby and Kristin smiling as he leaned against the vehicle. "You forgot the part where you will go out of your way to annoy me every day, and there will be ink splatters on every surface. All theoretical, but..."

"Maybe someday," Adam said wistfully, looking out at the valley. "But I would be an awful king." I could hear Kristin laugh in agreement, but I was more preoccupied with other things, like grabbing Luka's hands that rested on my shoulder and gazing up at him, seeing the light in his black eyes.

We would have a future together. Somewhere amongst those somedays, there was something for Luka and I. Whether it was in Greenable living peacefully, or somewhere else, always looking over our shoulders. Luka would always be mine.

"Artur went for a walk," Luka informed me, gently squeezing my shoulders. "I can't imagine he'll get very far. His mood seems to get worse with every step we take into the forest."

"I was just talking about the future," I told him.

"I know," he said, while pressing a short kiss to the tip of my nose, even though he was never fond of public affection. "You will get back to Greenable, Wren. Maybe not now, but someday."

"Is that a promise?" I asked him teasingly. "And will you be there? Perhaps you should swear it."

"Always trying to trick me," he said with a laugh, looking up from me as he shook his head. Luka smiled more these days, it felt good.

"Artur's taking his time," Winry noted in the background, tapping her foot in impatience as she broke the spell of high spirits that everyone had been feeling. "It's been a while since he left."

"Mhm," Luka nodded in concern, his eyes meeting Winry. "Hopefully, he did not fall."

Hopefully.

Everyone looked away, ready to go back to what they were doing, but then Lindy's fingers stopped drumming, and they did not start again.

"I do not see Artur along the tree line," Winry noted as I blinked at Lindy's features, the girl seeming to pause entirely. "Luka, what way did he go?"

Luka sat in the background, struggling to remember as I moved to crouch beside Lindy, my eyebrows furrowed.

"Lindy?" Adam asked, wondering what the commotion was. His voice trailed off as he looked and saw where Artur was, his mouth fell open at the same moment as mine. My skin felt cold as fear settled over it, and Adam's hand gripping my forearm to steady himself did not help it; he was just as pale and shocked as I was.

Down near the valley, where no human was meant to go, far beyond civilization—there sat our monk. Just feet away from everything, defenseless and with no excuse. Drunk.

He was always drunk. We shouldn't have let him be that way.

Just feet away from him stood the guards, capable of seeing him with the slightest turn of their heads.

"Wren, are you alright?" Luka asked when his attention returned to me, strolling over to where I stood. He stiffened, and then...

I knew what he would do before he did it, but I was powerless to stop him. The moment they saw Artur, the moment they grabbed him, the moment he undoubtedly let out a whimper—Luka was gone.

"—No!" The word tore out of me just as quickly as he took off, his long legs carrying him down the mountainside as I barreled after him, desperate to stop him. But he didn't stop, he didn't dare to. Instead, he went out of his way, running as fast as he could to save the pudgy little monk that had once tutored me, the dangers of the soldiers and the danger of what he was running into was lost on him.

"Luka—Wren—Don't!" Adam screamed after us.

CHAPTER FOURTEEN

My feet padded against the ground faster than I had ever moved in my life, acid burnt the back of my throat as my body hurtled after Luka's, practically tumbling down the hill.

Adam was not far behind and Lindy took off after him, shards of ice jutting out of the ground from her powers, threatening to trip Luka and I. My mind screamed indecipherable words as all that mattered was this all-consuming feeling of fear, the need to catch Luka and stop him, even if that meant losing Artur.

The urge to save the old man was intermingled with the need to save Luka, my only understanding being that if I reached the bottom of the hill, I could stop it. I could stop the inevitable. I just didn't know how yet.

Beneath my feet the ground turned slick, and I only felt the slightest sensation when my foot slipped, sending the rest of my body rolling down the hill in a tangle of limbs and clothing.

"Wren," Luka had barely said my name before he was caught in it as well, pulled in as I tumbled after him. Our hands desperately gripped for any purchase on each other that we could find, his hand gripping the back of my head as we moved down the rocky surface, cushioning the blows.

Down and down, a hoarse scream hit the air, scattering the birds in the trees. "Wren!" Adam did not come any closer, likely stopping with the realization that he could not catch up to us in time, not as Luka and I hit the bottom of the hill, the air escaping both of our lungs upon impact.

I gaped at Luka the moment my eyes opened, pain settling into every joint, my fingers woven into the linen of his shirt. He looked down at me in a similar way, as if realizing what had happened and the fact that we were mere feet from the camp, lying bruised and battered at the bottom of a hill. He panted in exhaustion, falling beside me in a quivering lump, my every breath shuddering as it escaped me.

He'd taken the brunt of the fall. I did not think that was accidental.

"Luka," I managed as I pushed myself onto my forearms, my body barely able to support itself. Somewhere up the mountain, Adam had begun to run once more, taking off after us, trying to get there before anyone else did.

"We have to get Artur," Luka said, unsteadily raising himself from the ground. "We need to get him before anyone else does."

We did. I shuddered, taking his hand as it was offered to me and letting him help me to my feet, my eyes darting around the trees. I hadn't heard a single sound, not yet.

"We need to move," Luka said, catching my face before I could look back at Adam, Luka's eyes were filled with concern as he regarded me. "They're going to find us."

They would, that much I was certain of. I nodded at his command, taking his hand into mine and forcing him to hold onto me, even if he tried to resist. "Together," I demanded. "You and I, Kinsley."

"Together," he agreed, his eyes moving along the trees, searching for somewhere, anywhere—We heard leaves crunch in the distance. Someone was coming.

My body was already too accustomed to reacting.

I shoved Luka against a tree, hiding him behind the thickened trunk of one of the older maples in the forest, my hands braced to either side of him, my eyes blazing as, upon seeing his mouth open, I pressed a finger to it. Our stare communicated one word, *quiet*. I barely breathed.

"You heard it right?" A voice spoke in the background, far too confident. Those soldiers always were. "He can't be out here alone."

I swore I could hear the blood rushing to my ears as the footsteps grew closer and closer, louder than any noise in the forest. Why would they bother to be quiet, they knew that they controlled the woods.

"There's always strange sounds out here though," another voice spoke, a woman. "These woods are teeming with Unseelie. Maybe we're wrong."

"A man like that doesn't get into these woods alone," the voice responded. "You heard him."

I was fairly sure that I could feel every breath that filled my lungs. I shifted my weight, trying to feel ground, and—

"You hear that?" The voice spoke. "Who's here? God, I pray it's an Unseelie." The footsteps came closer and closer. "But maybe if we're lucky, we'll get a little something more."

"Mmphf!" Suddenly I was the one up against a tree, Luka's hand pressed against my mouth, the young man leaning into my ear to quietly shoosh me. The soldiers were already beginning to look.

"Hello," said the female's voice, too pleased, too prideful.

"We know you're here, love. Might as well come out and get it over with. Are you Unseelie, or human?" Her footsteps were close, likely at the tree where Luka and I had just been standing. She veered around the side for us.

My eyes clenched shut, my shoulders rising and falling with every breath.

"There's something," the voice—a man, I decided—said. "Look at how the leaves are kicked up, it's something big."

This is going to be how I die, I decided. At this point, I would have given anything to have a chance at one of those boring deaths that no one ever thought twice about.

"There's no use using your magic, whatever you are," the woman spoke again, and I heard her gun click at her side. "We've been trained to spot illusions." My eyes shot open, taking in Luka's expression.

Not good.

Not good at all.

Luka did not look confident. His eyes kept flickering shut and, with them, his magic faltered.

My eyes moved down, desperate to look at the ground, desperate to look anywhere but up, desperate to pretend that we would be fine. But then I saw it... My skirt, flattened against the tree, just an inch of the fabric curling around the trunk.

An inch too much.

"Ah," she said once more. "You really shouldn't wear dresses, little girl. They make it oh so hard to run—"

A bullet hit the wood with a bang, splintering it by the side of our heads, and I couldn't help but scream.

Loudly.

"Oh what a wonderful monster you are," the man murmured, stalking towards us. "What kind of Unseelie are you?"

We would not stay still. To stay there was a death sentence.

In a second, I was at another tree, Luka standing behind the one beside me, every breath coming out too loud, too strained, too guttural.

"Hide and seek," the woman taunted, and I looked around the trees to see her, a middle-aged woman no older than fifty, her face weathered from the strain of war, her hand bracing her gun. "Come out, come out, little girl. We won't hurt you, much." I realized too late that I had lost track of her companion, unable to spot him beside her or amongst the trees. "If you are who we think you are, then we have a little surprise for you."

Desperately, I searched for him. The other soldier had to be somewhere, he had to be there—

"Boo."

The action was immediate the second he curved his head around my tree, instinct overwhelmed my common sense as I thrust my hand towards him with a flash of blue. I barely touched his skin.

He was on the ground, making a gargling sound. His hand was clutched to his chest and his eyes were wide as he realized—

"That's the one, Aida."

A scream ripped out of me and sent me careening backwards as a series of shots rang out next to me, knocking me from my feet. Five of them. The revolver had to be empty.

Luka's hands were on me before I even hit the ground, catching me and pulling me upwards in a stumble as the clink of bullets being reloaded in the chamber sounded in the air. More footsteps filled the air, more people approaching.

Luka pushed me out of the way as another bullet zipped through the air, making my ears ring. Bullets, more and more bullets, and then the crack of the wind—

"Luka!" I helped him up, pulling him towards me by his

shirt, our chests against each other as we stared into one another's eyes, our mouths open wide. "We need to run."

"Oh no, I just thought I would stay here," Luka's words tumbled out, the two of us stumbling together as a harsh wind broke past us, more people appearing, not just men with guns but Seelie and gifted humans too—

Suddenly the trees that had once meant unimaginable danger became the only place to hide. As we ran, the strange creatures of the night scattered, The Unseelie having hidden in the woods, but now facing the fact that we were dragging the soldiers they hid from back into the trees.

A whip of water, liquid and moving far too fast, shot past me. All I could think to do was swing my arms behind me, a large arc of blue firing out from my palms and sweeping across the ground.

"Argh!" It hit something if I had to guess.

I mustered another bolt of electricity with all I had, trying to make something larger, something that could hurt more than one person. My body throbbed with the effort, my hands burning as I swung them back once more, the crack of wood stinging my ears as it made contact with something, a trunk, and split it.

I could hear my heartbeat drumming away in my ears.

"Keep looking forward, Wren," Luka begged as I nearly ran into a tree, my eyes almost rolling back in my head in pain as I hit the side of it, sending my shoulder back.

The urge to scream hit me, but I swallowed it down. Not today. Not now.

Another large crash hit in front of me as I ran, my feet leaving the ground as wood splintered, Luka struggled to catch me and force me onto my feet as we disappeared behind another tree, both trying to catch our breath. The smallest cry escaped me as the thunder of footsteps continued, slowing only slightly as they tried to make sense of where we were, the splintering of the tree providing only just enough cover.

Luka's arms wrapped around my neck, his forehead falling on my shoulder as he shook with pain, my shoulder grew wet. I struggled to keep myself together, desperate to find some sort of escape, but the further we ran, the further away from camp that we got, and if we moved towards camp then it would be even worse.

"We know it's you, Miss Laurent," another soldier spoke, his voice echoing through the trees. "Your friend told us as much. You just confirmed it. He'll be glad to be rewarded for this."

"No," I shook my head from side to side, burying it in the side of Luka's neck as I spoke almost inaudibly. "No he didn't."

"We know that your little Unseelie friend is here, we know that you have Adam. There's no point in running, we know it all," the voice taunted, and I latched onto Luka's clothes, struggling to stay quiet. "He traded you for a bottle of booze and a chance at freedom."

"He didn't," I said, growing angrier. "He wouldn't. Artur wouldn't dare. We're friends."

"You can step out now and nothing will be done to you, or you can keep running and see what happens," the voice taunted.

It wasn't real. None of this was real. They wouldn't find us.

Luka gasped in pain as the footsteps grew closer once more. I became more determined to not let go of him.

"We can end this, little girl. You can do the right thing. We can do that, or you can face the end. Trust me when I say you don't want whatever is coming for you."

I didn't mean to. I shouldn't have cried. Tears just began to escape me in hot rivers, falling without my permission, nearly choking me.

"Wren," Luka's voice was soft, his hand raising to the back of my head, running over the knotted hair there like he had so many times before. "Wren," he repeated my name again, his arms tightening around me. "Wren, I'm still weak. I don't know what to do."

Where would we run? How much further could we go? Would Adam find us? Was Adam stupid enough to keep looking?

"I love you," Luka said, his voice desperate, holding me as close as he could. "I have always loved you." His hands were on me, moving constantly, almost irrational in their attempts to soothe me.

The forest was quiet. So quiet that I could hear our hearts beat. I knew that the quiet was bad, that it had never done me any favors. It practically rang out like a warning.

The soldiers were searching for me, my ears ached from their shots. It was only a matter of time, and it felt like there was too much to say and not enough words to say it.

I could not even begin to tell Luka what he meant to me, only nod my head against him, gripping him as if he might disappear at any second. I wished I could put it into words at that point, that it was still such a clear and easy feeling as the first time. Time had made it stronger, but harder to explain. Luka didn't struggle with words, however.

"I have wanted you for so long," Luka admitted, "and I have made so many mistakes with you. You will have to forgive me for those, perhaps when you are feeling particularly kind." His lips touched my neck and suddenly I wanted to be closer to him, as close as I could be. I wanted to bury myself in him and escape the world, to focus on him and him alone. "I am yours, I am always yours, Wren. I have always been yours."

Why did it sound like that? Why did it sound like the end?

I guess we were unlucky enough that it could be the end, that this meant death or something worse.

I could hear them growing closer. I knew that they were coming. I knew that the soldiers would find us.

Luka pulled away from me, his hands only moving from me to wipe away any evidence of tears from his face, the reddened rims of his eyes still giving him away, but I didn't dare to inform him of that. No, I could only look at him. I only wanted to look at him, and he stared in turn, memorizing me as well, clinging onto the details.

His hand rose to my hair, clasping one ink-stained lock between his thumb and forefinger, gently rubbing that spot with an unbearable kindness, his face moving once more into a smile, one of those smiles that only I was lucky enough to receive. A sad, loving smile.

"Wren, will you let me do something awful?"

I had no idea. I only wanted things to be okay, the two of us to escape. I nodded.

"You will never forgive me," he admitted. "I know that you won't, I know you. You will curse me with your dying breath, but I can live with that. I can survive knowing that." I didn't understand. "Look at me, look me in the eyes."

My eyes lingered on his, unable to look away, my arms still around his neck, hardly an inch between us. I felt his breath spreading across my skin. For a moment, I thought that he would kiss me.

He did not.

"Wren," his voice was silken, so sweet that I wanted to hold onto every word, my heart and mind filling with his voice. "I love you," he repeated, and I knew it completely. With every inch of my body, I knew that I was loved, that I had always been loved. "No matter what you hear, no matter how your mind screams to turn back—You are going to run. You are going to run until you reach Adam, and you are not going to turn back, you're not going to make a sound, you're not going to scream. You're going to let me do this."

Do what? My mind was blank, unable to think. What could Luka do? Why did I want to run? Why did my already aching muscles urge to move again?

Some part of me screamed, some part of me knew. He had only done it once before, but the feeling was so familiar that I could not mistake it. But my mind just couldn't accept it, maybe because it was him.

"You will get to Greenable," he said, and his eyes were brimming with hot tears. I wanted nothing more than to brush them away, than to look at my Luka and kiss his cheeks, making him smile again. The desire fell over me like the haze that was clouding my mind. *Compulsion.* "You are going to fall in love again. You are going to have a good life. You're going to be happy. I promise you, it won't happen right away, but it will happen. You will wake up someday and you will be surrounded by people who love you, Wren. You already have so many people who care about you."

I couldn't resist it, my hands reached up to touch him the moment the first tear fell, desperate to wipe it away. He didn't let me, instead catching my hand in his and pressing it against his lips with so much care. His kiss tingled against my skin.

"You're going to live past me, alright?" He said, and my mouth fell open to protest, but found itself unable to. "You are going to wake up some day, and you are going to forget me, and it's going to be okay. It won't be a betrayal, it will be what I want for you. That's all I could ever want for you."

"Luka?" That was all I could say as my mind rushed against itself, my thoughts desperately clawing at the edges, trying to reach some kind of understanding. That little word, his name, was the only clarity I felt. "Luka, I love you."

His eyes softened so much at that, I could hear his breath catch in his throat, see the regret cascading over him. "I love you too," he repeated. "I love you beyond reason and sensibility, Wren. But I need you to let go right now."

Let go? No. No, no, no. I trembled, the words catching in my throat, my body desperately fighting as I released him without my permission. A sob escaped me, a single tear crawling down my cheek, he leaned forward, pressing his lips to it.

"Goodbye, Wren," he said, his hand coming to rest at the back of my head, his thumb stroking just behind my ear. "I almost wish that we had spent less time fighting each other," he said, and his thumb tapped that space before it pulled away, lingering in the air as he looked at me with miserable eyes. "Run."

And I did.

CHAPTER FIFTEEN

THE WOODS PASSED ME BY IN A FLURRY, AND EVEN THOUGH I tried to fight it, I could not stop. When I fell, I just got back up again, moving even though I was desperate to stop, desperate to turn around and go back. The words just hung in my head, a sorrowful goodbye and a command to run propelling me far past my own physical ability in a direction I knew all too well.

The only relief was having them. Because so long as they stayed, a part of him remained. So long as I heard them echoing in my head, I knew he was alive.

And so long as he was alive, I knew I would find him. I might strangle him with my own bare hands when I did, but I would find him all the same. A part of me hoped that I would never run into Adam for that reason, because even if I was cursed forever, it was a better reality than the one where there was no sound in my head, no voice to tell me that he was okay.

But I couldn't run away forever.

The sun began to fall in the background, time seeming to bleed together as I kept moving in an endless haze.

I saw them pass me by, creatures with long floppy ears,

mossy skin, and yellow eyes. Unseelie, ones who were not given the opportunity to grab me. They were barely given a chance to know I was there. If I did not find Adam, they would find me.

And more than them, there was something else that I feared in those woods. Something else that could easily find me and capture me. Perhaps even break Luka's command. I couldn't help but look back as I ran, wondering where it might be in this large expanse of woods, if it was watching me and waiting.

If I would be cursed to see a bastardization of Luka's face rather than the real thing.

As the sky darkened, it became more of a chance. One moment there was light, the next moment the light was gone, the sun had fallen and the moon had slowly begun to rise, both hanging on opposite sides of the horizon as, devoid of thought and reason, I continued running. Running so much that my legs ached and my lungs screamed, the compulsion used on me far stronger than the one Luka had previously used on me, this time it was meant to stick with me.

A part of me realized that he probably figured he would be dead by then, not intending for me to wander through the night. But I did, my footsteps only slowing as the pain began to overwhelm me, but my feet still moving.

And I could not even complain. I could only look for Adam or wait for the worst. The darkness climbing in the distance painting a kind future in which the worse happened on my end, and not on Luka's.

But then when it seemed that my feet moved in circles, lost to the world, the forest seemed to whisper to me, speaking in a strange, foreign tongue.

A small blue light sprung to life, and my feet knew that that was the way to go. Then another, and another. Will o' the wisp, they led people to their destinies, those strange creatures that always seemed to spring into existence when most needed.

With them, my feet moved once more, my mind spinning but my body sure of where to go. So long as there was blue light, there was a path, and that path would lead me where I needed to go.

And then the world came to a crashing halt, going black. No noise, nothing, just the feeling of hitting something hard and then falling followed by the cruel sensation of landing on my back, but I felt so empty that I couldn't even process the pain. The urge to run, to do anything, left me.

"Wren," immediately hands were on me, trying to help me up, his voice booming in my head. "Oh god, Wren." I was pulled up by my forearms, still stubbornly refusing to open my eyes, to see whatever future sat in front of me. "Kristin, I found her!"

I knew it was Adam because the voice in my head stopped, Luka's voice. I didn't need anything else to recognize him.

"Open your eyes," Adam said, kneeling down on the ground beside me, still holding me up. "Wren, you need to open your eyes."

"No," I said, my voice tight, my eyes clenched. I couldn't. I could barely focus.

"Wren," Adam spoke again, giving my arms a furious shake. "Look at me, I need to see that you're not enchanted or anything. I need you to look at me. I can't take you with us if you've been compelled by one of them." He had no idea what had happened.

I hated crying. I always hated crying.

When Winry was little, she cried all the time, and my mother always tended to her. But whenever I cried, I felt like a burden. I never wanted it to happen, yet those past months... I was angry at the same time, it was building within me and slowly drowning out anything else.

"Hey..." Adam's voice was low, his arms around me immediately as I warily looked at him, unable to say anything. "You're okay, Wren. You're fine. You're home." He didn't know, he had no idea. "What's going on, Wren?"

I buried my face in his broad shoulders, wiping my snot across the fabric of his shirt. I could not look at him, I could not acknowledge that he was there. The voice was gone.

I heard footsteps approach, and I knew before they even spoke what they would ask.

"Where is Luka?" Kristin's voice, which was normally loud and enthusiastic, cracked. It was quiet and tense, suddenly fearful. "Wren, where is Luka?" He repeated.

I could not breathe.

"Where is my brother?" Kristin's voice broke, and I felt Adam stiffen as he realized what was missing. His mind must have picked up the pieces. "Where is my brother?" Kristin repeated, and there was a sort of desperation in it. I heard more footsteps approaching— Winry and Lindy no doubt— but I also heard Kristin fall beside Adam. "Luka."

"Kristin," Adam tried, but he could not stop Kristin from peeling me off of him and looking into my watery eyes.

For a moment, through blurry eyes, they looked so similar. Even though Luka and Kristin were nearly opposites in appearance, there were similarities between them. They had some of the same expressions when it came down to it.

It was like looking at Luka all over again.

I could not tell him what happened. "I'm sorry," it felt like such a frail and useless thing to say. Admitting it only ignited the fury in my blood more so. "I didn't want him to."

Kristin's face fell.

He got up from the ground, looking at me as if I couldn't be there, as if I shouldn't have been there. As if I wasn't real. Because he knew what I represented. I did not need to say what Luka had done.

"He did it, didn't he?" Kristin asked me, his eyes cast to the ground.

"He saved me," I whispered. "I don't know why. He should have just left me. He should have just run. I don't know why he insisted on saving me."

Kristin nodded, choking back a sob, every nod of his head feeling more and more like he was trying to convince himself more than anyone else. "He would be happy that you made it back then," he said, his hand clenched at his side. "I'm happy that you made it back to us," and if I didn't know that fae couldn't lie, I would not have believed him. Because the way he looked at me said it all, his eyes betrayed him.

It was clear that he could not bear to look at me.

"Kristin," Adam said, leaping to his feet just as my sister and Lindy arrived, catching Kristin before he could walk away. Adam's arms wrapped around Kristin, pulling him against him, both men equally matched in height. Hesitantly, Kristin's arms wrapped around Adam in turn—

"Wren," Winry barreling into me tore my eyes away from them, her arms around me as she knocked me to the ground, squeezing me as tightly as possible. "Wren, I thought you were gone. I saw you go into those woods and the soldiers going after you—"

"He had sold you before you'd even gone down the mountain," Lindy spat beside me. "He planned this. He is nothing but a traitor. He walked into their arms and the moment they let him speak, he demanded another drink."

Everything that I feared.

I could barely move. All I could understand was the anger beneath it all, threatening to consume me, lifting the ends of my hair into the air with its growing electricity. It threatened to spill out.

"We're going to get out of here," Winry began to babble. "We're going to go to Haldia, we're going to—"

"We're not going anywhere," I said, my voice not even sounding like it was mine. "I'm not going anywhere. Not without Luka."

"Wren, he's not here—" Winry began, and I could see her slowly try to figure out how to make me okay with that, how to get me to accept that. She had to get me out of there, she had to convince me to leave.

I couldn't.

"I am not going anywhere until I do three things," I spat, the anger in my blood had overtaken everything else. "I am going to get Luka back, kill that bastard king, and then I am going to skin Artur alive. I will settle for no substitutes."

CHAPTER SIXTEEN

"This is insane," Winry said for the umpteenth time, trying to convince me against it once more. "Wren, there is no logic to what you are considering doing."

"There is a sound logic behind what I'm doing," I informed her, pacing back and forth as I finally managed to pull Luka's belt tight enough around my waist, securing the pants and the bulk of the shirt that I'd stolen. I would not be caught out by my skirt again. "I am getting back Luka and getting revenge. There's nothing else to be said about it. Either you can join me, or you can sit back and watch, but I will not back down." In the background, the sun began to rise once more, Winry having insisted that I sleep on the idea and urging me into the car for the night.

Probably hoping that I would change my mind.

"We do not even know if he is alive," Winry protested, pushing off from the car door as Lindy looked on, far too willing to go along with anything. Winry would not let me go. "Have you considered that? The fact that by now, he may very well be dead?"

"He is alive," I snapped, nearly tripping over Adam as he sat on the ground, rubbing Kristin's shoulder reassuringly, his expression deeply strained. Kristin was beside himself, a fact that seemed to make Adam feel guilty, considering the fact that he hadn't been able to stop the two of us from going down there.

"How do you know," Winry screamed, shaking with anger, clenching her dress in her fists as she nearly doubled over. We had not fought so loudly since we were kids. "How do you know that he is alive, and this is not some hopeful delusion! Wren, I'm trying to take care of you, your mother would not want this for you—"

How did I know? How did I know?! "I can feel it," I screamed as if she was insane, as if she had insulted my very being. "I can feel him somewhere, I know that he is alive! I know it in my heart! He cannot be dead. He is not dead. Luka Kinsley is a thousand things but he is not dead."

"You have no way of knowing that," Winry growled, fierce tears bubbling in her eyes. "Trying to find him is dangerous, imagine if you do it all for nothing. You are my sister, I will not let you throw away your life for some delusion—"

Delusion? This was not a delusion. I knew it. I felt it in the fury in my bones, I felt it in every single gasping breath I took. I felt it in the electricity that built up in the air around me, small sparks floating as I stared her down, not even capable of justifying such a statement with a response.

He was not dead. He could not be dead. They would not kill him. Even though I was of no use now, and he had spited the King, they could not kill him—

I fought back the rage that brought sparks to my hands, the urge to scream that she did not know anything. She was the one who let me go in her place, who let me fulfill the contract instead of her. She was the reason that I was in this situation, and now she wanted to drag me to safety? To save me? If she was going to save me, then who was going to save Luka?

"I cannot do this if Luka is not with me," I admitted. "I won't."

"You do not know if he is dead or alive," Winry repeated, spitting on the ground in hot blooded fury. "Do not act like you do, because it is not possible."

But it was possible, wasn't it? It had to be. There had to be a way—

"—Actually," Adam's voice said warily in the background, pausing to take a rather large, nervous swallow. "She does."

Winry's face fell, all emotion slipping off of it. "What do you mean," she hissed. "What could you possibly mean?"

My mouth fell open and my eyes moved to him, taking him in with disbelief.

Beside him, Kristin turned, first in confusion, then in something more. His face changed, his shoulders dropping as something seemed to hit him.

"You are going to have to forgive me," Adam said, not just to Kristin, but to everyone. He reached towards the other man, squeezing his hand lightly before standing, once again swallowing his nerves. "I've known for a while, ever since I woke up with Kristin's mark across my lips. He said something to me just before he and Wren walked off, he practically told me."

Adam towered over me. He was there in front of me, looking as if we both shared a secret.

"You know, don't you, Wren?" Adam asked, his hazel eyes on mine, his body right in front of me.

"Know what?" I asked, alarm rising within me. What was he talking about? What could he be talking about? He acted like I should have been aware, but I was far from it.

"What promise did he make you?" Adam whispered, and I

only grew more confused. "What did he swear to you? Did you reciprocate, or was it one sided?"

"What are you talking about?" I asked, my mind rushing.

"He did not," Winry said quietly, disgust rising in her voice. "He would not— Luka would not claim my sister."

"—Kristin," Adam interrupted her, not daring to turn away from me, not even daring to blink. "You would know, wouldn't you? You would recognize it, you share blood— You know his magic."

And all of a sudden, Kristin was upon me, his hand seizing my wrist, his eyes snapping up to mine. I felt his fingers tighten.

The smallest gasp escaped Kristin, his head jerking to face Adam with eyes wide. "He didn't— Luka." I didn't know if it was shock or hope that resided in that look.

"What promise did Luka make you, Wren?" Adam tried again. "It's very important that we know. You need to tell us. Do you remember?"

Kristin let out a sharp inhale, his hands rising to my face, his fingers roaming it as I struggled to look at Adam, searching for something— "It's old, it's been there for a while. It's strong."

"I don't know," I said to Adam.

Kristin's fingers roamed to my bottom lip, peeling it downward and inspecting it, urging me to open my mouth as he examined my tongue. "Where did you put it, you fucking bastard..." Kristin murmured.

"He did not mark my sister!" Winry snapped in the background, almost drowned out by the way that the two men were consuming me. "Fae do not tie their lifespans to just anyone."

A strand of my hair came loose as Kristin let me snap my mouth shut, checking everywhere short of under my eyelids for something. My hand rose to tuck it back, placing it behind my ear like Luka had so many times before—

And then I knew. Without a single word, I knew. My

fingers stayed in that place, almost unable to move, every muscle in my body freezing. But when?

Kristin caught my realization, his skin going pale as he saw the confirmation that he needed, wrenching my hand out of the way and jerking my head to the side to look at what laid underneath. His hand tore my hair back, getting as close as possible. I'm fairly certain I heard Winry shriek in fury. "Behind the ear, it's so small I almost missed it," Kristin muttered. "He put it behind her ear."

"Where no one would find it," Adam said, his eyes closing as he gave a slow, pained nod.

Kristin threw his arms around me, his head resting against the side of mine as he took it in, proof that his brother was still alive. Proof that we could find him. He looked at the mark like it was some kind of holy deity, and perhaps to him it was. To everyone else it was something else.

A claim in Winry's eyes, one that made me Luka's. A cursed bargain to Adam, one which the King never knew of—and to Lindy, a thing that she was incapable of understanding. A fae mark placed God knows how many months ago.

For a fae to choose to mark their lover with a promise rather than make a bargain was worth far more than any devotion.

"That's why he couldn't put one on you when the King asked," Adam said bitterly. "That's why he was able to refuse. It's not that the King's crown is losing power as Theo believes, it's that that clever bastard Luka is so careful with his words..."

I wanted Kristin to move. I wanted to touch it, to somehow press it and magically feel his heartbeat under mine. Brilliant, he was utterly brilliant. One of the smartest and dumbest people that I knew at the same time. This is why he wouldn't make any promises or bargains with me, this is why he kept refusing, because he had already done it.

And if a deal need not be sealed with a kiss... My mind

went back months and months, to a small carriage where we sat pressed together, his fingers moving reassuringly over mine.

"Luka... Promise you'll stay with me," I muttered, the world seeming to jerk into being with that very statement. *Always*, he had said, his hands on mine.

Always.

He had promised to stay by my side. That had been his pact, not a two-sided bargain like so many fae made, nor anything for his benefit. He had promised to stay by me. He had even said it plainly, he could not leave me even if he wanted to.

"Tell me he didn't," Kristin said, pulling away from me. "Tell me he did not say that. He did not promise to stay by your side. That's a near impossible promise to fulfill." Because there were consequences for failing to fulfill a bargain.

And he was not by my side anymore, he had gone willingly.

"Wren," Kristin said furiously, gripping my shoulders and whirling me around to face him. "Tell me he did not promise that of all things. Tell me he promised something rational, or so highly irrational that he could not fail in doing it. Tell me that he did not word it like that."

I could not.

"Your brother has marked my sister," Winry growled, furiously trying to tear him off of me. "It is not her fault that he couldn't think of a good enough reason—"

"I'm not blaming her," Kristin hissed, struggling to hold onto me. "I am merely saying—"

"His foolish decisions are his own," Winry declared. "He is my friend, and he always has been, but whatever happens to Luka is his own doing. My sister is leaving."

"Like hell she is!" Kristin argued. "Every single moment that he is sitting apart from her without a plan to get back, my brother is likely suffering. You would have your friend die?"

"I would have my sister live," Winry proclaimed. "I don't care what that makes you think of me, Kristin. I do not need your high opinion to carry on in life." She was practically on top of me, desperate to pull me out of his grip, her nails digging into his wrists. "He should not have marked her, whatever his reason."

"Whatever his reason?" Kristin roared. "Are you in denial? Are you blind? Whatever his reason? You've lost your mind, Winry—"

"Well it is most certainly not love," Winry snarled. "Maybe lust, but I know my sister, and I know Luka—"

Hands shoved both of them back and away from me, knocking the two furious Seelie into each other with a snarl, a small Haldian girl forcing her way into the space between them and me, her hands tensed at her side as I was still frozen.

"You are utterly ridiculous," Lindy spat at the two of them in fury, refusing to move. "Look at you two, fighting. What is done is done. Learn that, learn that that is how the world works. Focus on fixing it rather than lamenting." A stream of curses, no doubt ones in Haldian, escaped the girl. "Dry your eyes and face the truth, you two."

"The truth?" Winry replied. "The truth is that Luka is going to die because he made a mistake, but I will not let my sister suffer the same fate! Regardless of whatever foolish ideas of heroism are in her head, we are leaving! This is dangerous! This is not what her mother would have wanted for her, and I am not going to humor such crazy notions as him genuinely being in love with her—To mark a young lady is not love. It is madness. My sister will live, and he can die, regardless of our friendship. I choose Wren, I always choose Wren," she sounded almost miserable at the last admission.

"You can not decide that your sister is worth so much more

than my brother," Kristin howled. If any Unseelie remained in the forest, I imagined that they were watching us.

"Winry, she has already decided—" Adam began.

"Of course you side with him," Winry snapped. "You would always side with him, wouldn't you?" My head was spinning with the fight.

"We are getting Luka back," the scream ripped out of me so harshly that my throat burned, my body nearly collapsing with the effort as I drowned out all of them. "I am getting Luka back," I said once they had quieted, my voice hoarse. "I am getting Luka back, I am taking care of this King, and I am hunting down Artur. Pay attention, because that is the only three things I will be doing. And if this mark means that he is alive and tied to me, then that makes it all the more easy." My body ached with anger, and for once, I could not hold back the electricity that spread beneath my fingers, burying it into my palms when I crushed them shut. "I am grateful for it," I spat. "I am grateful for Luka. Regardless of what fantasies you've convinced yourself of, my dear sister, this is not lust or delusion —I am as much his as he is mine. I have been his since you signed me over."

Winry looked horrified. I heard her breath catch, her eyes looking at me with complete and utter pity. Perhaps in Winry's eyes, to love was to lose. As a woman, all she ever had in capital was herself. The idea that I did love him, that I was capable of loving him more than myself—she looked broken. Because to her, her parents did not matter, Winry always had a different family. Winry always had me.

And now she didn't.

"You love him?" Winry asked. "More than you want to stay alive? To stay with me?"

"Winry, I am not like you," I said. "I love you, but I am not like you. I cannot choose myself over him. I cannot choose anyone over Luka."

"He's ruined you," Winry said so sorrowfully that I could barely comprehend it. Though a part of me knew that was not her true opinion, that she merely wished I was not like this, if only so that she could save me.

"I am glad to be ruined by Luka, then," I said, my fingers rising to that spot, the one that tied me to him.

For a moment, it looked like Winry would cry, then Adam pushed his way into the conversation, trying to divert our attention.

"There is no way to find him by mark alone," Adam said. "And I doubt that they would keep him in the camp, Wren." Ever rational, ever depressing. He squashed my hopes in one move. "It would be a hard thing to find him, mark or no mark."

"But fae marks are supposed to lead fae back to those they've made bargains with," I said, "so that they can fulfill them."

"And you are not fae," Adam said. "You are far from it. A skilled fae could find him with a hint of magic, but that's something they focus on in the military, not everyday life. I doubt that either Kristin or Winry have the experience."

From the quiet, hesitant looks on their faces, they didn't. Neither had ever even considered such a thing.

And so we had a map, and not a soul able to read it. Brilliant.

"There has to be a way," I began. "Someone has to have the ability."

Adam looked pained, unable to come up with a single name. We would have to find a Seelie to begin with, one with the experience that was willing to work with us. Surely he knew someone. Adam knew everyone.

But then Lindy straightened at my side, her round brown

eyes blinking as everyone else struggled to come up with an answer. And she moved.

Lindy tore off towards the vehicle, yanking open one of the doors and tearing a bag out of it, tossing it on the ground as she frantically began to search for something.

"Hey," Adam interrupted, taking off the moment he realized whose it was. "That's mine!" Not that Lindy cared, not that Lindy ever cared. She pulled a folded white square out of the pocket, one that I had seen before.

The newspaper. The one that Luka had bought so many days before. She opened it as she walked, roughly flipping through the pages until she found the article she needed, evidently having viewed the newspaper over Adam's shoulder at some point while he was reading it. Lindy was always nosy.

"Lindy," Adam began, shuffling behind her, confused as to what she was doing. "What have you got there?"

And then she shoved the newspaper at my chest, urging me to read it.

The article about me and my disappearance sat at the very top. I looked down at it, casting her a curious look.

"Read," she demanded.

"Wren Laurent has been missing for roughly three months now, taken from her home by what some believe to be a jilted lover, an Unseelie. She is believed to have had a previous relationship with the man, one that ended unfavorably and resulted in her abduction. Wren is believed to be travelling with the Unseelie..."

"Not that," Lindy shook her head furiously, her finger stabbing at the paper to indicate roughly which section of the newspaper the last paragraph sat at. "This."

My voice slowed as I read it out loud, the familiarity of the words hitting me. "The King's Army has been hard at work searching for Miss Laurent, believing there to be a possibility that her kidnapping was further motivated by the rising tensions between Seelie and Unseelie fae. A new captain has been assigned to head the squad in charge of finding Miss Laurent, an experienced tracker by the name of Nikolas Harding, who has recently been promoted to the rank."

Lindy looked up at me expectantly, waiting for some sort of response. I could only stare at the name in print, processing what it meant.

"Nikolas," Adam repeated.

"Nikolas," I echoed. Perhaps keeping him alive had not been such a bad idea after all. "But however will we find him? And if we find him, how will we convince him?"

"Luckily," Adam said. "I don't think he's moved, and I have a feeling that the wisps will guide us to him."

CHAPTER SEVENTEEN

He was easy enough to find. Largely because he was right where we left him, and also because, since he never seemed to fear anything, people were far too willing to talk about him, willing to brag about him just as he did about himself.

Because Nikolas Harding was rather impressed with himself. He had always been rather impressed with himself, always proud of what he could do. More so now than ever, since he had joined the army, fulfilling his destiny like his ancestors before him, he was on his way to becoming a hero.

And he would be a hero. Because Nikolas Harding had gotten most of the things that he wanted in life, nearly all of them.

Save for one girl.

A girl who he had never noticed before she became a member of nobility, a girl who he fancied himself to be a hero to. A girl who he had fallen deeply in love with, without knowing enough about her. A girl who he had showed pictures of in his wallet to the other soldiers, claiming her to be his love and also the one he hunted, the one who he would return.

And as he sat by the fire, he was doing just that, telling his tragic tale of heartbreak, unknowing that said girl edged around the camp, watching him with disgust in her eyes. Holding back the urge to gag, actually, when he took one last glance at his wallet before standing up, declaring that he would be off in his tent for the afternoon, reevaluating strategies.

I'd evaded him. He had been camped outside of the town we were staying at, Cambel, because he knew I was there. That much was clear, but I had somehow evaded him. And, having only been gone for a day or two, he had not yet had the time to find me.

Little did he know.

"Another one of those days, isn't it captain?" A soldier spoke as I tiptoed around the trees, trying to decide which amongst the tents would be his. There were some that were larger, but those could just as easily be for strategy or food. I looked for a hint of where he might have lived, my eyes desperately scanning the camp.

It would be central, wouldn't it?

"It has been," Nikolas said, his voice relaxed, a deep rumble dripping with charm. "No one's heard any news yet from up the mountain? Do you think Langley's gotten to the King yet? I am dying to get permission to move. You saw the Kinsley estate, I guarantee that there was not a spot of ink on the ground before she came there. It's practically her calling card."

"I guarantee that there was not ink on the ground before she came there," I repeated under my breath, mocking him. In the distance, if I looked far enough, I could see Lindy watching me, the others no doubt beside her.

Out of everyone, we had decided that I was the best bet. I already resented that.

"She's a lively thing, isn't she?" The soldier asked. "I just don't see how Kinsley can contain her, she seems like a spitfire, a girl filled with piss and vinegar. I can't imagine her willingly moving."

"She was a maid, once," Nikolas reiterated, "she's very susceptible to influence, the poor thing. I always worried about her."

Poor thing? Oh, they would be saying that about him once I got my hands on him. I moved closer to camp, stepping silently from my space behind the trees to crouch behind one of the tents, hiding just out of view.

"All of this for one girl," the soldier said. "I just don't see what's so special about her."

Lots. I could show that soldier in an instant. I rolled my eyes, quickly darting behind another tent, grateful that this one was taller. My eyes moved along the camp, looking for the location I needed. Nikolas's tent, Nikolas's tent... There had to be some sort of sign.

"She's an impressive young girl," Nikolas laughed, I swear my eyes twitched. I bet it was the first time that he had looked truly alive since what happened on the mountain, those moments when he got to talk about me. I tried not to think about that too much. "With lips far softer than any silk."

I'd kill him now, I decided. Forget tracking, I would murder Nikolas. But before I could solidify that idea and how I would execute it, something caught my eye—

Oh, he could not be so egotistical, could he?

"And she tastes far sweeter than any other woman," Nikolas said. "With a ferocity that you could not believe, almost feral, she kissed me like she wanted to devour me. All things considered, she probably did. I could feel her desire for me from the moment I met her."

He could be, I decided, sprinting for the entrance of the

tent and practically diving in because, on the side of it, there sat a family crest. One that I did not recognize, but the only one amongst them.

A dragon, rearing onto its hindlegs, lashing out at its attackers and winning, embroidered in silver thread. Below, a phrase in old fae, I knew enough to read: We Suffer No Losses.

And when I entered, I knew it was true. Because once inside, the tent was most definitely Nikolas Harding's.

It's rare that you can know someone so well that you can simply look at a space and attribute it to them, but there were few people as transparent as Nikolas Harding.

The oil lamps were already burning when I entered, likely lit by another soldier on a command a while before in order to ensure that the tent was warm. Very few books filled the tent, the few that were there being scattered and of all matters of military history, nothing outside of that. In the center sat a large table with a map of Whynne engraved on it and small pawns to move across it. Likely a family heirloom.

There were heavy silks about the tent, hanging in front of the tent flaps and beside the sleeping area for privacy, no doubt having been imported in by the Laurents. An engraved knife stabbed into the table, one that appeared to be used for carving despite its obvious expense, the whittled shape of a small Unseelie beginning to be carved into shape from the end of a stick beside it. Upon further inspection, the figures on the table consisted of a small, dress wearing figure with a high cut bob, two broad figures—one having a single flame carved into it, another figure in a dress with long hair, an almost wolf-like shorter figure, and one figure that was clearly male with ears carved into its sides as its only feature—those ears reached so high from the figure they almost looked to be horns.

I could not stop myself from pocketing the horned figure, looking across the way to see another broad-shouldered figure with a smile on his face and gills carved into his neck. I scoffed, flicking it over.

I continued to move around the room, taking it all in, looking at the scatterings of newspapers and some documents that I realized, with a jolt, were forgeries that I had made only a week prior. He had been hunting me. I turned one over in my hands, seeing that he had written down the location that it was bought from, a town just outside of the capital, and the date that the purchaser had gotten it.

Perhaps he was not as stupid as I thought.

I put it back down, slowly moving away from it and towards the bed, unsure what I was looking for or if I was looking for anything even, maybe I was just biding my time.

My eyes caught on the gun on the bedside table, a gun with an engraved handle boasting his name in golden paint. Beside it, an array of carved bullets sat, the chamber popped open and loaded until it was full. I reached for it despite myself, unable to stop myself from touching it—

"Well, goodnight to you too, Weathers," I ducked behind the bed curtains at the sound of his voice, the gun clenched in my hand as his footsteps grew nearer.

He entered the tent.

You know how sometimes, when you haven't seen someone for a while, they look wholly unfamiliar? That didn't happen with Nikolas. In fact, he looked so familiar that I almost felt sickened.

Older, just a bit, but war does that to a person. The rest of him was shockingly familiar, save for a finger on his hand that hung crooked against his thigh as he walked, likely having set too quickly for him to fix it after having been pulled out of the rubble. He had almost been crushed to death just a month prior. He would have died had I not insisted on pulling him out.

He sighed as he moved through the space, shrugging off the heavy jacket that so many of the military men wore and pulling at the belt around his waist, the one in which his holster sat empty. He must have decided not to fill it, feeling safe enough in his own camp, or perhaps comforted by the assortment of knifes hanging on his belt.

His fingers rose to his buttons as he moved around the space, reaching behind him and pulling the silk curtains at the front of his tent closed, more and more of his sweat-soaked skin becoming visible.

I threw my head back at the sight, staring at the ceiling as a silent alarm spread throughout me. He would not strip entirely, would he? I grimaced, moving to the edge between curtain and tent to look out at him once more, afraid that I would see more skin.

I did, but thankfully only his shirt was gone, discarded to the side in a pile as he began on his pants, his fingers stopping as his eyes caught on something.

The figures. Of course he would remember how they were set up, wouldn't he? Of course he would notice the missing one. That was just my luck, I didn't even bother to pray against it.

Nikolas looked at the table, his eyes flickering back up. For a moment, I thought of leaving. Perhaps I could have escaped.

His lips pursed. My hands held the gun so tightly that it hurt.

"It's you, isn't it?" Nikolas spoke, and I felt my breath catch in my throat, my body immediately pressed against the side of the tent, hoping that he would not find me even though I was the one with the gun in my hands.

"Which one of you is it?" He said, his voice careful as his fingernails dragged against the surface of the table, producing a soft scraping sound. "You know this is a very bad idea," he muttered, and I was reminded that this was his space, not mine. He knew where everything was.

And no soldier had one gun alone.

"Ah, shoes," he said, spotting me, his footsteps drawing nearer. Now or never.

I spun, the silk wrapping around me as I turned, catching on my arm and nearly going across my eyes as I thrusted the gun forward, my finger on the trigger.

I opened my eyes to see him staring at me, anger giving way to shock, which gave way to something else, his eyes softening ever so slightly as he continued to stare.

"Wren," he said my name gently, so gentle that it was almost inaudible. His hands did not rise, and he did not move any closer. "Wren, what are you doing?"

"I think it's very clear," I said, struggling to hold the gun up as the silk wrapped around me. A single step forward pulled some of the fabric off of me, bringing me closer to him. My body shook as I realized what I was doing, that I was holding a gun pointed at Nikolas of all people.

"You don't even know how to fire that," Nikolas said calmly, his eyes meeting mine. "You have no idea how to aim it."

"Try me," I murmured, keeping the gun on him. The trigger felt far too giving in my hand, like the slightest pressure would cause the weapon to fire. "Don't move."

"You're not going to kill me," Nikolas said, knowing all too well. "You wouldn't kill me, Wren."

"You don't know that," I said. "You don't know what I would do."

"I have been looking for you for weeks—"

"You think I don't know that," I snapped, finally forcing his hands up in the air, my mind screaming at me in fear of what I was doing. "You think I haven't realized that the army keeps closing in, Nikolas? You think I'm so stupid that I would not see you on that stage, having others kill for you? I'm not blind, Nikolas, and I'm most certainly not dumb."

"I didn't say that you were," Nikolas exhaled, his eyes closing as I waved the gun a little closer. "I'd never imagined that you'd come here— Not after what happened."

"I had no choice," I said, reminded by the fact that we were in the center of camp, and the others were waiting. Yet... Nikolas did not scream, he did not alert the other soldiers.

"We can do this the easy way, Wren," Nikolas said, sounding much like Adam when he negotiated with others and soothed them. "I can take you to the King and you can help, then you can go home. We can go home."

"I'm not helping the King," I growled, daring to step even closer, daring to touch the gun to his skin. I pressed it at the base of his neck, forcing him to look down at me, forcing his seafoam eyes to meet mine.

The worst part about Nikolas was that he was always handsome, even with the gills. I'd never really focused on it, but his dark red hair and blue green eyes were pretty, as was his carved jawline. He didn't look a thing like Luka, but he looked like something else, the type of man that girls draw when asked to dream.

It was a shame for him, because if he had looked a thing like Luka, I don't think I would have been able to hold the gun to him.

"What are you doing, Wren?" He murmured, his voice low and husky. "What are we doing?"

Even now, he wanted me. The realization hit me like a heavy stone, nearly knocking me off balance. He'd never even bothered to look my way as a maid but now, with his gun wrapped tightly in my fingers, he wanted me, a girl who was nothing like the one he had originally fallen in love with.

"I need you," I admitted, and that was the wrong thing to say.

He inhaled deeply, like he could breathe me in. Definitely the wrong words.

"I need you to find Luka," I continued, and he glared. Definitely not the words he wanted to hear. "You're the only person who can. You're the only Seelie I know who knows how to track—"

"Why, did he leave you?" Nikolas spat, beyond angry.

"They took him," I fired back, infuriated that he would suggest such a thing. "They took him after he sacrificed himself for me. He gave himself up so that I would be safe. I have a mark from him, he didn't want to leave me. He sacrificed himself for my safety."

"So that he would be the good guy," Nikolas growled, missing the point entirely. I could not have him go off like that, I could not have him argue with me. I was already beyond furious. "You should let him go then, let him become the martyr."

"You are going to help me," I demanded, pressing the gun harder into his chest. "We're going to find him."

"I would rather die," Nikolas declared, defiance burning in his eyes.

"That is very possible," I said in return, cocking the gun. I'd seen Nikolas do it before, unlucky for him.

The fact that Nikolas had the nerve to laugh. That he could look at me as if it was funny, as if any of this was funny. "You would never shoot me, Wren. You don't have the nerve," he said, dismissing me entirely. "You're not a killer."

He was right. He knew that all too well, from the moment I saved him he had figured it out. I was not a killer, I was not capable of killing. Somewhere out there, Mylene was probably alive, and I was okay with that. Somewhere out there, Camden was alive, and I was okay with that. I was no murderer.

I couldn't stop from lowering the gun.

"Just come with me and everything will be okay, I will make sure that you are safe. I will make sure that you do not leave my side, I promise you that. Either that or leave, I will tell no one, but I will not help you," Nikolas kept talking, he kept denying me. There was no way to fight him, not one that was easy. He would never leave the army. He wouldn't tell people that I was there, but he wouldn't be of any help either. "You can leave, or you can come with me. But that's your only option here, Wren. That's all there is." Was it?

"You're right," I conceded, looking down at the gun in my hands. "I'm not a killer, and there's no way that I can convince you to leave. Not all of this. You dreamed of being in the army, didn't you? This is what you wanted."

"That's right, Wren," Nikolas said, his hands slowly reaching for me...

"—So I'm going to have to force you," I declared, jerking the gun to the side, pointing it away from him, and closing my eyes.

A single shot fired.

"Wren, are you insane—" His arms were around me by the time I got another shot out, the man desperately trying to jerk my arm away. A scream rang out.

I had fired in the direction of the campfire. There was no reason for him to shoot, not in that direction. Not unless he was up to something, trying something.

"Wren!" He was on me, wrestling the gun from my grasp. I shot out the rest of the chamber, knowing that nothing would hit anyone, but also that a bunch of bullets would be damning in their own right. I couldn't help but let out a hollow laugh as he furiously tore it from me, looking from the gun back to me, horror on his face.

"I know you won't tell them I had the gun, Nikolas. I also know that there are no mistakes in the military," I spat. "If you leave now though, you'll be gone by the time they dig the bullet out of the ground. Before they see the name Nikolas Harding written on it and come to their own conclusions. The King's men don't like being shot at, do they? Especially not in their own camp. Such a thing would be read as mutinous, and you won't have an explanation for it."

A strangled breath escaped him as I leaned in, ready to inform him of an infallible truth.

"You can't lie." He couldn't tell them that I was there, nor could he explain the gunshots otherwise.

He could only stare, his mouth half open, the realization having hit him.

"You can't stay here, Nikolas. You can't be a part of your precious army, not when your squad thinks you fired at them. And you can't stay in the woods. Not alone." I shook my head. "Welcome to your dishonorable discharge, Captain Harding."

CHAPTER EIGHTEEN

He wanted to kill me, that much was clear, to the point where, for a moment as we ran through the woods, I thought that he might have tried. The fact that he didn't was surprising. But I guess, when you have nothing left to live for, killing someone just sort of seems bland.

He had not calmed down by the time we approached the lanterns on the hill, the lanterns hidden in the trees. In fact, I would say that he had done the opposite of calming down.

I think Adam only made it worse.

"Welcome back, Nikolas." That was not the greeting he should have given when we climbed up from the bottom of the woods, Nikolas constantly looking back as if he was contemplating a way to fix the problem and stay. "You know, it has been quite some time, but I really did miss you. I'm glad you agreed—"

Nikolas looked at Adam like he was a creature from hell. Actually, he looked at all of us like that. "I am not speaking to you," Nikolas spat, shaking his head as he walked past Adam, his hands clenched by his sides.

"To be fair, I think he might be telling the truth," I called after Nikolas.

A rude gesture was made in response to that. "I am not talking to you either," he spat, and carried on walking, no doubt figuring that the vehicle at the top of the hill was likely ours. He opened the door with a huff of frustration, falling into the car and slamming it shut.

He would be great company.

"I take it that he did not agree," Adam said, wincing as he looked after him.

"I'll speak to him," I said, stomping after him as Winry and Lindy only grimaced. "He's just a little put off—"

A furious yell erupted from the car, the sound of banging greeted our ears.

"Perhaps you should wait," Kristin grinned, standing nearest the car and placing his hand on my shoulder to stop me. "Maybe give him a little time to cool down, I'd like to talk to you anyway—"

"But Nikolas—"

"I'll talk to him," Winry said with a sigh, jogging up the hill to meet us. "I'm sure he'd rather see a friendly face, one that is a bit less involved. I promise not to conspire with him," she said upon my suspicious squint. "I wouldn't benefit from it to begin with."

I supposed that I had to believe her, considering the fact that Nikolas was absolutely beside himself with rage. Still, I looked to my sister. My smaller, shorter sister.

"I will be fine," Winry said flatly, bracing her foot on the car door and yanking it open with both hands, "Nikolas adores me."

I had never seen them interact before in my life. All I knew was that his friend Eli used him to get to Winry, and she had almost forgotten about him now that Eli served her no purpose.

"We're going to have to trust her," Kristin said gently at my side as the car door closed behind Winry, Nikolas making another furious sound of indignation. "And if not, I'm sure Lindy will take care of him." Ah, the furious Haldian.

I nodded, wincing as I heard a female voice rising within the car. Not good.

"You're only a tart!" Nikolas called furiously, to which I heard a resounding slap.

Lindy looked to the car in interest.

"I need to talk to you," Kristin reiterated by my side, his face dimly lit by the lights of the automobile. "It's something important," he warned, and I couldn't help but look over my shoulder in response to that, eyeing the vehicle behind me.

"More important than this?"

"Related to this, and far more important," Kristin confirmed, looking over to me with the slightest smile. Not a whole smile, not the type of smile that I was accustomed to from Kristin, but a smile all the same. "Come, let me start a fire for the others and we'll sit together."

In front of us, the fire blazed, Adam and Lindy sitting closest to it, the fur coat that Lindy had come in balanced upon her shoulders and Kristin's suit coat upon Adam's lap. Beside them, in the automobile, a soft light still burned from Winry's lamp, the murmurs of conversation still taking place. Luckily, they had calmed down.

And Kristin and I? We sat against the trunk so closely that our shoulder's touched, a small brown bottle that Kristin had hidden from Artur sitting in his hand. Every so often he would pass it to me, the stinging, bitter taste of alcohol burning my tongue as I took far smaller sips, always handing it back to him seconds later, earning a laugh from my disgusted expressions.

"Luka looks just the same as you when he drinks," Kristin said, finally pushing the cork back into the bottle, the sides of his eyes wrinkling as he grinned. "We can't have any more though, or at least I can't. I'm a notorious lightweight, and Adam would kill me if he had to haul me up this mountain because I got drunk off my ass and fell down it."

I couldn't help but smile too, looking down at my lap, thinking both of Luka drinking anything alcoholic and of Kristin getting so drunk he would fall down the hill. Apparently, it was such a frequent occurrence that Adam and him used to tell jokes about it.

"You look nice in his clothes," Kristin said quietly, seeming to attempt to gather some sort of strength. "I'm glad that you two are... Whatever it is that you two are."

"Are you trying to deny me like Winry?" I joked. "I think you could say we're more than friends," I said, wrapping my arms around my knees and letting my head rest against them, almost laughing at my statement. "I love him," I said with a sort of finality, it became easier every time I said it, "But everyone already knows that."

"We do," Kristin nodded, throwing his head back against the car as a soft chuckle escaped him. "It just seems like there should be more of a word for it than what's already out there, but I'm sure my brother would disagree. I knew he loved you since you and I came home drunk that one night from the teashop, and knew that he was in love with the girl he talked about when he came home from the Laurents from the first time he spoke of her slapping his knee after bandaging it."

"That's me," I laughed. "Wren Laurent, a very versatile maid."

Kristin cackled, his eyes remaining on the stars as he gripped the grass underneath him in his fingers, almost as if he was trying to remind himself that he was still there. "Can I see it," he asked after a moment, his laughter dying off. "The mark? Just before I speak, can I see it? I need to reassure myself that he's still here."

I obliged, brushing my hair out of the way and angling my head so that he could see it, letting his fingers pass over it as he swallowed, lingering for too long but not seeming able to do otherwise.

So long as that mark remained, Luka was alive.

I had thought that no one else in the world cared for Luka as much as I did. But Kristin? Kristin cared too much, he loved him. Luka was his brother, the only family he had.

"He's going to kill me when he sees me again for telling you all of this," Kristin muttered. "But then again, I guess I should be glad that he'll be there to do it." He sighed, satisfied with what he saw, ready to speak once more.

Before he could even begin, I thought to turn on my lantern. Just in case.

"It's a nice gift he gave you," Kristin acknowledged, looking at it briefly. "Ironic, but... I have to tell you a story, Wren."

I sat up eagerly, looking over at him. Any sort of story was good, especially if it helped to get Luka back.

"It's not a good one," Kristin admitted. "And I need you to swear never to tell anyone it for the rest of your life. Not even Adam knows. Only the King knows, and that is because the castle had to get involved."

Interesting. I nodded hesitantly at him, my eyebrows furrowing at the statement.

Kristin took a long breath, his eyes moving only briefly to me as he tried to come to a place to begin, then sliding away as he found it. Another breath, his shoulders rising and falling, and he was ready. His voice was even, but there was still a hint of hesitation, as if he was worried how it would be received. "My father was not a good man, Wren. I am thankful for the things that he gave me, my brother and the estates, but I am not grateful for him. I have some good memories of course, a lot of them, but I do not miss him. I loved him, but I do not wish that he was here."

Kristin kept going, his voice quiet so that no one else could hear as he began to dive into the story. This was a secret that was not meant to get out. "When I was four, my father purchased his second estate, the one that we stayed at just a few days ago. He told my mother that he bought it to get away and clear his head occasionally, no one really blamed him because their marriage was not a love match, and my mother was rather cruel too. He said that the location of the estate was important, and that he bought it for research. My mother was okay with that, she knew that he liked to do those sorts of things and said that it was better than far less noble pursuits."

Kristin wrinkled his nose before admitting, "but little did she know, it was for far less noble pursuits. You see, my father liked to research the Unseelie. He would go out into the woods and make notes, always going out with a pistol and a lantern in hand, always ready to take care of any problems. He went over much of these woods, he's the reason I'm not afraid of them, but eventually he found a place that he particularly liked. One that he eventually built the estate next to." He took a deep breath, struggling for a moment as more details came back to him.

"You don't have to continue, Kristin," I said.

"No," Kristin argued. "I do. I have to tell you." He shook his head at himself, at his inability to tell the story, pushing onward in spite of it all. "It was a pond near the base of the mountain, one that was awfully deep. The creatures in it tried to lure him under on the first day, not caring that he was Seelie, only that he had gold in his pockets. But one stopped them. One shoved him out before he could even step in the water."

"Luka's mother," I guessed.

"Luka's mother," Kristin confirmed, flinching at his brother's name. "She was kind. He came to visit her a few more times. He told me that he was in love with her, I was only four. He told me that that was why he did not often come home to my mother. My mother sent me to visit him that summer, but he would not let me go out to the pond with him. He promised me that someday, someday soon I would meet her. He told me that when the workmen came to our house to make some modifications, boarding up a few of the rooms. I believed him."

"And you met her," I said, nodding at him. Because he had to have, just by looking at his face you could tell.

"My father went out the next month with a large tank strapped to the back of his vehicle and a net made out of silk. He did not come back until nightfall." Kristin closed his eyes, struggling to calm himself. "He did not cut the net when he first brought her back. He did not bother to cut it for many days, he left it until it dug against her whenever she struggled. He put her in a tank in his office, and he would have me sit there and watch her. She looked human, very, very human aside from her pointed ears and green features. You could have mistaken her for a drowning woman, my father liked that about her. For two weeks she stayed in that tank..."

My jaw tightened, a desperate urge to ask what happened next flaring within me. I dared not think of Luka in any similar situations.

"And then he cut the net and he let her out, even though she did not wish to stand on land either. At night he would put her back in her tank. She did not speak, she did not look at me, and she did not want to be there. My mother had no idea."

That made no sense, "There were servants though, surely it must have gotten out—" I began.

"No," Kristin responded, shaking his head. "Everyone was sworn to secrecy. No one told. No one was ever supposed to know, because if they did, the Kinsley name would be tarnished. Especially if they heard what he did, that he forced her to tell him her name. Her true name. Something that a fae should have a say in most of the time... outside of certain circumstances. I found out that she was pregnant when she came to the estate..."

"With Luka," I said.

"With Luka," Kristin's voice trembled. "And my father wanted to keep him like a tadpole, but he could not breathe underwater. In fact, he detested being submerged. I'm thankful for that, I do not know what sort of life he would have had otherwise. My father was forced to bring him home and my mother was furious. The King told him that he needed to take care of the situation, lest the rest of Whynne find out what had happened and question the nobility. It was a stain on our family name. The King asked my mother to claim Luka as her own, even though he was not and she could not lie. The King made her sign the papers so that she could say it, she told me that she did it for me. And then Luka was ours, sent to that estate every summer until he turned sixteen and my father finally passed, his mother not living past his third year. He hated it there, especially once he became older. He always wanted to go home, to visit the Laurents once more, where they treated him with kindness and some semblance of respect."

Of course he did. I could only imagine. Though the Laurents did not want him to marry into their family, Lowell Laurent was undeniably fond of him. He threw a ball in his honor when the young man returned.

"When my father made that deal, he imagined that he would have several sons, and then it was just Luka and I. And while he loved Luka, he did not want to risk it getting out, the possibility of Winry choosing him and people knowing that the Kinsley heir was an Unseelie. The Laurents would kill us. But

Luka just kept going back. As we began getting older, my father began to try to figure out how he could change the terms of the bargain to exclude Luka, knowing that the Laurents would agree if he proposed them. But I couldn't let him do that, not under Luka's nose, I didn't want him to feel that unwanted. So I bribed my father, I told him that I would tell people he forced the morgen's name out, that he kept an Unseelie woman in the way that he did. To ask for a fae's name is such a cruel thing... He agreed if only for the fact that it would destroy us all if such a thing came to light. Though he loved Luka in a way, he cursed me until his dying day for forcing him to keep my brother involved in the bargain."

"And so Luka stayed in the bargain," I concluded, settling back against the vehicle as I tried to process it all.

"And by the time I knew that you entered the picture, my father was already gone. There was no way to modify the bargain, only work around it. I wanted him to be a part of the bargain so that he would feel wanted, even if he didn't plan to marry Winry. I didn't want him to think of himself as a monster. I was planning to marry Winry as intended for his sake."

"Why are you telling me this?" I asked, a distinct sinking feeling in my stomach as he spoke, the story beginning to rush over me. This was not a story that Luka would want me to know, that was true. This was not a story for me to hear.

"Because I need you to understand that I love Luka," Kristin said, "and that I, more than anyone, do not want to hurt him. More than that, I need you to understand what I'm about to tell you, and the gravity of what it means."

No. I knew before his mouth even opened. I realized it immediately. He knew it, he was going to tell me. "No," I said frantically, I could not have it, I could not hear it, "no, I do not want to know it—"

"You need to know it, Wren," Kristin said, calmly reaching over to me and peeling my hands off of my ears even as I frantically tried to cover them. "If the King arrives— if he says even one word to Luka, this is the only way to get him to stop. This is the only way to ensure that my brother does not end up having to do something that he does not wish to do."

"It won't be needed," I spat, trying to cover my ears. "I don't want to hear what it is, not if it's something like that. I want to know him as Luka Kinsley and Luka Kinsley alone, I do not want his true name. I do not need it—" The idea of knowing it, the stream of words that would bend him to me entirely...

How could anyone ever want that? How could anyone live with knowing that? It was different than coercion, I knew that, because fae didn't even have a chance to say no, not when faced with the King's word. They could only listen and obey. And if I had to say it to Luka, then that meant the worst. I could not stomach such a thing.

"Wren," Kristin said, his voice a warning as he firmly held my hands at the sides of my head, looking me in the eyes. I clenched my eyes shut, not willing to hear it.

"I can't," I said. "I can't know it. I don't want it."

Kristin shuddered, his hands releasing me, his mouth swallowing down the name. He sunk back against the vehicle with a sigh, because there was nothing else to do.

"I cannot hear his name," I repeated. "Not after what you told me." And he nodded, his eyes shutting.

"Then we can only pray that the worst does not come to pass."

CHAPTER NINETEEN

I DID NOT SLEEP.

My eyes were unable to close, my mind was unable to silence itself. All I could do was sit outside near the fire, and watch the others falling asleep around me. Eventually, Winry wandered out of the vehicle, her body curling around my side as she fell asleep. The smoke overwhelming the flames as the fire died down with the first glimpse of morning light, embers sitting in its wake.

I heard him before I saw him, his footsteps behind me, loud even though he had been trained not to be. For a single, blissful moment, I closed my eyes and pretended that they were someone else's.

"You know," said Nikolas, sinking into the empty space on the other side of me, avoiding touching Winry or I in any way. I didn't dare to look at him. "This is not the future I pictured for us when you kissed me all of those months ago. Not even close." I couldn't tell if he was smiling or frowning, I just focused on one thing.

"You're not angry anymore."

"No," said Nikolas, sprawling out beside me. I saw him nod from the corner of my eye. "I still am. I think I still will be for a while. I'm just coming to terms. I don't want to strangle you anymore though, so that's an improvement."

I let out a laugh, my chin once again falling on my knees, my eyes closing lazily.

"He must be kind to you," Nikolas said, his voice low and wistful. "Kinder than he is to anyone else."

"He's my closest friend," I admitted, silently wishing that he were there. I would have traded Nikolas for him in an instant. Actually, I would have traded a lot of things for Luka. Even the fire that kept us safe at night. "I love him," Nikolas had heard those words before, but I had to say it.

"I love you," Nikolas replied, his eyes on me. "Winry told me that if I did, I should stop being such a baby and help." He added, "even though you somehow single handedly managed to ruin my life in less than half an hour of being in it."

"It was a stupid dream to begin with," I told him, giving him a look. "Being a soldier was a stupid dream. Fighting in this war is a stupid dream, especially after you saw the King's plans. The fact that you continued to want to is utterly terrifying."

"I wanted to be a hero," Nikolas said, his hand running over his gills, rubbing the back of his neck. He looked so much like a boy again then, it felt like it had been a long time since he'd looked like that. "More than that, I wanted you. I still want you. I cannot help it."

"You can be a hero in other ways, idiot," I said, hitting my shoulder against his and choosing to ignore the other things he had said.

"Be careful, you still need me," he said, sinking backwards onto his hands. "I wish that things were always like this between us."

The grin slipped off my face.

"You love him," Nikolas repeated. Not with bitterness or jealousy, just as an admission of the fact. "Luka Kinsley," he whistled. "You could do better. I'll have you know that the name Wren Kinsley does not suit you."

I shoved him over. "And Wren Harding does?"

"It only sounds awful when you say it so unenthusiastically," Nikolas said from his spot on the ground, earning him a grumble from one of our still sleeping companions. "I keep telling myself that if I do this, you will eventually fall in love with me."

I had a feeling that whatever Nikolas felt would never change. Something about that was crushing.

"The mark," Nikolas said, closing his eyes. "If we're going to find him, I need to see the mark." Before I could open my mouth, he requested, "don't tell me any details, I don't think I could stand it." Fair enough. "I'm still fighting my own temptation to leave here without helping and let Luka die, don't encourage me."

I leaned towards him, angling my neck for him to see and pushing back the hair, exposing the raised patch to the cold morning air. He sat up, sitting beside me and adjusting my head so that he could see clearer, his fingers brushing against the spot.

"That's it?" He asked.

"That's it," I confirmed.

"It's tiny," he observed, brushing it once more. "No wonder no one could find it, it's barely bigger than a mole." Nikolas scrunched his nose, moving so much closer that it almost touched the mark. "It was there the whole time, wasn't it?"

"The King is going to kick himself," I said.

"Winry told me she's going to kill him," Nikolas said. "Not the king, Luka. Winry said she was going to kill him, and now I kind of see why."

"Why is there so much emphasis on marks like this?" I asked, cocking my head ever so slightly, accidentally pulling the mark away from Nikolas. "No one's fully explained."

Nikolas readjusted my neck so that he could look at the mark properly, stating, "you don't know what fae marks really mean, or you don't grasp it well enough. Well, it's not all bargains and deals for your souls, these things are actually quite important. It's more binding and claiming than any engagement ring could ever be and placing it out of sight says a lot more. Winry thinks it's almost rude. He's claiming you, but he doesn't feel the need to show others, it just shows that he's confident that you belong to him. In short, Kinsley is saying to the world that you two are permanently intertwined without even speaking it." There it was, just the hint of bitterness in his voice.

I straightened my head out of his grasp, blinking at the statement. "He just made a promise..."

"He did not just make a promise, there's no just about it. He purposefully made that promise and knew what it would mean," Nikolas said. "He was waiting to mark you again as soon as he could and took the first thing you could ask for to do it. He didn't care about the consequences." He did not ask what it was. He'd obviously been told by Winry. "Winry says that he will begin to die. I admit that the idea is appealing if it's true, but I'm sure you wouldn't agree. I'd thought that there was still hope for me yet, but you'd hate me if I tried to keep you away from him, wouldn't you?"

I didn't want to admit that it was a fact that Luka would die, because what if Nikolas changed his mind? But I guess my silence was confirmation enough.

The slightest, tortured groan escaped Nikolas, his lips pursing together. "I suppose this is how I will repay him for saving my life, though I thought the punch in the face was enough there. Or, I guess, I hoped."

I shrugged. "He didn't want you getting any ideas. I think it's safe to assume that all ideas left your head with that move."

"More than safe, you firing that gun has sort of quashed a bunch of hopes of mine," Nikolas confirmed, moving to sit in front of me, either hand braced on the side of my face. "Relax," he said, frowning as he took in my reaction. "I'm not going to kiss you, not now. Definitely not now. Maybe someday..."

"Not ever," I replied. "Definitely not ever."

He definitely didn't look pleased with that statement. "I'm going to read the mark. I need you to stay still."

Oh. I scooted closer to him, closing my eyes as I awaited it, wiggling just a little in anticipation. In a matter of moments, I would know where Luka was.

"Now, this is going to hurt," Nikolas began. "A lot."

"You have no idea the amount of pain I've felt these past few months," I said, opening one eye just slightly to look at him. "I've twisted ankles, fallen off of cliffs, been manhandled by a troll–Nothing you can do, short of stabbing me, is really going to hurt. Trust me, I was pulled from the wreckage of a car by old ham hands Adam just about four months ago, and I'm still doing fine."

"Alright, I'll humor you" Nikolas replied, his eyes wide and his teeth gritted. "Don't say I didn't warn you. This is not going to be pleasant." He did not lie. He was Seelie, he couldn't.

The pain was nothing short of blinding. I immediately tried to pull away from the shock of it, not expecting it to sting that way, or to even hurt at all. Nikolas grimaced as he pulled back his hands, his face apologetic but the fact that he was still reaching towards me confirming that he was not done.

"It's the location," Nikolas admitted. "If it was somewhere else..."

I closed my eyes, shoving my face into his hands before he could continue his criticism, my teeth gritting in pain. I didn't need to hear it.

I'm pretty sure that Lindy stirred beside me, waking at the sound that escaped me that time, because she was there when Nikolas pulled away, in the far too bright world that appeared the second my eyes opened. Her eyes drifted between Nikolas and I, asking a silent question.

"I got a little bit closer this time," Nikolas said. "Take a deep breath, we're doing this one last time."

"—Does it hurt the tall one when you do that?" Lindy asked, and Nikolas's hands were on me before I could echo the question, causing a small whine of pain to escape me, my body almost slumping over.

The answer was likely a yes, and I think he enjoyed that.

Nikolas said nothing as he held me once more, the throbbing moving throughout my head as his fingers pressed firmly over the mark, the Seelie magic in his blood stinging against my skin. I wondered for a second if it would be different since Luka was Unseelie.

But then Nikolas pulled away too quickly for such an idea to come to fruition.

"He's still on the mountain," Nikolas said. "Not the clearing where we went before, nor the entrance to the roots. Nowhere near that, somewhere higher. Somewhere where it is easy to get to him. Grab me a map," he demanded. "Quickly."

Lindy looked at him like he had sprouted another limb. "We do not have maps," she said, because why on earth would we have maps? We only had what was on our backs. "I can bring you a pile of dirt and that would look like your mountain, but I can not give you a map. I lack the ability to pull things out of thin air."

"Never mind," Nikolas said loudly, causing another person

to stir. Adam opened a hazel eye, his face coated in confusion as he looked our way. When he'd gone to bed, Nikolas was still swearing about all of us.

Now he was looking back, craning his head as far back as it would allow, his mind churning. "Of course, they'd leave a trail for you in the valley..." Nikolas began, running through what he did know about strategy. "So they would not want him to be far from it, not when the King still thinks that you are unmarked. Otherwise, you would not be able to find him, and they want you to think that you've found him."

Adam shook Kristin awake beside him, Kristin blinking sleepily, almost irritated as he slowly sat up. And then he saw Nikolas.

"Not the cabin either. Nowhere near the cabin, the trees don't match, and they had trouble enough digging it out after the landslide. Those rocks almost ruined that half of the mountain, we never did find Mylene."

A part of me thanked God that it was not the cabin.

"Near the castle then," Nikolas said, his fingers tracing the mountainside as he spoke. "Between that and the valley, so that the King and Camden can stop and pick him up on the way if they've not yet lured you out. They've been busy with preparations, and it's hard to duck out—"

"Especially when you have to admit that you're leaving to torment an Unseelie," I spat. "It sort of spoils the mood, doesn't it?"

Nikolas ignored me. "So, they've likely not gotten to him yet. The trees have a little dip right there," he gestured so that I and everyone else could see, "and it's between the castle and the valley. They wouldn't want to put him in a heavily wooded area, especially considering the fact that he's Unseelie and the King believes that they're all in cahoots, so they would put him there. In that little area."

"A hike," Winry noted, having woken up while I wasn't paying attention and not even bothering to get up as she watched him work. "I am so tired of walking and moving in general. My feet are bleeding."

"You're going to be at a disadvantage too," Nikolas whistled. "They'd have the upper hand. High ground."

"Unless we had a diversion," I said, my mind already moving. "Unless we do something so utterly stupid that it distracts the guards in the camp and keeps them busy."

"We'd need more than one diversion," Adam said. "We would need something to lure them into the woods, and then something so utterly distracting that it would keep them there." It sounded impossible.

But I owed it to Luka.

And I had come up with far stupider plans.

"But what are we going to do?" I said. "Or rather, you. Because I am going to get Luka—"

"And if Theo does come," Kristin began.

"The King will come," Adam said, his voice certain of it. "That dip that you indicated in the trees is not that far from the palace, and if any commotion breaks out, it will carry. There will be no avoiding the royal family hearing. Not with how tightly I know the royal army to keep their shifts. And if the cage is made out of iron, as fae cages often are, it would not be quiet to open without the key."

"Then we face the King," I said. "And we put a stop to this business once and for all. Whether or not that means his head on a pole, I don't know yet, but I'm eager to find out."

"You're only a human," Nikolas said. "He's the King of Whynne, the Fae King of Whynne. He can control all Seelie and Unseelie, humans too. It is more likely that you will not win. Compulsion is a powerful tool."

"And we should be scared of him for that?" Lindy asked,

rising to her feet. "You fear words? They are nothing in the scheme of things."

It sounded so utterly ridiculous when she said it like that, even knowing the truth of the situation. We did fear words. We did fear what could happen. But it was such a ridiculous thing to fear in the end, even if we could not resist them.

"We fear Camden," Adam tried to rationalize. "Have you forgotten? She's vindictive and vengeful, utterly insane. She's at the King's side, the most powerful man in Whynne, and willing to use him for all he is. She's unstoppable."

And finally, Winry spoke. Her voice was cold and unwavering, informing him of something that she had tried to tell me before. "Camden is only a Seelie. Yes, she is a woman, which is quite a powerful thing, but at the end of the day, she remains only a Seelie. Unless we stop her. Right now she is just the same as Kristin and I, but if we keep putting this off then one day she will become more. One day, they will forge another crown with both pieces of the fae trees. Are we really going to let that happen? Because rest assured, I am just as much of a tart looking for a suitable marriage as she is, and I am of no danger to you." She shook her head, spitting, "but if you put a crown on my head, I could be."

I could feel her words in my bones.

"We're getting Luka back," I said. "And if this is what fate demands, then we are handling the King as well. I will not lose twice... After this, Artur should sit in his bar quaking in fear, because I will come for him. I will not forget."

CHAPTER TWENTY

The mountain looked almost beautiful from where we stood originally, very near to the base of it. Though winter was beginning and the leaves had long since left the mountain's assortment of grey and white trees. And knowing that Luka was there, amongst that break in the trees, made it all the more beautiful. In fact, for those short moments, it was breathtaking. The most beautiful and frightening thing I had ever seen.

But you find that when it is not just you, and you are no longer at the bottom, things can turn out to be far more of a vertical incline than you remember, and the forest that you once swore was working with you, seems to work against you.

Especially when there is a large, heavy vehicle beside you. One that you need to use all of your strength to push up the face of the mountain.

"I get it now," I said with a nod. "I finally understand why he only wanted one car going up the road." Because it was so steep. Because an extra one or two thousand pounds made it steeper, and most tires slipped on damp, decaying leaves. This was why there was never anyone behind the King. "If this falls, I hope that it runs me over," I declared.

"We could always leave the car," said Nikolas impatiently, far too unwilling to continue. "I do not even like Luka that much."

"We are not leaving the car," Winry hissed behind him, desperate to pull her weight, she pushed as hard as possible. "We are nearly there, and the car is half of the plan. Without it, we have nothing."

"It is an awful plan," Nikolas began.

"And yet you could not come up with any others," I rebutted, because it was an awful plan, and there was no way it would work. "I thought that you were meant to be a strategist, Nikolas." But since it was the only plan that we had, and my plan in particular, we were going with it. We needed a diversion. This was the diversion. This would distract them.

"Besides," Kristin said while stuck behind the car, pushing the trunk and the bulk of the weight with every inch of muscle in his body. "We have Lindy. She's supposed to be lucky." Kristin had evidently held onto that little statement by Adam for a while.

All eyes turned to Lindy, gritting their teeth. The girl only shook her head, walking in front of the car and guiding us where to push with large waves of her hands.

"Lucky," Kristin repeated, desperate to hold onto that little promise. I suppose, all things considered, she was a little bit. Not enough to justify the importation of a young girl from a foreign country, but enough to say that I was glad that she was there.

"We just have to get it up there," Adam said, changing the topic from her back to the plan. "Once we get it up there, we do as we planned, Wren runs like hell, and we... do as we planned."

"This is suicide," Nikolas whined, throwing his head back. Heroics were far easier in the army. "Torture and then suicide. I will never forgive any of you."

"You are always welcome to go back to your squad," I grunted, shoving the car with my shoulder as hard as I could. "I'm sure that they would give you a warm welcome."

I think he growled at that.

"We are just feet away," Adam spat, quickly using his forearm to wipe away the sweat that plastered his forehead, causing the car to slip down ever so slightly before he frantically began to push it again. "If you could all manage to not start fighting for five minutes..."

We were. We most definitely were close, you could hear the soldiers' voices on the wind and smell their campfires. A small plateau awaited just feet away, a break in the trees not so far from their camp. We didn't know that it was there, we just guessed that there had to be something nearby.

And there it was, glorious. Lindy spotted it almost a mile down. I had never felt my heart beat so fast.

Because it was working, we were going to do it. And with one final shove, the last piece slid into place.

The car, once very nice, had seen better days. The forest was rough on it, as it was all things, and in the sunlight one could see the dents and scratches in the black paint. It was far from pristine now, and it was sitting there, ready to be used. I had to take a moment to admire it.

"You need to go," Adam said as the others grinned at their victory, his voice hardly audible. "I did not want to say so in front of the others, but with our luck, the King will be down here any minute. We cannot waste time. You need to move, get Luka and we'll try to get out before he comes. I don't feel like dying today."

"I'm suddenly nervous," I replied, my voice catching. "Perhaps don't mention dying."

"I don't think you have ever been nervous a day in your life," Adam replied, looking away from me, a hint of undeniable fondness visible on his face. "You're coming back," he said, his voice confident. "I don't care how you do it, but you're coming back."

"And I'm bringing with Luka," I said, pulling a length of ribbon from my wrist and securing it around my hair, pulling it away from my neck. "I'm not coming back if I don't have Luka."

Adam nodded, sure of that fact, his eyes still on everyone as they looked at the car and grinned at their success. I wondered what went through his head, if there were any particular thoughts that stood out, if he was as inwardly afraid as I was, just afraid to tell everyone else.

But his head was level, and his shoulders were squared. And with one last look at him, I took off, moving as fast as my feet would allow, the forest giving into me as I ran. Lone Unseelie, creatures with webbed hands and huge glowing eyes, mocking smiles and impossibly sharp snouts, watched as I passed by, moving out of the way, seeming to know that they could not stop me.

I found my way by sound alone. Navigating through the woods by the sounds of moving soldiers, men engaged in constant conversation and work. All I could do was pray that it was not the forest tricking me, and that Nikolas was right. This was the place.

A hint of burgundy and blue greeted me in the distance. Just a flash of it. The colors of higher and lower ranking military men. The colors of hope. I closed my eyes as I saw them, not willing to face the truth if they were just an illusion, my body somehow dodging the trees blindly. Maybe it was dumb luck.

So much of my life had become that.

But then I opened my eyes again and the camp grew closer and clearer, more solid. A thing that I could grab, and I felt my body thrum with anticipation.

My footsteps slowed and I used the trees around me to support me as I navigated the uneven terrain around the camp. I had to go to the other side, because if I tried to enter from the way that I went, then once the distraction happened, they would see me. That wasn't what I wanted.

What I wanted was to find him.

I knew he was there. I could feel it in the mark behind my ear, undoubtedly shaped like a small bird as the one before had been. But it was easy to convince myself that that was only want speaking, that desire had clouded my judgement. I wanted to be sure, but there was no way.

All I could do was keep moving and wait. It would not distract all of the guards, but it would distract just enough of them that I could get through, I believed. It would at least scatter the bulk of them. I just had to wait for the sign.

And then it went up, soaring above the trees, a single ball of flame hitting the blue sky. No one would know to look for it if they had not been keyed in to watch for it.

My hand rested on a tree, I braced myself against it once I saw that sign, preparing for what would come next, a series of events. One that we had discussed at length, one that I was not confident would work.

There were many soldiers in the camp, so many that it seemed like they were shoulder to shoulder. An assortment of all ages and ranks, the majority of them gathered around one area, a large tent. They lounged outside of it, looking bored but unable to do anything else. It was their assignment to keep that tent as safe as possible, ensuring that any outsiders did not get in.

The plan had to work.

The sound hit the air. A loud, metallic honk, one that forced their heads up. Then, another. The men looked to each other in confusion, attention gotten. The whole camp was alert, the sound echoing louder than it really was against the empty trees.

"Come on Adam," I muttered as they all stood there, looking off to the distance, squinting at the woods. "Give us a show."

It was like a match striking. There was no subtlety about it, no preamble. It just happened. One second nothing, and then, through the forest, the loud pop of flames. I knew that the car was nothing but fire then. Phase one.

The men looked with wide eyes to one another, clutching their rifles in their hands without any clue of what to do next. A few started to move, a slow crawl towards the woods, but then the flames grew.

I could not understand what they screamed, just that it spurred the others into motion. They were running, the camp was clearing. They were going to see what it was, save for a select few. Phase two.

I adjusted the cloak around my neck, hiking up the folded over trousers and adjusting my belt. Then I lifted my cloak, tucking my ponytail into the back of it and hoping that my shirt drooped loosely enough. I had to look the part, if only for a moment. I needed them to not recognize me.

Only two stood guard at Luka's tent, the others circled the small encampment and were so spread out that they would not be able to catch me if I darted in. I just had to stay calm. I tried to steady myself, but that type of thing never worked. I just had to learn to deal with my crushing nerves.

"Here goes everything, Kinsley," I murmured, striding forward. "I hope that you're worth it." I knew that he was.

. . .

I HAD NEVER BEEN A GOOD ACTRESS, OR A GOOD LIAR. I think that is why so many fae were fond of me, because I was one of the most transparent humans they had ever met. But at that moment, I knew that if a single soldier's eye landed on me, daring to question me, I would become a talented liar. I would convince them that I was undoubtedly meant to be there, a new recruit sent up the mountain and into the frying pan. A little bit of pity never hurt anyone.

When the first guard saw me and only nodded while I was near the camp's perimeter, I could not believe it. I think my heart raced a mile a minute, barely comprehending the fact that he believed it. He believed me, how badly was the King training these guys? And then the next one did too and I moved on through the rows of tents, my eyes down if only to make sure that I would not trip.

"Oh my god," I breathed, still moving, always moving. It was working. I couldn't believe that it was working, and it was almost time for phase three to keep the other men from doubling back. "Luka, I'm going to see you soon."

I clenched my eyes shut, holding my fists so tightly that my palm could have bled for all I knew as I hurried through the tents, listening for that sound.

It needed to happen, and soon, because otherwise they would come back. The large tent was close, so close. I could feel the mark on me warm, not burning, but forming a comforting heat. He was in there. I knew that he was in there, I knew then that it wasn't some comforting delusion, but the truth. I would see Luka again.

Whether I would join him in being trapped in there remained to be seen.

And then I heard the creaking of wheels turning. So old

and uncared for, so strained by the curse of fire. It was a quiet sound, barely there. I was a few miles away, I might have even imagined it.

But I knew that the automobile had started moving, and that now, at that very moment, it had begun to slip down the mountain. Soon it would actively fall...

Commotion. Confused men. I could hear them. And then the thud of hundreds of footsteps on wet earth, following the vehicle. Would they be stupid enough to follow it all the way down? Would it go far enough to keep them away?

"Do not hit a tree," I mumbled. "Do not hit a tree." That was the last thing I needed, for the car to hit a tree right away, giving them an opportunity to turn back.

I had to move fast just in case.

The entrance was right in front of me, two young men unenthusiastically guarding it. They looked up at me with lazy eyes.

"Hey, you got authorization to go in there?" The guard hadn't even begun to stand before I touched him, sending him backwards with his mouth opened wide in surprise.

"Wait a second—" The other one began, my hand swept out in his direction before he could finish, his body slumping over when the current hit him. I was getting better at it.

Two men shocked and downed. I had only seconds before someone saw what I had done.

"Please be the only ones," I whispered, grasping the clasp of my cape. "Please, for just once, let things go right." I pushed aside the flap, stepping inside of the tent, my eyes immediately met with darkness, complete darkness. Even with the small bit of daylight poking in behind me, I did not see a lamp.

They kept him in the dark.

The realization hit me, practically punching me in the

stomach. Of course they did. Had he even seen sunlight the past three days? What else had they done to him?

Suddenly, I did not want to remove my cape, instead holding it tightly, close to my body. What if it was not just him there? But soon people would spot the guards and come... I let go of the flap behind me, closing my eyes and ripping the necklace out from underneath my shirt, my fingers struggling to find the knob.

One turn, two. Click. Light. Dim, but useable light.

I opened my eyes to see it, watching as the flame burned away in my hand, only providing enough light for me to see immediately in front of me. Thankfully, no guards stood inside. I could walk in without fear.

I walked across the tent, taking in the assortment of things scattered about, the maps that hung on the walls and the lumpy rugs placed on the uneven ground. Mismatched furniture sat around the room, gathered like seating for an intimate lecture. It would be used by the King, I knew. The décor confirmed it. He would sit there and look upon Luka and feel that he had won... If Luka was even in there.

My eyes moved around the tent, the lantern illuminated the space inch by inch as I crept across it, looking in every direction. He had to be there. I knew he was there. If he could only make a sound or say something! Why was it that Luka never opened his mouth when I needed him to? He couldn't make the whole rescuing thing easier for me?

And then I saw it.

Rusted and aged, halfway hidden in the corner behind a tapestry as if it were some ugly statue or something, something that they didn't wish to look upon rather than what it was. A cell. An iron cell.

Luka.

I looked around the absolute mess of a tent, searching for

what I needed, hoping that someone was stupid enough to leave it out. No dice.

Science, then.

I moved to the cell, not daring to look inside yet. I could feel my heart in my throat.

Iron is magnetic. The lock was iron. Luka had given a long demonstration on magnetism once, when we were still in the Kinsley estate and secrets were still being kept as secrets.

"I hope you are proud of me, Luka," I whispered, closing my eyes. "I have worked very hard." I shoved my hand against it, channeling everything that I had into it, the concentration being nearly painful. I heard the lock give way with a click.

And there it was. One last door, one last step. The terror of not knowing what would be inside. I hesitated, I hated that I hesitated. "Luka?" I asked but received no response. There was no easy way out.

I gathered all my strength and pushed open the door, hoping beyond reason.

CHAPTER TWENTY-ONE

At first, I could only hear my breathing. Constant and pained, scared. Nothing else.

And then there was a wheeze.

A solitary wheeze. The noise of someone or something struggling to survive.

"Luka?" I stepped in further, even though my mind begged me not to, even though reason protested entering a cell without checking to make sure that the door would not close behind me. The indignity of it all hit me. The absolute and utter insult. Because there was something so demeaning about it, locking him in an iron box and leaving him in the dark.

I was angry, far too angry. But I couldn't help it.

"Luka?" I said his name again, adjusting the knob of the lamp around my neck to create more light. A miserable sound responded to it, a figure towards the back of the cell pulling in its long legs to flinch away from the light. It hit me then that it must have stung if he hadn't seen light for days. My hand flew to the knob again, but I was hesitant.

The woods were full of Unseelie.

How could I trust that it was him in there? What if they had placed another Unseelie in the cage, and he was somewhere else? How could I believe that nothing would happen to me? I should have left it on. But then, what if it was him? What if I hurt him?

My hand rose to the knob, turning it completely off, my eyes shutting with the motion once more, afraid of what I might see. I took one step into the darkness, then another, trusting beyond reason that nothing would happen to me.

"Luka," I said his name again, trying not to sound unsure. Any uncertainty would have been damning, both to him and me. I dropped down as I neared where I thought he was, feeling blindly.

My hands landed on a limb. I grabbed it, my hand moved up it. I searched for his chest, looking for any sign of life. I could feel the warmth coming from his skin, but that didn't mean much, not if something had recently happened.

"Luka," I whispered his name once more as I pressed my open palm to the heat in front of me, feeling what thundered below the flat surface. A heartbeat. One that grew steadier by the moment.

And then I was on my back, blind with not a single ounce of air in my body, someone else on top of me, someone else's heart thundering above mine. Someone hopefully just as scared as I was.

We struggled for just a moment, me trying to reach for what I believed to be him and him trying to shove my hands away, to shove me away. He used everything he had to peel my hands off of him, stabbing them towards the ground and trying to get me to stay there. I tried to grab onto him, to take him down with me, but I couldn't, not when his nails dug into my skin and he gave a final jerk, pushing down to the moist ground below, his hand shoving at my chest at the same time. My head bounced against the soil.

The awful realization that it might not be him hit me.

And I could say nothing. Not as the hands slowly grew tighter around mine, pinning my hands far above my head, the owner moving their legs to either side of my body. I could only open my eyes, not seeing anything in the darkness, just hearing and feeling. I was trapped, completely and utterly trapped. I could summon electricity, but a part of me feared the consequences that would arise depending on who or what was above me.

"Please," I said. "Pretty please, Kinsley." *Be him, be Luka.*

The chest above mine moved in sync with the rise and fall of my body, and I wondered if the person could see me. Had they adjusted to the night as well? By the second, they felt firmer, more real. I had not realized at first how frail they were, how lightly their body pressed against mine. Slowly, the weight above me was getting heavier.

The back of my mind screamed with fear. I began to struggle, trying to get my hands out of whatever it was's grip. My legs kicked below it, useless with the way I was pinned, a single, enraged cry escaped me as I struggled to get out, the back of my mind screaming that there were guards who would very soon be looking for me. Whatever was in that cage, it was not human. Likely some Unseelie they'd caught outside of the camp.

"Let go," I hissed, trying to throw one of my elbows up to get out of its grasp. "Let me go!"

The being only grunted, struggling to keep me down until I rocked my weight violently to the side, shoving it off of me. Immediately, I tried to scramble away, getting halfway there before the hand grabbed my wrist once more, my foot connecting with its stomach in the struggle as I clawed at the lantern around my neck, struggling to grab it and turn it on.

The light came suddenly, the knob turned all the way around, feeding a flame so bright that I recoiled, as did the thing approaching me, its teeth audibly snapping shut as it shoved my other hand down, silently trapping me once more.

I tried to reach for the bars to give myself some leverage while blinded, my feet kicking furiously underneath it, a silent scream caught in my throat. My eyes squeezed tighter, the light stung. But it was to my advantage, the only thing I had, so I opened my eyes.

At the same time that he did.

His eyes were on me, his mouth open. He looked at me as if I was not real.

"Wren," his grip loosened only slightly. I stared in turn. He moved one of my hands to join the other, his fingers wrapping around my wrist as he looked down at me, horrified. "Is it really you, or is this just another terror?" Terror?

I flinched as he reached back behind my ear, recoiling from the touch. Other things knew what was there. Other Unseelie. The Gancanagh.

He trembled as he felt the raised skin, his fingers lingering there. "Wren," he repeated. My ears rang when his skin touched mine, the mark throbbing. He closed his eyes, looking relieved.

He looked fuller somehow, more alive, and, taking in my terror, he winced. He grabbed my wrist once more, forcing my hand to move as he needed it, pressing my fingers against bumpy, long since damaged cartilage. "Wren," he repeated once I'd realized, and then his arms were around me, tight and unyielding as he clutched me to his chest, another shudder ripping through his body as reality came to me.

"Luka," saying his name felt like a relief, my arms wrapped

around his waist, desperate not to let go as he pulled me to my knees, hunching over to bury his face in my shoulder as I pressed my head against his collarbone, my ears ringing. I was practically in his lap, desperate to be as close to him as possible, to feel as much of him as I could. "It's really you. You're here," I could have cried. I tried not to.

"Please tell me that you did not just walk into a cage in the middle of an army camp for me," Luka muttered, holding me so impossibly tight that my whole body ached. "More than that, tell me that the door did not lock behind you."

"I have done far dumber things in the past few days, Luka," I admitted, moving even closer, practically throwing myself on top of him.

His lips pressed against me. My neck, my shoulder, my ear —any skin that he could find. Anything that was not covered. "Wren," he repeated. He was unwilling to let go, unwilling to even pull away, like I might disappear at any moment. "You shouldn't have come back." But he looked relieved to see me all the same.

"Greenable," I replied, resting my head against his neck. "You promised me Greenable."

He pulled away at that despite my protests and his eyes on mine as he told me, "I did not promise you Greenable." Ever willing to argue.

"No," I said. "You did. You promised that you would stay by my side."

The emotion slipped off of his face as he realized, his jaw going slack. Uncertainty filled his gaze.

"Right where I couldn't see it, Kinsley?" I asked, tilting my head at him so the marked ear stayed higher. "Knowing how badly that I wanted it? You're cruel."

He was sheepish, so suddenly shy in an utterly endearing way that was absurdly unfamiliar to me. "If you knew and you were coerced, there was no way to stop you from mentioning it..."

My lips pressed against his, my hands holding his head firmly in place as I poured everything I had, all of the emotions of the past few months, into that single kiss. His hands rose to my waist, only capable of resting there as I practically pushed the two of us over, basking in the fact that he was there, and he was alive.

"You could die," Luka said as I kissed the corner of his mouth, the gravity of our situation hitting him the moment I pulled away from him. "Wren, you should not have come here. You could die."

I shook my head frantically, my arms tighter around him. "I know. I've actually been told that nearly a hundred times by now."

"Wren," he tried again, his arms loosening, the fact that we were both stuck there setting in. We were both in that cage. He did not resist kissing me again, his eyes closed and his mouth unrelenting as he savored one last embrace before pulling away. "Wren, we need to go. We have to get out of here."

I nodded against him, just happy to see that he was there and to know that it was really him. I pulled away, but it felt difficult, like one of the hardest things that I could ever do. He cupped my face, stroking my cheek before finally getting up, his hand held out in my direction as he begged me to take it.

I slapped my hand into his, taking in the way that the light from the lantern reflected in his eyes, the way that his features were so familiar, he was still him. It had been only days, but it felt like centuries. Time tended to move slowly when you were worried about someone. The rising urge to grab him again and hold him close built in me, a stupid, girlish urge to kiss him once more and tell him nothing but sweet words.

That died away when I stood and the world was no longer Luka and I's alone.

"It shouldn't have been this easy," purred a female voice. "You shouldn't have just walked right in. I almost feel bad for you now..." With a single click, the tent was thrust into light, a familiar figure near the entrance. Not of the cage, she wasn't that quick or quiet, she couldn't even touch the door. But the tent.

The princess. The soon to be queen. Camden.

"Oh Wren, you really do make things too simple," she hummed. "It's such a shame."

CHAPTER TWENTY-TWO

I HAD NOT IMAGINED WHAT IT WOULD BE LIKE WHEN I SAW her again.

Of course her face had popped up a few times in my nightmares, when I speculated what the worst could be. One time, I had even seen her out of the corner of my eye when sleep deprived and immediately assumed myself to be dead, sent to the lowest pits of some sort of hell, forced to confront her as a punishment.

But there she stood, perfect as always, not a speck of makeup out of place, her eyeliner so sharp that it could have drawn blood with the slightest touch. Dressed in white, an ungodly specter, the toll of a death knell.

And she only looked at me, her brown eyes meeting mine as her head slowly tilted, daring me to say something as she stepped into the tent, every single footstep sounded like the beating of a war drum. Closer and closer.

She had never bothered to fight me before, though the gleam of want always shined in her eyes. For all she hated me, for all I feared her, she thought me beneath her. Perhaps I was just not as formidable of a foe to her as she was to me. I think she liked to believe that I was so inconsequential, I should be almost invisible to her. I was so far beneath her in her eyes.

And I thought her too far above me, so far that she was primed for a fall.

I could only hear the murmur of sounds outside, the noise cut through by the sheer silence that absolute terror inspired in my mind. Something was happening, I couldn't be sure what. My mind couldn't pick out the details, not when faced with her.

"I have been looking all over for you," she said, her voice almost a tsk, chiding. As if she thought the situation to be funny.

I supposed it was easy to think such a thing when you had the upper hand. Every game of war was funny when you were on the winning side.

"Why are you alone," were the first words to tumble out of my mouth, my eyes moving behind her, looking for someone to follow her. I had so rarely seen her on her own. Surely the King would soon follow.

"Because you don't warrant any additional company," she said. "Save for your little plaything." I had no doubts as to who she was referring.

"He is not a plaything," I spat immediately, feeling Luka's hands in my cape, he was already looking for a way out, already formulating a plan, especially now that I was there and he had something to fight for.

"I'm sorry about your mutt, then."

The ball soared past her before I could even think about it, hurtling into a cabinet behind her with a great crash, the sound of china shattering within it hitting the air as she took a single step to the side to avoid it. The sparks of the electricity reached for her face but did not touch her. Her eyes remained on me, unimpressed.

"Wren," Luka's voice warned me, but my hands were already raised, my pulse already quickening. I felt the energy coursing through me. We needed to get out of that cage. Then, out of the tent. Lastly, out of the camp.

As soon as possible.

But Camden stood in the way. "You're so reactive," she said boredly, taking another, long stride towards me, almost as if it were a leisurely stroll. "You should learn to control your temper, but I suppose humans are prone to moments of impulsiveness."

I pulled out of Luka's grasp, stepping towards her and thrusting my hands forward as I moved out of the cage, another bolt left my fingers but missed again, she was too quick. She moved closer, still seeking to close the distance between us. Her face screamed of danger. I was struck again by the fact that I had never fought Camden before, nor paid attention to her when in the midst of things, then my eyes noticed her hands.

Her palm was flat towards the earth. She was not ignoring me entirely. She was planning.

"—run." The word ripped out of me without a second thought, the ground leaving me all at once before I had time to process it. I was brought back to another time, another place, another mound of dirt wrapped around my ankle, a set of thick roots in its midst—

I swung my hand up as I heard Luka say something, unable to make out his words, just the fact that the sting of blue sparks poured through my fingertips, cutting through the air, moving before she could touch me... Then she grabbed me, dodging again with expert precision, the fact that she could last so long against Adam finally explained by her speed alone, and then the explanation ripped away from me with a scream as she bent my hand back.

Way back.

Nearly shoving me to the ground as she did it, her face still not moving. I did not even think, my foot swinging upwards, connecting with her.

I felt my foot connect with her gut, her body grunting as she pulled away and stumbled backwards.

Now we were even. Now it was a real fight. I scrambled to my feet, desperate not to be the one stuck on the ground.

"What's the matter," I spat, grabbing my wrist as I looked at her, my shoulders bobbing up and down as I struggled to focus, to keep panting and consequentially keep thinking rather than sinking into pain. Tears already pricked at the corners of my eyes. "Do you not like it when other people fight back, Camden? Are you too used to forcing their heads back down, waiting for them to bow first before you make your move? I'm so sorry, princess. How rude of me."

She snarled, her perfect, straight white teeth revealed with that simple raise of her lip, her eyes bored into mine.

That was good. That was where I preferred to keep them. Wherever Luka was, it didn't matter at the moment. Just that Camden was focused on me.

"You know your friends are out there right now," she spat. "We saw them from on top of the mountain, saw your little trick, and we sent the guards down to pick them up. We'd been keeping an eye out, we knew you were coming. You're so predictable."

"What an astonishing observation," I spat, readying myself just as she did. "However could you have guessed? Wren will come back to Luka, the man that she loves. Wren will come to get him, to rescue him from our clutches. My, you two must feel brilliant." I shook my head. "Oh, of course you do, since you have never known a day of love in your god forsaken, miserable life. The idea that someone might care enough to come back for another person is so novel to you, isn't it?"

I should have anticipated the wind that nearly knocked me over. I shouldn't have been surprised that the sharp whip of it smacked across my face, knocking me off kilter as I continued to cradle my left hand, the realization that it may never heal the same hitting. Pain ripped through my body.

But I had to keep moving. I had to keep going. I glanced to my left and realized that I did not see Luka. He was gone. Hopefully completely. I couldn't look for him longer than a second, all I could do was hope that he got out.

If I could have done only one thing, it would have been that. Make sure that Luka left.

But I knew he didn't. He wouldn't.

Another disapproving sound and an additional gust of wind was sent, slamming me back, smashing me into the cage. The sheer force of it rattled my bones.

"Speak again of love and all of your wonderful little joys," Camden dared me, stepping closer to me, her hand on my throat as she seized me from the cage, pinning me back against one of the thick tent poles at the center. Her eyes practically burning holes into mine. "Tell me all about it, I should love to hear such things from your lips before you die."

"Then you have a longtime to wait," I spat, actually spat, my saliva falling on her face. "Because I do not plan to die today. Sorry to disappoint you."

It was the first thing to make her actually react, her other hand reaching up to touch it as she realized what it was, and that it was mine. "Humans," she hissed, as if it were typical of our entire species. Suddenly, both her hands were upon me, my feet dangling in the air, her nostrils flaring. "You are nothing," she snarled.

Her hands were too tight around my windpipe for me to speak. All I could do was give into nature, the primal part of my brain reached up for her hands, clawing at them desperately. It seemed like I kept ending up like this, pinned by my throat.

The difference was, even at the hands of the Unseelie, I did not teeter so close to death.

"I know all about you," she sneered. "Every last detail." Her nails dug into my neck, stabbing into the skin, encouraging warm liquid to pool at the surface. "You are nothing," she repeated. "Born to a whore mother in an unimportant town, your father a local farm boy who wanted nothing to do with you. Given a life only out of pity and some misguided obligation to your mother, meant to scrub floors for the rest of your days. Nothing important, nothing special. A *human*. One that has spent all of her time amongst the fae, away from her own kind. They call that a taken human, you know," she whispered to me, as if it was an interesting fact and not another taunt. "One that has been stolen by another world but does not belong. One that will always just be thrown amongst us, never quite fitting in. Just taken from their world."

She sounded so angry at that, the fact that I had dared to be a human of all things. What a vile, ugly thing to be.

"You were only adopted out of necessity, to keep the Laurent's pitiful bloodline pure and allow them to hold onto their delusions of being nobility. They had no desire for you, no care for who you really were," her voice trembled with rage, I think it was only increased by my unmoving legs, by the way that I did not fight back and instead simply stared back at her. "Your beloved tried to weasel his way out of your deal, neither him nor his brother wanted to marry you. Yet you stand here and you act like you are important, like you matter in the grand scheme of things. You have been nothing but an insufferable little gnat buzzing in my ear. You are nothing. You have never been anything but an object of convenience, of occasional entertainment for the fae. A human kept for a purpose, to dance for the rest of our amusement and to give us a story to tell when we were bored. Nothing more."

"And yet I'm still alive," I managed, despite my restricted airflow. "Still alive and still here, buzzing in your ear. Even though you think I've served my purpose." The edges of the world seemed to turn black. "Buzz. Buzz." I felt tired, so tired. My body felt weak.

A dry chuckle escaped Camden, as she quietly said, "squish." Her fingers tightened, the dark edges seeming to grow larger, to take away more of my picture of the world. A realization hit me.

Oh. After all of this time, after all of the fear and uncertainty, I was finally dying.

And then it was torn away from me almost as quickly as it came, the ground suddenly reaching for me.

No. Not reaching, not moving. I was moving. I was falling to the ground. Maybe that was a part of dying. Maybe you fell through the ground when you went to hell.

I didn't think such a thing would feel so solid.

I landed in a huff of air, my ears ringing so loudly that I could barely hear, a splintered piece of wood fell beside me, the hem of Camden's dress just barely visible.

"You'll pay for that, Kinsley!" Camden swore, the wind slicing through the air like a knife. I blinked blearily, staring at the wood before me. The one stained with her blood.

And then realized what she'd said.

Kinsley.

Luka did not have much in the way of physical gifts, it was not in his nature as an Unseelie. But he was there. She was looking at him, facing him. Attacking him.

Whatever energy I had doubled at that moment, nothing

else mattering to me when compared to that realization. I smashed my hands together, whipping them in her direction, a gash of blue firing from them.

I had to protect him.

Air. That was my next focus. Air.

I could breathe it, I could taste it. I struggled back into a sitting position, letting it pour in past my bruised throat, letting it rattle in my hollow lungs. Another thing whirled past me, narrowly missing me.

I heard a whistling sound in response as I struggled to lift my head back up.

Luka. Something had fired his way. Something had narrowly missed him. She was fighting, he had lost to her before. I had not even seen the battle, even though I knew that he had put his all into it, stalling her long enough for me to tussle with Adam and slide through the fence into the woods, a bag full of empty notebooks at my side.

My hands were on the pole behind me as I dragged myself back up, the weakened, broken wrist of my left hand making it feel almost impossible. I could barely use it anymore, I would have no aim—I flinched as I tossed it her way anyway, another bolt of blue leaving me, seeming to take a slice of my soul with it.

I would continue to fight. It was a brief set back, but I would fight. I would not go down without a fight.

"You," Camden snapped, her foot stomping down on the ground, a ripple of earth moving beneath the ground in my direction.

I used the pole as leverage, swinging to the other side, my eyebrows raising as I realized how successful I was, that I had somehow managed to evade her. It was truly shocking.

"No," Camden growled as her eyes tore away from mine,

stealing off in another direction. "Get out!" She shouted, her hand slicing through the air.

Luka.

I didn't even think, lobbing another ball of electricity, an almost mist-like thing catching it before it could hit Camden, her burning eyes moving back in my direction.

"That's right." I said, pushing away from the pole, stalking towards her. "Keep your eyes on me." I could almost see the fire pour out of her pores. "I'm the one you want. Not him."

"You're nothing," she repeated, and I barely had the time to react before a rock sliced by me, cutting not only my shirt, but the skin beneath it and burying into the wood of one of the cabinets behind me. "I'm a general's daughter, the bride to the King, and you? You're—"

"Wren Nettles," I provided, the electricity swirling out of thin air and finally hitting her. Finally leaving a mark on her perfectly pale skin. "I'm Wren Nettles. Daughter of a whore, former maid, and lover of the Unseelie. Perhaps you should tell me all that you know of love and joy, I would hate for you to die with such cruel words on your tongue at the hands of such an inconsequential little gnat."

"Oh please," Camden sneered. "You haven't the stomach to kill me."

"Try me," I replied, and I fired all that I had towards her, the bolt ripping through the side of the tent.

CHAPTER TWENTY-THREE

I KNEW THAT I HAD MADE A MISTAKE THE SECOND THAT long, tattered ribbons of the tent remained, opening it entirely to the outside world, her body falling back with them, collapsing against the ground.

Not dead. She had been so utterly right about me, she was not dead, far from it. But she was, however, incapacitated. The opening in the side of the tent had revealed the dangers outside, the fighting continuing all around us. Scatterings of Unseelie escaping from the forest, battling alongside the few weary travelers that had come to their home to fight the King.

I had forgotten what the King had done to Adam, and I had forgotten one other thing.

The rain.

Adam was the one who could hold his own against the King, the one who had managed to fend him off. And now there was rain, a downpour.

And Camden was on the ground in front of me, barely breathing. Her pink-painted eyelids dropping, her body limp.

Everything that I had feared, sprawled out in front of me. Creating a new horror. One that I could not anticipate.

"Wren!" It wasn't just Luka's voice that rang out, but Adam's, Kristin's, so many others—I couldn't turn quick enough.

"You." The voice boomed in my head as I bounced against the ground, my shoulder hitting the packed soil, my mind still spinning from the lack of air. I had just been knocked what felt like a thousand feet back, my back hitting one of the great trees, my eyes nearly rolling back into my head.

And then I realized that it was a tree.

Really realized.

The domain of the fae, outside of courtrooms and lavish balls. The place where they came from, there they controlled the world around them. Danger.

The roots of the tree squirmed beneath me, reaching towards me, trying to trap me, forcing my back against the trunk as one wound around my leg, trapping me. Horror, absolute horror broke through me, and Adam was far away.

Lindy even further, managing more people than him, freezing more than he could manage with the rain pouring the way that it did.

I saw Luka's mouth move, he began to run to me before he was forced down to the ground with a careless shove of the King's hand, the magic gripping him as the King kept moving closer and closer.

There had been many things that Adam had done right in his fight with the King, managing to stay away from the woods was the most prominent amongst them. Because though the Unseelie lived there, though the Gancanagh reigned, Theo was still King, and his crown was made from those trees. He still controlled them.

Even if the forest was living and breathing, seeming for a

moment like it was trying to rebel against him days ago. Trying to trick me into saving it. Now it had betrayed me, wrapped around his fingers. Perhaps it didn't have any other choice.

"I asked for very little from you," the King spoke, so much distance between us, but not a care visible as he strode up to me, slow and unfettered. "In fact, I asked for next to nothing, and this is how you repay me? This is how you repay my kindness? You know, I had fancied that I would give you mercy the next time you came to court, that I would fix your little perversions and set you up with a proper Seelie fae, but look at you," his boot was under my chin, tilting my head up to look at him. "You disgust me."

"I am not the king who is destroying his country," I said.

He let his foot slip from under me, allowing me to fall forward. "I am doing what I have to to maintain control, to deal with these Unseelie rebels and the way that they try to take what's not theirs. The way that they have always done that. I'm sorry that you do not understand."

"There are no Unseelie rebels," I spat, "just the love of your life, taking advantage of your fears, driving you further and further into madness while she creates a war in your head that does not exist. All for her to land on the throne—" His foot snapped across my face, kicking the words out of my mouth, causing me to choke as blood, fresh from the sharp pain in my nose, flooded my mouth.

"You do not speak of her that way. You do not speak of your queen so cruelly—"

But I had to. I had to rationalize with him, I had to make him see sense. "You're scared of the Unseelie because of something that happened to you, and she knows it. She made you more frightened. She took advantage of you, she blew things out of proportion," I should have been glad that it was his hand that slapped across my face then, stinging with brutality. It was far kinder than the foot.

"Learn," the King demanded. "Close your mouth and learn your lesson, before I make you. You do not speak of your future queen like that—"

"There are bad people in every group, bad actions in every species. There are humans who murder as well as Unseelie, but she didn't focus on that for you, did she? She cherry-picked, she told you the stories you wanted to hear, the stories that other members of your kingdom would want to hear. Because it was good for her. Good for you to be afraid, good for others to feel the same as you, to justify the way that you felt. Your mother hated Unseelie, and you? You were afraid of them, she didn't finish the job and you couldn't get the country together enough to put together the pieces," I spoke fast, so fast that the blood just leaked out of my mouth, I couldn't be bothered to swallow it. He needed to hear me, he needed to hear reason.

Smack. My eyes closed again, a soft cry escaping me.

"Wren!" A voice screamed in the distance, desperate to draw near, desperate to claw his way closer. "Don't touch her!"

"She was convenient for you," I said with a sway, "someone who further justified your fears. And you were convenient for her, a prince. A King. A man with a title so strong that no one would ever look down on her again."

"You are Unseelie trash," The King growled. "A lover of monstrous things, perverted by their magic. Delusional beyond imagination."

"And you're a coward."

I could not imagine how I looked, hauled up by him, hanging from the collar of Luka's ripped dress shirt, my hair pulled back from my face, forcing the King to see more of the carnage. More of what his delicate little flower of a bride had done to me. I wondered if he would even realize that I had come to the camp in pristine condition; she was the violent one, not me.

"I should sacrifice you to them," Theo said. "Slit your throat and throw you off a cliff dressed in white, leave you to be a bride of the forest, just as Camden suggested. Then they'd be happy, appeased, if only for a moment. That awful thing. The Gancanagh."

"Do it," I dared him, sounding like a child. I had always been a reckless, careless thing. I had always started fights and dived into trouble. "Throw me to them. Give me to the forest. Then you can lie in your bed at night, wondering. Hoping that I do not come for you. I will, you know. Even if I die and you level this forest, I will come for you."

He shuddered, his hands trembling in my collar.

"Can you do it?" I taunted. "Can you kill me? You know, Camden just mocked me for not being able to kill her."

He looked at me like I was this alien thing.

"You can't, can you? You've always relied on others to do your bidding, you've always been soft. That's why Adam's still alive, isn't it? You're soft." My eyes held his, my hands raising to clasp his wrists. "He told you that he loved you, did you even know what that meant?"

He looked at me, trembling, afraid to agree with me. "He's the same as you," Theo said, his voice breaking, his body not wanting to agree. "Camden told me. He's the same as you, ruined. That's why he said it. He was told to. He can lie. He's become bitter and cruel now, maybe he always has been. He said that just to get a reaction out of me, and it meant nothing."

I breathed, the air shaking as it came out of me. "How could you ever say such a thing about Adam?" I asked, gaping at him, beyond astounded. "Out of all of the people in this world, Adam. He was your friend. The only true one you had."

"He belongs to you and your lot, the people that this forest has ruined," Theo whispered, but even as he spoke, there was an air of doubt. "Camden said it. She cannot lie."

"Camden is a fae, Theo. A whole fae," I said. "There is no one else who knows better how to bend the truth. You know that, Theo. You know that she's tricked you." I could see it behind his eyes, he knew. He was perfectly aware, yet he kept me there, hanging from Luka's shirt, the fabric having slowly become untucked from underneath my pants. Somewhere, somewhere far away, Luka stood. Watching.

Waiting for the worst.

"Theo," said a voice on the wind. "Theo," it repeated, so soft and sweet, like a lover's embrace. Like a desperate cry for the one that you adored to hold you. That was the worst. That was the danger.

Her confusion, her mock innocence. Her voice breaking, sounding as if she was ailing, as if she needed him. How long had he been alone? How long had his parents been gone? Twenty years, I had heard. Even to a fae, twenty years was a long time to be alone. To a human, twenty years felt like an eternity.

Twenty years without an equal. Twenty years alone. Twenty years as the king of this country, likely with no one to turn to. She knew.

She saw a lonely man, one who only lived off of courting the giggling, preening young ladies of the higher court, and she knew that he wanted more. She saw him, his only friendships coming from the Harlow line, a line which he had shaped himself. One which he could never be certain of whether they actually cared about him.

Even when Adam said that he loved him, meaning far more than friendship.

And Camden destroyed it. She dug her way in. She preyed upon his fears.

"Luka," I said in a soft, strangled voice. "He tells me not to be afraid of anything. He laughs at me when I am ridiculous and he teases me. He is always serious, but he does what he can. When he sees something to worry about, he tries not to make it any bigger, nor more pressing than it has to be. He hides newspapers with pictures of the woman he knows I'm afraid of."

"I don't care to hear of your love story," The King replied through gritted teeth.

"I just want you to know that there is another way. That this is not normal, that you don't have anything to be afraid of," yet as the Unseelie tore through the men, fighting for their lives, I understood that he could not see it that way. "If she loved you, she wouldn't want you to live your life in terror."

"Theo," Camden called in the distance, a wail. "Theo, please. Please, before she hurts me."

Me, the one battered beyond belief.

"Look at me," I said, shaking my head. "Do you think I can hurt anyone?"

"I didn't think you could before," the King admitted.

"I just want to be with Luka," I said. "I don't want to be a hero, Theo. I don't want to hurt Camden. I just do what I have to, I've just done what I've had to. You and the rest of the world are what intervened. You and the rest of the world are what made me your monster."

Pain. Ripe, aching pain tore through him with that statement. He didn't want to hurt anyone, he didn't want to be the villain in anyone's story, just as I didn't want to be the villain in his. "But now you are," he said, his eyes raising from me, looking past me, looking through the trees. "And he wants you." I knew what he meant. I knew that he meant the Gancanagh. Maybe he even saw him. "You belong to the Unseelie," he said. "You are a danger to society."

"I'm a teenage girl," I said. Because, at the end of the day, that's all I was. Just another girl, one on her way to adulthood. I was so close to adulthood that I could taste it.

I could only imagine what I'd do if I lived.

"You can't kill me," I repeated. "You don't have it in you."

"And I can't let you go either," said the King. "Because he is there, and he will claim you if I do."

"He won't," I began. "The Gancanagh won't. He's here to watch over us, he's here to stop what you're doing, he's here—"

No. My eyes closed. "We should send a message," a voice rang out from behind us, churning my stomach. A voice that was delicate but resolved. A voice that tried to sound as if her cruelty was something that had been created by others, as if the world had made her awful rather than the fact that she was shaping the world around her.

I heard a soft grunt beside her, the sound of Luka hitting the ground.

"No," I begged. Why had she grabbed him? What would she do? Was she going to make me watch her kill him? Did she bring him to the edge of the forest to end it all—

"If you can not kill her, then they should know. Know that we won't allow any of this, we will not allow the Unseelie to steal away any more girls, bending them to their will. They should know that there are consequences to their actions." Camden sounded so soft, so convincing, as if she were genuinely worried. "We cannot have more humans in Whynne end up like Wren. It is something that we just cannot allow."

The air turned cold, only a cloud of air escaping the King at first, the man finally releasing me, allowing me to topple to the ground. "You're right," he said, utterly convinced. Desperate to believe. "You're right, we need to do something. We need to save people like her."

"We need to set an example," Camden said, shoving Luka

forward. Luka winced with the action, then winced again as he met my eyes. "Unless there's someway that you can stop this situation from escalating, Theo."

The King couldn't even look at her. A deal was out of the question. He could only let her push Luka forward.

"He should be the one to do it," Camden said.

And the look on Luka's face said it all. He already knew. He was completely aware.

He tried to move away when the King grabbed him, the words he spoke to him were not something I was even capable of thinking, but his hands were tied, literally, and we were alone. "Kill her."

We were all alone when his eyes glazed over.

CHAPTER TWENTY-FOUR

THIS WASN'T HOW THE STORY WAS SUPPOSED TO END, WE had only just found each other again.

We had just fought for each other, tooth and nail, and I had risked everything for Luka. There was supposed to be a happy ending, that was how stories were supposed to end. But a long time ago someone had told me that there would be no fairytale endings in the story of Luka and I. Someone had told me that there would be no happily ever after; the King. It was the King who made it that way.

The King who watched as Luka's ties were loosened, his eyes still on me. The only kindness they could give me was the chance to run, the King stepped back from me, his eyes silently urging me. But what good would that do?

"Luka." An example for the ages. This was the new version of the Princess and the Pond Scum, one of the bastardized fairytales of Luka's youth. This was the Maid and the Unseelie, and it did not have a happy ending, just a thousand notes in the margin to shoot down any questions when a curious child asked why.

Why didn't she run?
Why didn't she do anything?
Why didn't she fight?
Because she couldn't. Even if she knew she had to.

CHAPTER TWENTY-FIVE

"Wren." Luka said my name, and it was a warning, a plea.

A message from someone who was barely there anymore.

I could only shake my head as he changed, becoming someone I didn't know, someone I couldn't know. Someone who stood there with the King's voice echoing in his head, trying to shake it off, trying to become himself again.

Sick.

This was sick.

The King and Camden both knew it, of course. They both knew that, for all the King ranted about perversions, this was it. There was no going back.

And for a moment, I remembered when Kristin offered me Luka's name, his true name. I remembered how I rejected it, telling him that I didn't need it. Did I still feel the same way now, or did I wish otherwise? I couldn't answer. The reality of my situation was too difficult to comprehend.

And even though I had steeled myself against it, even though I had promised myself to go quietly, something caught on the breeze. Or maybe it just caught in my head. An urge to run as fast as I could, to move before he snapped into it.

To rewrite the story.

Because for all that I adored Luka, for all that I had wanted him...

I really, really didn't want to die. I couldn't put my finger on it at first, and then I realized what it was. I remembered that something, something the King didn't know about, sat behind my ear. Something that bonded Luka to me. That promised he would go with me wherever I went. He would die with me if I didn't do something.

"We could make a trade," the King said. "You could give me your powers, all of them, and we could stop this right here. We don't have to do this—"

It was appealing, but...

"No deal," I said, wincing at the fact that I so much as said that. I wouldn't take his deal, I wouldn't trade with him. I wouldn't give up my powers, just as I wouldn't give up Luka. This was where we sat as a result, at an impasse.

Or not an impasse, not even close, because the moment the King nodded, I was off, all thoughts of nobility out of my head. Self-sacrificing was made for someone else, and me? I wasn't a fan of it. Not if there was even the slightest chance that we would both die.

I barely made it to the encampment before he was upon me, trailing close behind me, trying to grab me. Luka moved fast, far faster than normal. All I could do was duck and weave, not running in a straight line because if I did, Luka would surely outrun me. He had six inches on me, at least.

I turned back, immediately regretting my decision. I fired off a spark in his direction to slow him down.

"Wren, what are you doing?" A voice shot through the crowd, I think it was Kristin. I couldn't answer him. I didn't know how to. I wasn't trying to hurt Luka, not yet. Actually, I was trying to do the very opposite, but you try to explain that to people. It's hard to say that you're not actually trying to kill someone when you're flinging magic their way.

And then I slipped and Luka seized the opportunity, trying to take me down. Not getting it, not understanding why he shouldn't. Because the voice in his head, the voice of the King, told him that he was meant to kill me, that there was no other way.

So I swung a fist at the side of his jaw, my hand at his shoulder giving him another shock.

"Wren!" A voice called out, but it didn't matter, not at the moment, not as I struggled to get myself back up.

I was injured beyond belief. I'd not been healed. I would not be healed so long as Luka was like this. There would be no fae magic for me, but even though I was weak, I would not let Luka kill me. Of all people, I would not let him do it.

"I'm going to find a way to snap you out of this," I promised. "I'm going to find a way to get you back. Maybe if I get you to the woods—" His hand swung in my direction and I screamed, ducking out of the way, sinking back into the mud. "Listen to me! Luka, listen to me!"

"Wren—" The second Luka was upon me, the voice spoke. Not his nor mine, but Nikolas's. Nikolas seeing me, Nikolas not knowing what to do.

Luka on top of me.

I screamed, shoving Luka down even though he did his very best to reach for me, my body completely covering his, pinning him underneath me.

"No guns," I shrieked, practically begging. "No matter what, no guns—" I couldn't have Luka shot, not again.

Luka's hand gripped the collar of my shirt, yanking me downwards, ripping a few buttons off in the process. His forehead pressed against mine, his hand holding me there while his other hand reached.

I gave everything I had in me to pin that one hand down, both of mine shoving it to the ground, my eyes stuck looking into his, our brow bones practically touching, and then...

A flicker, just a flicker of that awful place, the one that he had showed me only once before. I felt myself begin to sink into his illusions, like I was being pulled under the water. I let go of him, the shock filling my body before I could do anything about it, and then his hand escaped me, flinching in pain. I had not meant to do it, but I couldn't dwell on it.

I smashed his hand down just a moment later, meeting his gaze as I forced it against the ground.

"Don't," I warned, but he couldn't hear me. I knew he couldn't. "Luka." I just wanted to say his name, I needed to hope beyond hope that he would hear it.

He would die too, I had to remind myself. One false move and he would die too.

"Luka," I repeated his name again. "Luka, Luka, Luka. This is not how I pictured things going," I said, "you need to snap out of this. You need to listen to me."

His furious gaze held onto me, and I knew what it was like then to be hated by him. Because at that moment he looked at me with something so angry, so bitter, and so venomous that no other word came to mind than hate, and I just had to bear it. Because I wouldn't say what it was out loud, the fact that he despised me at the moment.

"I love you," I whispered, sitting there on top of him, unsure what else to do and flinching when another horror poured through my mind. "I love you, Luka. I'm not stupid enough to try to kiss you at the moment, but I love you. I don't want to hurt you."

"Please," was his only response, his voice begging me to

help him. Another, awful terror tore through my mind, curling my spine and allowing him the upper hand, my whole mind fading away as I tried to focus on anything else, any sort of memory to protect me.

Anything but darkness, large and endless, the feeling as if I might fall at any moment. The feeling that if I screamed, no one would hear—

I opened my eyes again, finding that I was on the bottom again and he lingered on top. But even then, I wasn't completely sure that that was true and not an illusion, because there were strange bits that bled in, little oddities that I did not understand. Odd looking Unseelie, soldiers frozen in horror, and him.

The look on his face almost begging me to do something. Almost desperate for me to move, but angry all the same.

No, I decided, feeling pained by his weight above mine. *That was reality.*

"Kill her," Camden's voice rang out in the background, a demand. Not one with the same cherry coating as the King's, but one that was still forceful in its own way.

His hands were braced on either side of me, holding my hands down, his fingers crushing mine. His eyes held mine, begging for me to do something, to shove him off, to put him out of his misery. "Please," he repeated, and there was just a flicker of something in my mind, not horror, but a small memory. I held onto his hands.

The two of us laughing in bed, me moving closer to him, stroking his wrist. Him tightening his arms around me, placing a kiss at the base of my neck. Greenable. That stupid city mentioned once again, the two of us promising each other. Our only goal.

Home.

One of his hands pulled back against mine, trying to move

my fingers. I think he would have done something if I had let go, but instead he just pulled at it, halfway trying, halfway not. He did not want me to touch him, he did not want my memories to hurt him. There was more commotion, more sounds in the background, but he was there with me.

"Greenable," I said, because I could think of nothing else, and his eyes closed slowly, almost blissfully. As if he were imagining it right there. "You and I." My hand pulled away from his, even though it was dangerous, even though it was risky. I reached for him and I touched his jaw, his soft skin.

"Do as you were told," Theo said miserably somewhere, and another blast of horror hit me as I held Luka's face, it was so powerful that it churned my stomach.

I would die of fear, it appeared. Every illusion ripped through me, tearing me apart.

I was sure that someone was calling my name somewhere. That someone was demanding that I throw him off, that I fight. For a brief, terrifying moment, I almost considered it. I considered sending a wave of electricity through him, shocking him just enough to get away. But then I remembered that only hours before, he had been locked away, kept in the dark, nearing death.

I just couldn't do it.

I tried to focus on the good things, if only because they pulled me out of that cloud of darkness.

The two of us sitting on the couch together, my legs thrown over his lap. Watching him read through his books, the urge to touch him so strong. Grabbing him from behind and burying my face in his back when he thought that I was asleep, relishing in the way that his hands stroked mine when he realized that I wasn't. Looking at him through the window of the cabin and grinning when he caught my eye. Dancing. Laughing. Feeling as if his smiles were mine and mine alone.

That crushing realization when I realized that I loved him so many months ago while he sat below me begging for forgiveness, and every bone in my body wanting to scream when Kristin pulled me away from him—because no part of me wanted to hurt him. No part of me was ever capable of hurting Luka.

His face came back into focus for a minute, every breath that he took tearing through him. His eyes grew red, I heard the front of my shirt tear further, another button popping off.

"I'm sorry," he whispered, and death felt so blissful for that second, in the sweet illusion that followed it. "I'm so sorry."

Because for the shortest moment in time, I was someone else. Someone watching a young maid slide around the hall. Someone clutching his chest, hoping that she would not turn because then the ache that he felt would be overwhelming. Deciding to leave that night, deciding that he could not stay a moment longer looking at his brother's broken face when he told him. *Do you love her?* Kristin asked, not wanting him to go, seeing through his every illusion. *I can't say,* Luka replied. He knew.

He knew. *I have to go, it's for the best.* Not for him, but for her. She would never have a proper life with him, she would never love him, and even if she did, he couldn't damn her to walking beside him.

And he wished it did not have to be that way.

Horror. Gut wrenching horror. Something so terrifying that I could not feel anything, the blackness of magic rotting in my stomach. No sound, no light, no feeling, nothing.

Absolutely nothing.

It filled my mind, consuming me. It wasn't real, it couldn't be real, but I couldn't escape it.

I could only drown in it. Try as I might, I could not feel Luka or anything.

This was death. This was what he knew of death. The illusion was luring me in—

Then the world snapped back into place, there was light once more.

"Stop." It sounded like his voice, but Luka's mouth did not move. It was that cherry-coated, sweetened sound of compulsion. "Stop now." The world around me seemed to spin. I could not tell where the words were coming from, just that they were there, and they were real.

Luka stared down at me, and I couldn't place his expression.

His unfogged black eyes looked at me and only me, his mouth slightly agape, he didn't seem to be breathing, but rather the air was pulled in and out of him by some unseen force.

No more horrors came. Nothing. I had braced myself for more, readied myself for more, but they were not there. I could not move, nor could I speak. I did not want him to leave.

He was the only thing remaining besides the buzz of soldiers and the hint of something else filling the air, but not mattering. There was just Luka. He was a blessing.

I felt something, something wholly bitter leak out of me, the taste repulsive, but I did not dare to cough. Because, perhaps, if I coughed, he would run. But if I stayed still, if I stayed silent, then he wouldn't. Then I could look at him.

I desperately wanted to copy all of his features down like I had with so many documents before, and ink it into my memory.

"Wren," he spoke my name, his voice strangled, his hand moving to my face, cupping my cheek within it. He was so horrified that I felt sick, he was looking at me as if something integral had broken within him. "Wren, say something."

I couldn't, I could only stare. The rain still fell heavily around us, rolling off his head and making his features look so much softer, the look on his face became something so much more beautiful. I felt holy, like I was having some sort of religious experience, even though I'd hardly ever gone to church, nor prayed to any god.

He was back. He was there with me.

"Please," he said as my hand roamed his face, my thumb feeling the skin of his lips, my mind amazed at them. "Please, say something. Don't be quiet now, Wren, you always talk. Please just speak to me."

But what would I say?

"The girl is dazed," someone else, also sounding like Luka, said nearby. The Gancanagh. "Give her to me."

No. I did not want to go anywhere else, not then. Not ever. I just wanted to remain there, with Luka and Luka alone.

"I would rather die," Luka spat at the other voice, not even bothering to look away from me, his hands lowering, pressing just above my chest, feeling my heart beneath them. Relief coated his features, he held me a little closer.

Someone stepped closer. Someone wearing something unusual, a sort of finery that I had not seen. Perhaps clothing from the old court, the original fae court. Intricate patterns embroidered onto a pair of breeches, silvery white thread sewn into delicate patterns of flowers and fauna, looking almost like a spider's web spun into silk.

"You're here to collect your tribute then," Theo said in the background, and I knew then why I heard Luka's voice twice. It had left the woods. It had dispelled the magic. It was the Gancanagh. Just as much a monster as Theo, just in different ways. "Your fascination repulses me."

"I am not fascinated, the woods merely take kindly to her," the creature replied. "Give her back, stop this fight permanently, and we can live in peace. Step down and I, the true King of Whynne, will take mercy on you." I realized then why the noises had died down; the fighting had subsided with the Gancanagh's appearance; he was such a terrifying and formidable creature at that moment that no one could continue. Reality was setting in around me, at any moment fighting would begin once more.

At any moment, someone would decide that I was meant to go with the creature.

I stared up at Luka, slack jawed. He looked like he'd sooner tear his own throat out.

"No one is taking her," another furious voice ripped through the crowd, caring very little whether he had a crown or the woods to assert his authority, nor that the rain had rendered him almost useless—his magic was fire, after all. Flames never fared well in the rain. "You will not be taking her anywhere, and you will not be doing anything more. This ends now." Adam.

"You're just a silly little human," I could not tell which king, either of woods or Whynne, spoke.

And I didn't care.

"Wren," Luka said, giving me the slightest shake. "You need to say something now. I need you to blabber on, do what you always do, let the words tumble out of you. Please. Please show me that I have not broken you. I can't do this—"

"I do not blabber," I managed hollowly, my eyebrows furrowing at the statement, if he wanted me to speak, he was going the wrong way about it.

Those four words broke everything in him, making him peel me off the ground and press me to his chest, holding me desperately, as if by doing so, he could stop the world around us. His arms were crushing, far tighter than any hold he had given me while trying to kill me, far tighter than his hold on me in the cell. I could barely breathe, but I raised my arms around him all the same.

"No," he said, "You do not blabber. My apologies. My apologies a thousand times over," he spoke quickly, hysterically. "You only speak, and I adore every word. Please keep saying more, please. I beg you to just keep talking to me."

"Why does your throat not hurt from lying right now?" I wondered out loud, the pressure in my head releasing as more black bile leaked out of me. The remainder of his illusions.

He laughed, shaking his head against my neck before pulling away, brushing the vile liquid from my lips without a second thought. All around us things continued, but for that moment, there was only him. "Your voice has never sounded so sweet, Wren. I could listen to you talk for hours."

And I could have too, if Adam had not moved forward beside us, stealing my gaze.

CHAPTER TWENTY-SIX

"What are you?" Spoke the Gancanagh, marveling at the man in front of it as its features morphed once more, finally becoming visible to me as Luka pulled himself off of me, moving to the side, pulling me onto my knees.

In front of Theo and the Gancanagh stood Adam, fire balanced on his fingertips.

"I am the only person who cares about this country, it seems," Adam said, Kristin's hand on his shoulder, his mouth whispering Adam's name as a warning in his ear. "And I hate to inform you, but you will not be collecting whatever you've tricked yourself into thinking is owed to you. You and Theo do not deserve her, nor do you deserve the Kingdom of Whynne."

The Gancanagh paused as its face rearranged, seeming to consider Adam, a sickening grin sliding across its features. For a moment, I thought that it would taunt Adam once more, appearing as Theo. But it didn't, maybe it was out of pity. Instead, it let its features continue to shift, moving until it landed on one face—Not that of another, not the face of any person that I'd ever seen, but the strange, blonde haired, slotted-lipped man that I saw in the woods. I realized then that this was either his true form, or his favored one.

"Are you proposing a dual amongst kings?" The Gancanagh asked.

"He is not a king, he is a boy," Theo snarled beside the creature.

Adam laughed, looking to his former companion with contempt. "I am not a boy, Theo. I am twenty-three. Just three turns older than your soon to be wife."

"You are young, compared to us fae," Theo said, his voice catching, his eyes on him, begging Adam not to do what he was planning. "You have no idea what you are doing."

"I think he has idea enough," I spoke, moving onto my feet. "I think he has more of an idea than anyone."

"Of course you do," Camden spoke vilely, looking at me. "You are one of the reasons he is ruined."

I snarled, taking a step towards her before Luka could pull me back as he tried to keep me from engaging.

But Adam was only amused, wholly humored by the fact that she would say such a thing. "Ruined?" He grinned. "You would say that I'm ruined? What other fun things do you tell yourself to fall asleep at night, Camden? Do you joke to yourself that you will be a benevolent queen? I have bad news for you if that's the case."

"You're just a human," Camden sneered, dismissing him, every bit ready to attack him herself. "A walking match, one that will not work in the cold and wet. You should be thankful that Theo wasted his time on you."

A sound of amusement escaped Adam, his smile only becoming slightly strained as the realization of what she said hit him.

"Adam," Kristin warned at his side, his hand on Adam's shoulder. Adam's eyes met his for the briefest moment. "I won't watch you fall, I can't save you twice." He knew what it would mean, what the risk was.

He would lose.

"I'll fight beside him then," I said, taking a step forward as Luka grew stiff behind me. "I believe in him, just as everyone else does. I believe that he should be king, so I'll stand beside him."

"You have already been bested once, girl—" Camden started.

"Me too, then," Kristin interjected, caring very little for such a duel, and all of the soldiers, the ones who stood to the side began to mumble uncomfortably, shifting awkwardly, perhaps wondering whose side they should be on. Who had the best chance of victory? A soldier would like to know if only so then he didn't betray his King.

"Me as well," Winry said, pushing through the crowds, her shoulders shrugging. "If you're going to take my sister."

"A dual is meant only for the parties who would stand to gain—" Theo began.

"I will too," Luka said. "If it is for both Adam and Wren," he said, earning more of the King's ire. I heard the softest, most amused sound escape from the Gancanagh.

"—That is enough!" The King snapped before Lindy could step in, not a single member of his guard or army, nor the girl behind him so much as moving forward to join him in battle. "It'll be three ways and three ways only, or it will not be at all. So unless you," he whirled around to face me, glaring at me, definitely regretting the fact that he had spared my life, "plan to become king, then you shall stand to the side and watch. The same goes for the lot of you, if you think yourself so capable of winning on your own merit and leading this country, then please step forward. But if not, if you know your place and the way that the world is supposed to be," Theo said, his eyes slipping to Adam. "Then step back."

Adam made no moves to do any such thing, unwavering in Theo's storm. "Then, shall we?" Adam asked, watching Theo. "I will warn you though, I have bested you once, and I have no qualms about beating you, forest king. Not if it is for Whynne."

And the Unseelie, who had previously been kicked and taken advantage of by the young king, looked back at Adam with a smile. He had previously tried to claim him, previously tried to take advantage of his weaknesses, but now he did not bother. He did not change his shape and instead looked upon Adam with something akin to respect. "It would be an honor to fight against you, human. Out of all people, you have held my interest longest." And since his tongue rendered him uncapable of any untruths, I knew it to be a fact.

"When this is done," I said, looking over to Camden as she stood beside me, her eyes focused on the area cleared out at the center of the camp. "I look forward to seeing you in shackles."

"And I look forward to seeing you flayed alive, scum," Camden spoke through gritted teeth, watching the spectacle before her with squared shoulders.

The men entered the cleared space, or rather, the two fae and one man entered the space. All three looking from one to another and sizing each other up. It struck me then that never before had a human faced a fae, not in recorded history, not in a dueling ring. Such a thing was only reserved for those with true powers, which, up until recently, did not include humans.

But now?

Adam looked every bit as dangerous as the other two, every

bit as daring and foolheartedly brave. Maybe more so, knowing that he was human and cursed with frailty.

He did not have the power to heal in an instant. He could not call others to do his bidding, yet he stood there all the same. Daring them to tell him otherwise, daring them to say that he did not belong. It was clear from the look on Theo's face that he did not think Adam should be there, but he said nothing. Not when confronted with both Adam and the soldiers of Whynne, the ones that he showed his best face to, the ones that looked up to him—Now everyone was watching them.

Everything that Theo had rode on a few short moments. On his ability to either force his friend to surrender, or to do the unthinkable. What would he do?

"Have you ever thought to yourself that just five minutes in a library has evolved into this?" Luka hummed in my ear, holding my waist, his thumb looped around one of the belt loops. "I often wonder what might have happened if you just left me to sleep rather than forcing me awake." There was a hint of fear in his voice.

And it struck me what a strange thing that was to think of.

"I did not force you," I whispered, my eyes turning towards the field. "You woke up willingly."

"Because you loomed over me, looking at me as if I were your possession, and you'd come home to find me broken."

"You were as much mine then as you are now," I shook my head, turning just as the battlefield raged to life, a flame flickering in the dying light of the afternoon, waiting in Adam's palm. For what, I did not know. There was no countdown, no guards to separate them if things got too rough. They all stood apart, unmoving. In a true fight, no one wants to throw the first punch, that was to be at a disadvantage, because then the other person could do something unpredictable.

But Theo did, directing a powerful gust of wind at the

Unseelie, focusing on him rather than Adam. Because that was the easier way to go, far easier than facing his friend.

And Adam took advantage of that, tearing after Theo.

I had not gotten to watch the first fight, being instead otherwise preoccupied. I had only walked up towards the end of it, catching the final moments before Adam lashed out at Theo. I did not know much about Adam, I did not know that he was graceful as well as quick. He was elegant in a way, a trained killer. Of course the King was quick and far more refined in all his movements, age having played a hand in that. But he was different than Adam, he lacked the raw strength that Adam had.

And he relied more on magic than Adam could. That was the difference, Adam was a man of strategy and execution. Theo was the type of man who didn't like to get his hands dirty, the type of man who sat and gave orders. He rested at war tables pushing around wooden figures of his enemies. He planned battles that others would fight for him. Adam did not. Adam was not the type to stand on the sidelines, nor the type to sit back and watch. Adam was the type to run ahead of the troops. That was why he had held such a prominent place in the military, he had earned it.

And the King of the forest? The King of the Forest was chaos personified. He was a wild, untamed thing. Someone who never thought of such ideas as strategy, or his limitations. Someone who simply fought. There was also a sort of nobility in that, an underestimated elegance, because all he knew was to win. And was there anything more bold and plainly royal than assuming that you would win? I could not think of anything.

Adam ran at the other two, his hands swinging, the fire forming an arc. An arc that moved and singed. Theo tried to concern himself only with the King of the Forest, only with the unfortunate unseelie. But he did not realize that Adam would sooner grab him than anyone else. That Adam would wrench him back by his collar, slamming him to the ground.

Adam's foot slammed down on Theo's stomach as he pointed his hand in the direction of the Gancanagh, sending out a pillar of flames. I stepped forward, my mouth agape as I tried to see more clearly, but Luka's grasp pulled me back. It was as if he feared that I would run in at any moment, and when Theo grabbed Adam's leg, pulling him down to the ground as he attacked the Unseelie with a mighty gust of wind — it seemed like a warranted fear.

Because I wanted nothing more than to run and stop him from hurting Adam. The King gripped at Adam's collar and pulled him up, his fist slamming against Adam's face. There was no magic to it, it was personal, just as it was when they fought before, tumbling across the mountainside, trading blows over Camden of all people.

I feared that Adam would hesitate, that he would see Theo's face so near to his own and a part of him would break. Love doesn't change that quickly, not in most cases. I worried what would happen. I worried that Adam would lose his nerve.

I would not let Theo or the Gancanagh reign over me.

"Adam!" Kristin's scream tore through the crowd as he shoved Camden aside and practically threw her to the ground in the process, pushing himself even closer to the front. "Adam!"

Was Kristin trying to distract him? I could not see screaming Adam's name doing much good. Or at least, initially I couldn't. Had Luka not done the same for me a few times before, his voice bringing me back to reality. Adam's head twisted, his eyes looking across the valley to Kristin.

His hand slammed up, shoving the King's face away, shoving the man he once loved far from him.

Just in time too, since the Gancanagh grew near, stalking closer and closer.

Adam whipped his arm out, a stream of fire shooting towards the. He pushed off the ground with his other hand, not even looking as the Gancanagh fell with the blow. Adam stalked back to Theo, another ball of fire shooting from his hand in the Unseelie's direction as Adam seized his longtime friend by the collar, taking advantage of how thin the King's frame was in comparison to his. Adam watched as Theo kicked at the air. Theo whispered something to him. Whatever it was, Adam did not like it.

He slammed Theo to the ground, whipping his body in a long, fluid motion so much like snapping a rag, his eyes cold as Theo arched away from the ground.

"Do not compel me, it won't work," a small voice spoke from in front of me, reading his lips as Adam spat at the man. I had not realized that Lindy had even moved, much less that she was standing next to me. I suppose it made sense though, Kristin was near and she always drew close to both him and Adam. "The King tried to charm him."

"A mistake," Luka said as the look of imminent victory slid off of Camden's face. The King was losing, at least for the moment.

Adam grabbed the back of the man's collar, swinging him up and dragging him behind him. He kept moving, he kept stalking. Next, he approached the Unseelie King, determined to ensure that his victory was realized. The Gancanagh only looked up at him, blinking at his nearness. I supposed at that moment that it would try something, that it would have a last chance trick up its sleeve. But it only looked at Adam. It looked at Adam and what he had done, what he had accomplished. Adam dragged Theo behind him.

"What would you do to the Unseelie," the whole forest

seemed to ask, its question echoing amongst the trees, its voice so loud that all could hear it. "Would you treat them as he has? Would you sit in your castle in fear of them? You have hurt them before, all at the request of another, what would you become on your own?"

These woods were the Gancanagh's, and he belonged to them just as much as they belonged to him. He had done everything in his power to fight for them, I realized. Terrorizing me and those around me, but still trying to save the forest from the future, the future that Theo had planned.

Adam only looked at him, as if silently stating that he already knew, as if the answer was obvious. The forest had given him the magic. The Unseelie were a part of that, as were the Seelie. The forest had birthed not just them, but him too. He was not like the King, who saw the others gifted with magic from the forest and wanted them dead.

I also knew that Adam feared them. I knew that he had justified harming them, stating that they had done the same to us. But there is always an array of good and bad in this world. I had tried to explain that to Theo, the fact he couldn't reduce everything to black and white. There were grey areas, there were good Unseelie too and bad humans. Even worse Seelie, if you heard the tales that Kristin told. No one was wholly right or wrong in our situation.

Adam had once told me that I was a good person, or that he believed me to be. Because I was going to do what I believed was right. Because I was going to do something to help Whynne, or so he hoped. We barely knew each other then, but I had already made my decision about him. At that time he was someone who sat back and watched the atrocities that happened in Whynne; I did not believe him to be capable of being good. I didn't tell him, but he must have known.

But the Adam I knew now? He had gone with me. He had

fought for Luka of all people, put his life on the line and abandoned the man he loved when Theo had shown his true self. He did not try to offer me solutions, new Seelie to replace Luka or titles and gems to numb the pain if he were to be taken away from me. He understood me, he sympathized.

He saw me running without Luka and he grabbed me, holding me as tight as possible when he knew. He humored Lindy, letting her tell him all the things she hated about Whynne and treating her just the same, even though it was his home and the land that he loved. He still showed kindness to Nikolas, and found humor in every awful situation he found himself placed in. He dealt with Winry's unending whining.

And when the Gancanagh looked at him, thinking only of his home, of the way that the world had worked against him—Adam kneeled. He offered more than just his hand, he got down to the Gancanagh's level, looking the Unseelie in the eyes as if it were an equal. Unfearing and unwavering, not bitter for the pain that it had caused.

A part of me was forced to think that he was not angry that the Unseelie had tried to use him before, that night in the woods just a month prior. That it had donned another's form to taunt Adam, nor that it stole the people he cared about from their beds in interest of its grand plan. He treated it just as he would me or anyone else, maybe even kinder.

His hands wrapped around the Unseelie's and he pulled it to its feet, nodding at it, nodding at the woods around him. And the Unseelie looked to him, to the gathering of soldiers by his side, and to the woods behind him. And he nodded back, giving Adam's hand the slightest squeeze, and then he stepped back, bowing his head.

To The King of Whynne, Adam Harlow.

CHAPTER TWENTY-SEVEN

The camp erupted into applause as Camden stood on her own, not a single soul beside her. No one would dare move near her. A few hundred feet away, Theo laid unconscious in the dueling ring; unable to help her.

And now he had lost his crown. The only thing that she had ever wanted from him. I almost thought that she would approach Adam next, feigning kindness, feigning love.

But she did not, she stood alone. She did not try to put on another act.

She was all by herself, just like she was when Winry first met her and the other members of nobility laughed and danced around her. Just as she was when she was only a girl, not determined to be queen. When she was nothing, just as I was.

Everyone else rushed around her, eager to greet the new king, to start a new beginning, but I hung back, Luka waiting just feet away from me.

And Winry stayed too.

You are a monster, I wanted to say. *You deserve to be alone.*

But I didn't speak.

"I remember you," Winry said, walking up to Camden. "I remember when you came up to me at the ball, when I was young and you were one of the girls in the beautiful ballgowns, dancing the night away while my bedtime still lingered." Her hands were on her shoulders, her face was kind. My sister chose to speak to her, perhaps knowing that no one else would. No one would give Camden the time of day anymore. "You could have been so much more than this," Winry said. "You could have been so much better."

Camden just watched the scene, her head shaking in disbelief, the soldiers gathering and cheering. "I wanted Whynne to thrive," she said. "I wanted it to become something more, to take its proper place in the world. We lived under a selfish, philandering king. Was it so bad to think that I could change him?"

"And were you successful?" Winry asked, her voice gentle. "Did you help Whynne? Did you become more than the girl standing at the edge of the party, wishing that she was a part of it all?"

A whimper escaped Camden, her eyes falling from the celebration.

"You'll be thrown in the dungeons," I said, finally finding the words, finally finding the strength to approach her. My sister looked back at me, casting me a look. "You know that it's true, that you will not be able to run. Even if you try now, the Unseelie in these woods will find you. They know what you've done, and they know who you are. They'll kill you."

Camden sighed, looking utterly defeated. I wanted her to fight, I wanted her to turn around and try something with me, maybe even attempt to compel me, but she didn't. "You're so much better than me now, worth so much more," she said. "Does that not make you happy?"

No, I wanted to say. *Because I will still see you in my night-*

mares until the day that I die, wearing your pretty silk robes and playing at being queen.

"Did you ever love him," Winry asked. One last attempt at kindness, one last try to show Camden some form of sympathy. Some form of understanding. Because Winry was one of the only people in the world who could understand Camden's ambition so well, and the shackles of courtship that she turned into tools. I think my sister thought that if Camden could say that she loved Theo, then I'd feel pity for her.

"Sometimes," Camden said. "I would try to believe that I did. I would value his kindness, his confidence, and the way that he did not let other people step on him. I tried to be like him. But ultimately, I despised his lack of ambition, his refusal to push the status quo. Whynne could have been a great country, if he were not at the helm."

"Whynne would have been a great country if you were not standing behind him," I replied, looking at her. "If you did not guide him towards cruelty."

All the fear that I felt for her left, she was no longer this mythic beast. She was just a woman, nothing more.

One who had manipulated love and fear to craft a kingdom, now watched that kingdom move past her, evolving into a new one. A kingdom that hated her.

"We should go," Luka said, pulling at my arm, knowing that if I looked at her a moment longer, even more of what I knew of the world would shatter. I never imagined a world where I would pity Camden. "We should congratulate him."

I nodded, looking to my sister. "Winry?"

She shook her head, moving to Camden's left. "I'll stay with her," she said. "Make sure that she does not try to run, especially now that she knows the consequences."

A good idea, I looked at my sister, her petite form and her tiny, child-like features. Camden would consider running, I knew, but she would not succeed with Winry watching over her.

Kristin and Adam's arms were around each other's shoulders by the time that we reached the group, the two men grinning from ear to ear. The former king was nowhere to be seen, long since dragged off and taken away. If I had to guess, I would say that he was shoved into an iron cage. One that sat in a tent half blown open. One that sat far away from Camden and all of her tricks.

Theo was far away from the festivities that had begun to take place, far from the laughter that had broken out. The new king was telling drinking stories. Ones of hauling a man into a taxicab, the same one who hung beside him, and yanking his shoes off one by one the moment they got through the front door, the other man having only had a few mixed cocktails then falling drunk.

By the next day, the rest of the kingdom would learn of their new monarch, of the beginning of a new Whynne.

Off to the side, a Haldian girl sat, holding a crown looking to be made of gilded sticks and twigs—an ugly thing. Something that didn't even belong to her, nor any land that she was a part of. Something that had always been meant for Whynne.

"Lindy," I said, Luka and I drawing nearer, the slightest chuckle sounding in the back of his throat as he took her in, the way that she looked at the crown with utter contempt in her eyes.

"He gave it to me," she said with a scoff, looking down at the thing in her hands. "He told me that I should break it. It's an hideous thing."

"That is a crown that several people have died for, Lindy,"

Luka informed her, unable to hold back his humor. "Hardly worthless."

"And it is an unfortunate, disgusting thing," she proclaimed. "Devastatingly ugly. In my country we would never wear such a hideous, prideful thing." I had no doubt that she was right, just knowing her.

"Yet you haven't destroyed it," Luka said.

She looked sheepish at that, peering down at the crown once more, looking as if she wished that she had hidden it. "What if he needs it someday?" She asked, speaking of the crown and its ability to command the fae. "What if something were to happen and he wished that he still had it?" She was worried for Adam, worried that he would fall into trouble again.

"It won't happen, Lindy," I said, sinking to my knees beside her. "So many things will, but that? No. He will never wish for it, I'm sure."

Lindy frowned, unconvinced.

"Adam has become The King of Whynne, you will become an ambassador, and I will do just as I planned to," I told her. "Life will go on and things will continue to change, but Adam will not need that crown. I am sure of it."

She nodded hesitantly, looking at it with a sort of finality. Her hands gripped the sides of it and she closed her eyes, as if afraid. But she was going to do it, she had decided.

And in a single motion, she snapped it over her knee, the crown fell apart so easily that it was almost unbelievable, tumbling to the ground as if it was such a plain, ordinary thing.

And then, because it was truly extraordinary... it rotted. Quickly. One second it was there, the next second it began to decay, being reclaimed by the land of Whynne. The wood turned to mulch beneath us.

And that mulch changed too, just as all things in the forest did.

One second, the crown of Whynne sat. The next, a circle of mushrooms. It was so sudden that we could barely process it, just gape at the ground.

Whynne had taken the crown back.

For a moment, Lindy looked shocked. In fact, I was confident she would never stand again.

Things like that evidently did not happen in Haldia.

"Let's go back to the party, Lindy," I encouraged, offering her my hand, desperate to move on. "We should join the others." My eyes still rested on the circle beneath us, the unsuspecting toadstools.

"You're right," she said, standing up to join Luka and I. "I should join the large, pointless party." Pointless, just as all things were in Whynne to Lindy.

We guided her back, Lindy's hand fitting in mine as she looked around, almost appearing younger, and we approached the revelers. She disappeared instantly, and I knew that she'd been dragged off by someone, Kristin likely, and forced to tell stories of her home country to the admiring crowds.

I had almost forgotten that we were the heroes now.

"It feels strange, doesn't it?" Luka said, hanging back at the edge of the celebration with me, looking at everything before him. "This is it. It's over. Everything that has happened is over."

"You almost sound wistful," I said, standing beside him, letting my head rest on his shoulders.

"I can not help but marvel at what we have done, but I wonder what lurks ahead," he said. "What punishments will there be for Theo and Camden, and what will Adam do with the country?"

"Do you truly wish to know?" I questioned, looking over to him in curiosity. "Do you want to stay here and find out?"

I knew the answer, he looked positively nauseous at the idea without even saying anything. He looked positively nauseous just looking at the crowd before him. He did not want to celebrate, he did not want to sit in the castle and pretend that he was glad for the adventure. Just as I did not. Just as I did not wish to reminisce longer than needed.

"We'll go home then," Luka said, catching the knowing look on my face. The words sounded so strange coming from him. "We'll leave tomorrow and go home, I'll go back to the Kinsley estate and you will... perhaps come with. Perhaps you could stay there all of the time instead of at the Laurent estate. Though, it will be scandalous—"

"It will be," I said with a nod, "People would know what we are, that we're lovers. The two of us living together, two unwed people in the same house, and people will talk. But I don't mind."

Luka nodded slowly beside me, looking away from me, his voice teasing. "I seem to remember a contract," he said, and I spun around to face him.

I could feel my eyebrows in my hairline.

"Invoking it would be a great way to ensure that Kristin gives me the Greenable estate," Luka said slyly, referring to the bargain which originally dragged me into his life. "But I do not believe that I would suit being head of the family, I do not have a head for business, only for scholarly pursuits."

"Are you...?" I asked, looking over at him in astonishment, a frustrated huff escaping me when I realized that he did not look back my way, only continued to hold onto me, his thumb brushing where a small bird once sat on my hand.

"Of course not, I do not have a ring," he pointed out. "Nor your father's blessing, nor have I notified my head of house." He continued, "but perhaps someday. I'm happy with how we are for the moment."

"For the moment?" I asked, my voice raising, incredulous. "So you will then? You are? We are? Or— Are you asking me, or are you just teasing me right now?"

"Whoever knows how I shall feel about it the next day, or perhaps the one after that," he teased, earning my ire. "Perhaps you will just have to wait."

"Kinsley," I swore, shaking my head at him.

"Wren," he tsked. "I do believe that we have one last thing to do."

"Do we?" I asked, squinting at him. "And what is that?"

He cast me a sly look, "I believe that we should say goodbye to the king."

CHAPTER TWENTY-EIGHT

HALF OF THE TENT WAS GONE, THE REMAINDER TIED IN ON itself by the soldiers. They tried their best to close it, a few pieces of rope holding different parts of it together. All that really managed to do was keep the back half of the tent together. There was no doors or windows to it, nothing to let in much light—not as the sun began to set on the horizon. You just had to bring in your own torch and hope that that was enough. It seemed ironic, the king who was once so afraid of what lurked in the dark was now trapped in it. But, perhaps the irony was lost on everyone but me.

Adam hadn't come to see him yet. I was sure that once he had, the room would be lit up. I had to admit that a small spiteful part of me was happy for the time being, because Theo had done the very same thing to Luka.

Now he sat alone in the dark too.

"Have you come to taunt me?" A voice spoke from the darkness, unseeing, but already knowing. Already well aware of who would visit him. "Is it Adam, my dearest friend? Or is it

Wren, the girl and her Unseelie?" He scoffed, "I would not be lucky enough for it to be Adam."

"You're not," I said, the tiny lantern from my neck held in my hand, illuminated when nothing else was. I hadn't bothered to ask for another torch, the Unseelie were no longer something to fear. Or, at least most of them weren't. "It's me."

"Ah, Wren," said Theo. He knew immediately. "One of the heroes of Whynne, and Luka, I presume."

Luka was there, standing right behind me, his hand on me as usual. He had insisted on being there, that I should not go alone. No one should have entered the former King's tent on their own, save for Adam.

"To what do I owe the pleasure? Are you done dancing and singing and celebrating the fall of my family name out there, have you now come to mock me as well? It's so kind of you to come." His voice was ripe with sarcasm, his eyes fierce with anger.

I sighed, ignoring him as Luka and I drew nearer to his cage, sitting down in front of it. Beside me, Luka dug in his pockets, searching for something. I tried to keep my eyes on Theo.

"How does it feel to be alone?" I asked, not expecting that he would throw himself at the bars, snarling, touching them even though they burned his skin. I had not thought that he would be so willing to hurt himself, not to get at me.

Every inhale he took was labored, and his eyes were practically slits as he glared at me, his skin scalding against the metal. Fae were weakened by iron. "My true subjects will find me, girl, and you will regret your actions. You will regret not taking my deal, maybe not now, but some day."

"I won't regret it. And as for your subjects? I don't know if they will," I muttered to him, gripping the bars and leaning in.

"You should hope that Adam takes pity on you, because I most certainly wouldn't, not after all you've done."

"People will look for me—"

"And they will not find you. I don't care what Adam decides, if he gives them even the slightest opportunity to save you, I will take care of you myself," I threatened. "I may not be a killer, but if you and Camden were to step out of line, I could find myself more than willing."

"Awful, dreadful bitch," Theo spat, his saliva splattering across my face. I only scowled, almost unaffected.

"We could have been friends," I told him. "You could have been saved. I tried to help you when we were out there, I tried to save you. You could have still been king."

"And what does salvation look like to you?" The former king growled, releasing the bars of his cage. I could see his blistered and burnt skin. Perhaps he was more fae than man. "Do you wish me to love the Unseelie as you do? To kiss their sweet little faces and wish them the best? Perhaps to turn a blind eye to their monstrosities?" He asked, blinded with his fury.

I did not feel the need to respond.

Luka, however, did.

Luka didn't speak, but he found what he was looking for in his pocket and pushed his hand quickly through the iron bar, hissing as his skin brushed against it.

It was a small thing. Just one of the hard, blueberry cakes the soldiers were making outside as the celebration went on. Luka had grabbed one when we'd passed the soldiers, I'd thought he'd eaten it. It turns out that he'd saved it, perhaps thinking of the king well before we entered the tent.

"I am not an animal," Theo proclaimed, glaring at the hand that reached out to him. "I will not be fed like a dog. Especially by the likes of you."

"I do not want you to be hungry," Luka said, and there was

something there, something under his voice. A hint that they had not given him the same kindness. "Take it, please. I do not wish to put it on the ground if you change your mind... you're worth more than that."

"Don't tell me what I'm worth, Unseelie," Theo snapped, slapping it out of Luka's hand. "I should have killed you when I had the chance." Immediately, sparks rose on the tips of my fingers, my eyes warning him as Luka drew back his hand.

"You do not touch him," I informed Theo. "You do not touch Luka ever again."

"Where is Camden," Theo howled, choosing to ignore my statement. "Where is my fiancée? When will you bring her to me? When will I see her? Where has she gone?"

"Away from you," I said, reaching for Luka's burnt skin with a tsk. "You will not see her again for as long as you live."

"She tried to plead for amnesty," Luka explained. "She insisted that she had no part in it all. Luckily, Adam did not believe her. Luckily, no one believed her."

Theo could only stare.

"No," he said. "She would not. She would choose to be beside me, you are merely trying to keep her away from me."

"She didn't love you," I informed him. "She never loved you."

"You're lying," the former king said. "You and your Unseelie are lying. Camden adores me."

"We're not," Luka said, casting him a weary look. "Though I wish we were. I cannot think of anything worse."

I had never seen a man look so broken before in my life. It was as if, at that moment, almost all of the light died out of Theo's eyes. He did not have a single spark of defiance left in him. None of his subjects had come for him, and now he knew that his lover would not as well.

"It gets cold in here," Luka said quietly, beginning to pull at his jacket, not yet done showing pity to the man. I cast him a warning glare, wishing that he could put it aside. But there was something more to him, something more to the cage. Something he dared not to speak of.

He had experienced hell in there over the course of the last three days, but he would never tell me what exactly that hell looked like. He was just trying to ease Theo's suffering because he knew what Theo was about to go through. It made me feel a surge of possessiveness, a want to hold Luka and take him away, to keep him from this. Luka deserved so much more than this.

But ordering Luka to be locked in a cage was not the only cruelty that the King had inflicted on Luka.

He'd taken away Luka's dignity and reduced him down to nothing more than an animal when he asked them to put Luka in that cage. Then he'd tormented and neglected him. Then, because that was not enough, it was never enough, the King had forced Luka to do something awful, to hurt me.

And when Luka pulled back from me in those moments, having nearly killed me, I knew that Theo had broken something in him.

But Luka still took his jacket off for Theo, he still made to shove it through the bars before I snatched it out of his hand. He still looked at me and begged me to do it.

And because it was Luka, and I could not say no to him, I did.

I pushed the jacket through the bars, averting my gaze before the King could look my way. I let my hatred and disgust for him be implied.

"Luka," I said, dusting the iron off of my hands before reaching for him, cradling his jaw. "We should go, people will start looking for us. Your brother will want to see you."

He nodded, the tiniest hint of regret playing upon his

features. But, following my request, he got up, offering his hand to me.

"I need to speak to the King alone for a moment," I said quietly, allowing Luka to pull me to my feet. "You should wait outside."

Luka looked from me to Theo, then back. "What if he..." The unspoken word was compelled. What if he tried to compel me?

My lips pressed briefly against Luka's forehead. "I think after everything I've been through, not even that crown could convince me to bow to him," I said, caressing his cheek. "I'll be only a moment."

Luka cast a wary look back, but nodded all the same, willing to humor me, just for the moment. "Just a minute, nothing more. I'll come back for you if it's any longer."

"Just a minute," I agreed, letting his hand go, watching as he slowly walked out. He looked over his shoulder one last time, his eyes still holding that inkling of fear.

And then I was alone with the former king. The man sitting on the ground, nothing left of his life. Nothing to do except wait, nowhere to be, no one looking for him. The King was reduced to a prisoner and nothing more.

All of his luxuries would be gone. His castle, his cars, his army. He had nothing in this world. But most of all, for the first time in his life he was completely powerless, dependent on the whims of another.

After everything, he was just a man, half-Seelie, half-human.

And I had only one thing to say to him.

"You should be glad for people like Adam and Luka, because I would leave you to rot. I would let you wallow in the dirt. I would not offer you jackets or muffins. I would not even bother to sentence you. I would leave you here in this cage, until you had rotted to nothing more than toadstools and mulch," I said. "Be glad that they are here and that it is not me, because unlike Camden, I am capable of love, and I am more than capable of revenge too."

Theo only sighed, the slightest whimper escaping him as he pulled his legs into his body, wrapping his arms around them. He was trying to hide it, the flush of shame, the sound of tears. But I knew. He looked like a petulant child, one that had been scolded by his nursemaid and was now furious with the consequences.

This was our former king. The former leader of Whynne.

I picked up the jacket that Luka had tried to offer him through the bars and bunched it in my fist, throwing it at his back with furious force, enraged by him. How dare he cry, how dare he act like he was the victim now. I had given him a chance, and he had repaid me with cruelty.

The jacket hit his side, falling back down into the dirt. I could not help but feel just a little bit of pity with that. Now he had only a dusty, dirty jacket for his blanket. Still, a small, vindictive part of me couldn't help but feel like it was more than he deserved.

Another part of me was afraid that his cruelty had somehow worn off on me.

CHAPTER TWENTY-NINE

"There you are," a deep voice spoke once I was alone, Luka having left to speak to his brother for the time being, a quick exchanging of words as the night came to a close, the older Kinsley brother still trying to get Luka to stay. It was just Adam and I then. "You know, I really thought that you would come up to me and congratulate me. I looked around, almost the whole night, but you weren't there," Adam said.

"I didn't want to force my company on the new king."

"It is hardly forcing if I am the one who seems to constantly seek out your company," Adam laughed, moving beside me and eyeing the dwindling fire that sat before me, his gaze sliding over to me with an amused sigh, likely wondering how my mind had become so busy that I let the fire burn down.

"Well," I said as he snapped his fingers at the fire, and brought the flames roaring back to life. "Congratulations, my king. Do not expect me to bow or even take a knee," I joked. "It's been a long day."

"I would never ask that of you," he said in mock offense, looking at me with humor.

"Now that you are king, you should think to pull that dishrag off your face," I joked. "Surely a king can afford razors," he swatted at my thigh, shooting me a playful glare as I teased him. "Do you enjoy looking like you've lost a bet? You know that thing is repulsive."

"Now you are testing me," he said, still charming, still handsome—Still everything that he had ever been, even with a kingship to his name. "A thousand years in the dungeon alongside Camden, effective immediately—Unless you apologize."

"Ah," I said. "She'll be awful company."

He chuckled, sitting cross legged and leaning far too close to me as he asked in that beckoning, convincing voice of his, "so, Greenable."

"Greenable," I nodded, shaking my head at him. I already knew what he wanted to say, what he wished he could ask.

"I suppose I can not convince you to stay up near Chines, can I? You and Luka will not be members of my court?"

"You could not pay me enough to stay near this mountain," I proclaimed. "Nor do I think Luka would even think of it. With my luck, Mylene would come crawling out of the rubble to kill me."

"A shame," he joked. "I'm sure Camden is going to need a court ordered torturer and your name really was the first one to come up for the job. I only had to think for a second, remembering all of that time I hung out in seedy taverns, babysitting drunken monks and having lightning bolts lobbed my way every so often before I thought of you. Camden really will be missing out on the best of the best." He shook his head, "she will simply have to stay in the cabin that I assign, left out in the middle of the wilderness with no one to bother. What a shame that will be."

Ah. I nodded, agreeing with his round about way of explaining her punishment, appreciating the humor. I could only guess which cabin she would end up in, or how many Unseelie would be lurking in the woods, watching her. "And Theo?" I asked, because he was the hard one, the one that I didn't know Adam was capable of punishing.

"Force to stay in the palace, left to wander the estate," he said. "I did not want a martyr, nor any rebellions." It was a lie, a bold-faced lie. He did not want to hurt him, he did not want Theo to suffer. Not Theo, who he had once loved so much. Adam couldn't stomach it. "I could not even look him in the eye, nor could I stand the idea of taking his home away from him," Adam admitted, speaking of when he finally visited the tent just moments after us. "Hopefully, someday I'll be able to," he said, growing quiet.

"Luka said that Kristin is staying in the capital," I said, not a fan of the silence, I glanced over to him to watch his expression, a sneaking suspicion having long since formed.

The problem with Adam was, he was far too clever to not realize what I was doing, instead looking away from me. He said in feigned interest, "oh? He didn't mention that." Even though they spent the whole day together, even though they had not left each other's sides. Adam knew, of course.

"Yes," I confirmed, looking over at the two Kinsley brothers, Kristin already beginning to fret over Luka as the younger brother looked on, annoyed.

Kristin caught me watching them as the two were talking and his eyes flitted from Luka to me. Kristin's face lit up as his finger rose in a not-so-subtle point for his brother, wanting him to know that I was watching. Luka was surely embarrassed by it.

"Apparently he has some sort of business up here, something concerning the gemstone business that cannot be taken care of in Greenable. Though how he managed to do such things before outside of the capital these past three years is beyond me," I clarified.

"The fact that he is willing to leave his estate in the care of his brother and you is beyond me. I would never leave you two alone," Adam replied, informing me that he knew of my now fully realized plans. "But apparently he is quite fond of you, though he worries that you will try to kill his brother again at the slightest provocation. Still, I believe there is no need for worry."

"Not in Greenable," I said, almost laughing as Luka finally gave in, tossing a look over his shoulder in my direction, his ears flushing purple when he looked back to see me staring at him, his whole body practically pivoting to look at Kristin. "But if Kristin is in Chines, then I worry about him. There will be no one to make sure that he gets home, no one to lie on the staircase with him when he gets drunk from only a thimble full of alcohol. Whoever will care for him?"

"You can just say that you've figured me out," Adam proclaimed, raising an eyebrow. "You need not taunt me this way. Might I remind you, I'm the King now—"

"And you have fallen victim to him tricking you a thousand times over," I said. "Making a nonsensical deal with you that you will never fulfill." In a low voice, akin to Adam's, I added, "still not fond of each other, I see."

"I am not yet tricked," Adam said, swatting at me. "And I am not yet captured, I still have much more of this life to live. But I am interested. Very, very interested," he said with a spark in his eye. "I suffer from a weakness for blonds. That is the most to which I will admit."

"Winry will be so disappointed," I said. "She was eyeing your grandmother's library."

"Alas, she will have to settle," Adam said, moving to stand

as the two brothers broke apart, throwing a wink in my direction before jogging past Luka, his shoulders nearly brushing Luka's.

Luka raised an eyebrow, looking behind him at the newly crowned king, a silent question on his face.

My eyes met Luka's, my face softening, taking in the oversized jacket that hung around his shoulders; Kristin was a mother hen in his own right. I was lucky that he had not yet forced me to change, Luka's stained garments still hung off of me as a reminder.

If I took them off so soon, I might have forgotten. I might have awakened in the tent and not known what had happened until I stepped outside. It would all seem like a dream. I didn't want that. Not yet.

"Are you going to bed?" I asked, taking in his expression. I did not dare comment on Kristin's jacket.

"Yes," he said. "It will be a long drive, it's pretty hellish going over these hills. I don't think it will be possible to sleep, not then. Perhaps when we get home, but it's late and I am far too exhausted to be petty and turn down the tent I was offered."

"Mhm," I nodded, clasping my hands together to keep them warm. I was not tired, not yet. I didn't know when I would sleep, or if I could sleep. I did not want to face the night yet, not when the terror of the day still loomed over me. "I'll come to bed soon," I said, looking at him. "If you'll let me."

"No," he said sarcastically as he bent down to look at me. "I had thought that you should sleep here. Outside, alone." Taking in my wrinkled nose, he laughed to himself as he bent down beside me, his lips pressing against my forehead. "Come when you are ready," he said, his voice kind. "I will be waiting for you as always."

I caught his shirt, wanting him to stay just a moment

longer. I wanted to keep looking at him and remind myself that he was truly there. After all, we had only just reunited that day.

"I am not going anywhere," he reassured me, caressing my wrists. "I will be in the tent, Wren. I swear. I would not leave you now, you've not even begun to yell at me for compelling you in the woods."

Right, that. My face fell, a glare breaking through.

"That's what I figured," he replied, pressing his lips against my wrist, the bone still aching but healing with every brush of his lips, the healing magic of fae spreading underneath them. "Wake me before you yell at me," he said. "I would love to pretend to hear every word."

I SAT ALONE AFTER LUKA LEFT, STILL THINKING FOR A long time. Still processing the world around me. In the span of one day, so much of what I had known had changed. But other things still remained true.

And so, I sat, unpacking what I knew. Unpacking the fact that just a few years ago, I would have been scrubbing floors, and the fact that that would have been a very lovely, less terrifying way to live. I thought and I overthought, going over so many things again and again to the point where I almost felt overwhelmed by myself.

When I was fifteen, I had not imagined this. Never in a million years, would I imagine fighting a king or being stolen by the Unseelie. Let alone the existence of people with magic in their hands and no fae blood to speak of! Being tricked into a fae bargain not once, but twice—Three times, if I really thought about it. My god. Things really had become a mess.

And the more I thought about it, the more overwhelming it became.

The fact that I was not dead felt like a grand mistake at the hands of the universe. Like something that I really should have celebrated. I had fought a troll! I had jumped off a cliff—Actually, I had been forced off of a cliff. What had happened to the original idea for my life? When had things begun to spiral out of control? Girls like me were supposed to be courting stable-boys while reading novels we'd stolen from our master's collections that would raise our mother's eyebrows.

And there I was, friend to the King! Asked to be a part of the King's inner circle—the court, no less!

How could I even begin to process it when I thought about it like that? It was overwhelming. I needed relief.

"So," said Nikolas as he settled beside me in front of the fire, most of the festivities having died down, most of the people having fallen asleep as we drew deeper and deeper into the night. "Tomorrow."

"Tomorrow," I replied, already knowing that he knew. Already well aware that Kristin couldn't keep his mouth shut, voicing his disappointment that Luka and I would choose to leave so soon, finding escort down the mountain with one of the soldiers who was determined to go home. It had not been hard to find one from Greenable, the kingdom's second largest city.

"You're leaving," Nikolas said.

"I am," I said, nodding. The air was thick and uncomfortable, but fitting. Nikolas and I had a strange relationship now, so very different from the one that we had once knew. So very different from both of our delusions of love. I had thought at one point that he would be it for me, a chance to join society, to finally belong— But he wasn't.

And I wasn't it for him either.

"I know that you're hoping for a miracle, that I'll say that I've moved on from you, or that I'm in love with someone new. Perhaps you hope that I will say I'm happy for you and hope you want me to be happy too," Nikolas said. "But I'm just not that type of person, and I'm sorry for that. I wish I could be."

"It's who you are," I said. "An insufferable, useless fish. One that dances for too long and has the worst sort of luck in the world."

He smiled, shaking his head as he leaned back, the night sky painted above us, the Unseelie still hidden in the trees, and the world peaceful for once. A genuine smile was across his face, boyish, but no longer innocent. I remembered that first night, the one where I had believed that I could love him. The one where he had chosen to listen to me.

"If it is not awful, and selfish, and rude," he said. "May I ask to be your friend? Though I have done so many things wrong, and I am no hero—will you still humor me and pretend to be my friend. It's hard not to admire a girl who has both waved a gun in my face and bit my bottom lip so hard that it drew blood."

I laughed, patting his leg. "I can bite you again."

"Ah, but it will not be the kind of bite that I like," he replied with a grin, his smile only fading slightly when he added, "and I will no longer think you are lying to me when you tell me that you kissed Kinsley."

"No," I said, still finding humor even though he did not. "I would hope that you would not."

"The two of you," he said sadly, a hint of jealousy in his tone. "In the Kinsley estate, unsupervised. Who knows when I will see you again, he'd likely have my head if I dared to step on the grounds." He tried to push away the thought but couldn't succeed. Instead, he said, "Adam told me I can still be a captain, which is all well and good, except that I will be sleeping side to side with other soldiers. Meanwhile, Luka will be sleeping next to you."

I looked at him and winked, a cattish grin sliding across my face, even though a hint of guilt still remained. Though he did not truly know me, he loved me. And even as I turned out to be not as he expected, he continued to love me. I did not make excuses for him not giving up on being with me, and I did not begrudge him for loving me. It felt like a gift.

"You know, I had a checklist," I said, tutting as I leaned back, letting go of my legs and reclining as I looked up at the night sky. "Just a small one, I believe I told you of it. I have mentally crossed off two things on it."

"Oh?" He asked with an air of interest, looking my way.

"But one still remains, one impossible, unbelievable thing— It's very important to me, Nikolas. I believe I need help with it."

"And what could that be?" He asked, his voice brimming with hope.

"Well, you see," I began. "I need to find someone, but I have no hope of doing so. Someone who is good at disappearing, who will likely eventually head towards the sea." Nikolas's eyebrow rose. "Someone who double crossed me for a pint of whiskey," I said. "I heard he's desperate to leave the country."

"Someone who you cannot find," he noted with interest.

"A certain, slimy little monk who I would very much like to have words with," I admitted. "Actually, I'd prefer to skin him alive, if I were being honest. But perhaps withholding his booze would suffice."

He laughed, knowing exactly who it was.

"Do you know a good tracker?" I asked.

His lips pressed quietly against the apple of my cheek. Nikolas, for once, fell silent. He pulled away, his face overjoyed, his teeth gleaming in the moonlight. Not a hero, not by his own standards, but something else. Someone forgiven. And if I had to choose a way to end things with Nikolas, that was it.

The two of us sat side by side and, just as we had done months before, we talked endlessly about anything and everything, about things other than war or the future, about ridiculous hobbies and frivolous things. Knowing that the next day would be a goodbye, not forever, but for now.

CHAPTER THIRTY

IT HAD RAINED.

At almost the exact moment that the automobile had pulled away, it rained. The car sped away and we stood at the gates—getting absolutely pelted with rain. Rain so thick and heavy that it immediately soaked through to our bones, an unbreakable curtain of rain. Rain so heavy that Luka had immediately ripped off his jacket, shoving it at my chest to hide what was behind my now almost transparent white shirt.

Rain that had made the imposing gates of the Kinsley estate seem that much taller, and the ride home seem that much longer. Rain in which an underinformed maid scrambled for fifteen minutes after we had arrived, as she struggled to get the gates open for her returning employer and the girl who stood beside him, eyeing the stained shirt and men's pants that the girl stood in.

She immediately ran to get a towel and alerted the other maids that their long-awaited masters had now returned, leaving the two of us standing in the foyer blinking as heavy, thick droplets of water rolled off of our clothes and plastered our hair to our foreheads.

Luka made a sound as he stood beside me, grimacing at the thick, unmovable grime that had coated his skin. Seeming to debate with himself for a moment before finally pulling another face and snapping his fingers, choosing the lesser of two evils I assumed. A small breeze moved by, and I looked back to find him dry, still dirty but utterly dry, his hand running through his now frizzy hair.

"You know, you could dry me too," I complained and he sighed, rolling his eyes before leaning forward, securing a single button of the coat that hung loosely over my shoulders as he once again kissed my forehead, the same air moving around me, rendering me dry too. Still dirty, still disgusting; but dry.

He pulled back just in time for me to catch sight of the maid returning, her eyes widening and the towels slipping from her hands, the young woman immediately bending over, scrambling to pick them up and avoiding my gaze.

I blinked at her, tilting my head. Confused as to what had startled her.

"I... Um..." She swallowed it down, shoving the towels in my direction, even though both Luka and I no longer needed them.

"Marni," Luka spoke. "Maybe you should grab Mariel and ask her to put out some clothes for Wren; she will be staying here from now on, after all."

"Right," she said quickly. "The young... Miss," she said hesitantly, eyeing Luka, looking as if she was trying to figure something out. I didn't know what it was, she had seen me plenty of times before.

"Mine," he had said flatly, perking her up entirely.

"Yours," she repeated excitedly, handing the towels to him and scurrying off, practically bolting through the corridor. I didn't understand at first, not knowing what could have excited her about my appearance this time versus the last.

And then I realized.

Oh. I had been that very girl before.

"I timed myself poorly," Luka said with a hint of amusement, "she now has to tell the whole estate that I have a partner, and more than that, that I thought to kiss her forehead in the hallway. That's a large development in their eyes." He took my arm, dismissing the occurrence, "Kristin speculated that they might have even had a betting pool."

"A betting pool?" I asked, glancing over at him in interest.

"The odds were not in my favor," he replied, ushering me forward. "So, if I had to guess which one of them, I would say that Mariel is likely feeling like a very lucky lady tonight."

I laughed, leaning my head against his shoulder as we began the extremely long trek up the stairs, my body already beginning to pull towards the guestrooms, finally ready to change and wash away all of the grime.

My eyes roamed around the room as we walked, taking in the far too familiar rooms and the fact that they looked so absolutely ordinary, as if they had sat waiting for us for just a few sweet hours rather than months. It felt like the house itself had spent the past few months expecting me to come storming through its hallways once more, or for Luka to pull me around the corners. Like we had never left.

"No," Luka spoke as we reached the top of the landing and I started more obviously pulling him to go back down the hallway where both his room and my preferred guestroom sat, his hand reaching around me to grip my other elbow and pull me away, redirecting me with a simple tug. "Not yet."

"I smell rotten, Kinsley," I said, raising an eyebrow at him and looking back over to the much beloved sleeping quarters. "Surely you do not prefer this."

"And whose fault is that? I seem to remember there being plenty of opportunities for you to get clean," he said, unimpressed with me. "You just so happened to turn down every one of them."

"In hopes of a nice, warm bath," I replied, wrinkling my nose at him. "Excuse me for not finding pleasure in the idea of a kettle heated over a fire being poured over my head."

"Be patient for five seconds," he said, pulling me along behind him. "Only five, nothing more. We have something important to do, I can promise you a bath after it."

"If you say any sort of work—"

He cast me a look, silently, playfully scolding me but nothing more.

"Fine," I agreed, letting him lead me, the hallways feeling familiar but unfamiliar at the same time. All of the small turns and tight corners had become lost to my memory from a sheer lack of being there, but I still knew it just as well as I ever did, I could still anticipate every turn. Which is how I knew that, for the moment, he was messing with me.

Purposefully trying to confuse me.

I cast him an irritated glare but humored him all the same. He led me to a small, rather unimposing door, his hand closing around the doorknob before he turned back to me.

"Close your eyes," he commanded, and I was so amused by the fact that he was being even the slightest bit playful that I followed his directions, closing my eyes and letting him guide me, his hand pushed at the small of my back until I had entered the room in front of me, one of his hands moving over my eyes as I tried to step carefully around him, hiding the room from sight on the off chance that I might peek.

He pushed me forward, just the slightest pressure on my back, and urged me to keep walking, my body moving until something pressed right under my ribs, something long.

"Alright," he said, standing behind me, his fingers swiping down my skin, away from my eyes. "We're home."

Home?

My eyelids fluttered open, taking in the sight in front of me and immediately I understood him, we *were* home. Not the estate, but the place within it, the sprawling library with two desks, one large and imposing, the other small. The sofa that filled the space between them, making it feel cozier. The large windows that looked out to the world, a place where I had once stood and wished to be anywhere but in there, suffering through his company. The library.

Our home. The place where Luka and I had spent most of our time together.

Our things were still strewn about across our desks like we would return at any moment, the items that we had forgotten to pack in our haste to leave. An assortment of pens and paper, a few scattered to the ground when I had decided to sit on his desk to try to charm him.

I beamed over my shoulder catching him looking at me, taking me in. I was already smiling so wide that it hurt, but the look on his face forced my grin even wider, a laugh spilling out of me.

"Every single time you look at me like that, I am overwhelmed," he said. "Every thought that I have leaves me. It is a cruel and awful thing for you to look at me like that, because I am defenseless against it."

"Because I'm so happy with you?" I laughed, turning to face him, "because you make me happy?"

"Because I am in love," he said. "Because I can not believe that, out of all of the people in Whynne, you would look at me that way. That I am lucky enough that you love me too."

I felt my bravado leave me. All of a sudden, I was facing

him. All of a sudden, his arms were braced on either side of me, his face there, so close to mine.

"You look starved," I whispered, not speaking of his physical appearance, but of his expression, of the way that he looked at me, ravenous.

"I am starved," he said, his voice low. "I am left constantly wanting."

"It is a cruel and awful thing for you to say that," I said, taking a single step towards him. "Because I am also constantly wanting... Even more so when you were gone."

"I should thank you then," he said carefully. "And even more so, apologize for the time that I was gone... If you would allow."

I thought my response was obvious. The smallest, briefest peck of his lips, daring him to do more, daring him to make good on what he had implied.

He was upon me. Not waiting any longer, not holding back in the slightest. His lips pressed against mine, hard, demanding, and definitely not unwelcome. Far from unwelcome.

My arms wrapped around his neck as he reached for my back and just underneath my knees, sweeping me upwards into his arms, whisking my feet out from under me. His desperate, frenzied kiss was so different from that of our reunion. But it morphed with every step as he carried me down the stairs, changing from need, overwhelming and aggressive need, to passion. Devotion. Dedication. The unending want, the same desire that flowed through me.

A tenderness was exchanged between us as our touches drew out into longer, softer caresses. Desire was different than passion, different than caring. It was a completely different beast, and though I had known it and indulged, what Luka and I exchanged was something I could not define, something invisible between us that pulled tightly when he sat me back down on the edge of his desk, pulling back and looking at me in an indescribable way.

"You," he said simply.

"You," I repeated, looking back at him, already reaching for him again, aiming to hold onto him. I wanted his contact, I desperately needed it. Anything to touch him once more, anything to be constantly reminded that he was there and he was real, that Luka Kinsley was standing across from me in the library again, looking astonished. "We made it," I said. "We're home. Greenable."

"Greenable," he agreed, still gazing at me with that ever-consuming look. "We're in Greenable."

"Together."

"Together," he repeated and, without a second thought, I threw my arms around him, pulling him in and holding him close, thinking about all the ways that things had changed.

Thinking of how I had sat at the desk across from his, cursing his name. Thinking of how I had hated him so much, was so desperate to avoid him yet also so desperate to please him, and how he sat back in his desk watching. How Luka, the Luka I knew, had caught me in the hallway, despite probably hoping to avoid me and find a way to both solve his problem and have a swift journey back to Audon. Thinking of how he managed to catch me and save me from falling time and time again, sometimes despite himself. Thinking of how he lied, and the consequences it inflicted upon him.

Thinking of the way that he had left for all that time and came back, still wanting me, but unwilling to force things.

"I have one last thing to show you," he said, pulling away from me, his lip twitching upwards.

"And what could that be?" I teased. "Because I think that I have everything I could want right in front of me," I said.

"Close your eyes one last time," Luka requested, stroking my cheek.

I could only laugh, rolling my eyes but doing as he asked. I leaned towards the edge of the desk as I felt him draw near, waiting for him, thinking that he would kiss me. Instead, his hand brushed past my waist, reaching for something from the inner pocket of Kristin's coat. I frowned.

"Hands out," he demanded, halfway chuckling at me. I huffed, doing as I was told.

And then I felt a weight in my hands. I did not even wait before opening my eyes, immediately curious.

Abel's Fairytales.

My eyes widened, looking down at it. It had been so long since I'd seen it, I'd assumed that it was lost in the cabin. There was no way that it could be the same copy. Surely the other one was just as battered and torn.

Luka leaned over me, taking in my surprise with a click of his tongue, his fingers flicking the cover of the book over, exposing the first page. "Kristin grabbed it at the last moment, shoving it into his pocket. He was always waiting for the right moment to show me."

"To Luka, you are not alone in this world," I read aloud in disbelief, almost incapable of processing that it was there in my hands after all this time. "Love, Wren."

"And I do love you," he admitted quietly into my ear. "More and more every day."

EPILOGUE

Six Months Later

"You're relentless," I hissed, smacking Luka's hand away before he could continue to steal more from me. He had taken only a sip, but that was enough. Actually, that was far too much, all things considered.

It was just before six in the morning.

Not a holy hour by far. Not an enjoyable time of day in the slightest.

Luka only rolled his eyes, reaching across the table and choosing to pour a cup for himself instead, noting once he had his cup raised to his lips, "perhaps you would not need so much if you had not awoken so early."

"Perhaps I would not have awoken so early if someone had not pulled me out of the bed before the sun had even risen," I noted with irritation, ignoring the fact that the reason he had woken me up was that he slipped on a pile of papers that may or may not have been mine by the side of the bed, placed there with the hopes of being productive in the morning.

Those hopes were now dashed by an early morning.

Waking up early almost always ensured that I would get nothing done.

"You're not a morning person," Luka noted, taking a long sip of his coffee. "I'll try to ignore your mood."

"I am a morning person," I argued, grabbing my cup and practically gulping the remaining half down before pointedly slamming it on the table. "This is not morning."

Luka sighed in amusement, looking at me from across the kitchen table, still not having explained why it was he was even awake at this hour. Or why he had been waking up early for the past five days. Every time I tried to ask, he circumvented the question, or squinted at me and asked if I was sure it really was that early. As if the dark blue sky of his barely qualifying 'morning' was not a dead giveaway, nor the maids chattering—I'd befriended them all, he couldn't escape me.

But he kept his secrets.

How he managed to evade the household staff was beyond me, the maids knew everything. A part of me felt as if he might have bribed them. Luka was up to something.

"I spoke to Lowell Laurent again yesterday," he said conversationally, a flicker of amusement in his eyes as I continued to fight the temptation of sleep, the coffee having done nothing to wake me. I would know his secret soon enough. "He said that Winry has really missed you. Perhaps you should visit her soon."

"I see her nearly every day."

"I know," Luka chuckled, shaking his head at me before finally taking pity on me and instead of continuing to steal from me, pushing his cup across the table to me. "If you're going to be awake," he said.

"Mhm," my eyes slid down to it, noting that the cup was nearly full. Peace offering accepted.

Behind me, Mariel, the oldest maid and therefore the defacto second in command after the Kinsley's rather absent butler, appeared with an assortment of letters in her hands as well as a single, tightly wrapped parcel.

"Ah!" Luka straightened, immediately perking up, his eyes landing on the package amongst her arms. He looked at it expectantly, indicating to her that she should place it in front of him.

"It's not for you," she chided, shaking her head at him before setting it down in front of me. "Kristin sent a package for Miss Laurent instead."

Luka's brow furrowed. He looked like he would have liked to argue otherwise, perhaps he would have if I were not there.

I perked up, looking down at the parcel in front of me with surprise, Kristin's last letter hadn't indicated that he planned to send me anything. But, there it was. A large, clumsily wrapped package, one that he'd wrapped with butcher's paper of all things, the bundle held together with a twist of string.

Luka watched me carefully as I unfurled it, his eyes never leaving the package and his body looking rather strangely like a lion poised to pounce. He was on it before I had even moved the first soft cardigan out of the way, seizing a small pouch from underneath it.

"What's that?" I asked, peering over the table at him. I strained to see what was in his hand, a small black drawstring back with the name Luka clearly placed on its tag. The parcel in front of me was completely forgotten.

"Nothing," Luka replied, hurriedly shoving it into his front pocket.

My eyes narrowed.

"Look at what Kristin has gotten you," Luka insisted, pushing the packet a little bit closer to me. "He said that he was sending you a gift, and that he'd packed some treats as well."

I frowned. "Kinsley."

"Laurent," he replied evenly.

"What is in your pocket?"

"Nothing is in my pocket," he said playfully, his eyes roaming away from mine. Since he didn't specify which pocket, the lie was forgiven.

"I saw you put something in your pocket."

"Did you?" He asked, speaking as if such a thing could not have possibly happened.

I stood, glaring at him the whole time as I approached him and stalked around the table to his chair. He merely looked on in amusement, both of his eyebrows raised and his lips pressed together, not daring to make a sound as I stood in front of him, glowering.

"Your pockets," I said, presenting my hand to him.

"One of them is completely empty."

He was testing me. I was not even halfway awake and Luka was testing me. Fine, if Kinsley wanted to play a game, then I would play a game. I held his gaze and plopped onto his lap, still facing him and being all too uncaring about how the maids would speak about our unabashed affections for the rest of the morning, Mariel having only just left through the door and another set of eyes no doubt taking her place. My hands braced on his thighs, my face demanding.

"Good morning," he said in amusement, his hand raising to the small of my back, his eyes glinting with a hint of a challenge.

Luka. Kinsley.

"Miss Laurent," he said as I pulled at his pants, trying to get to his pockets. "I should inform you that you are behaving rather improperly for a young lady."

I scoffed, as if I would care about that. My hands found the small velvety bag, pulling it out of his pocket and brandishing it victoriously, the pouch hanging from my finger by its string. I had barely the time to grin obnoxiously in his direction before it was snatched out from under my nose, Luka lifting the bag high up above his head with a decidedly annoying chuckle.

Of course he had to be absurdly tall.

Immediately, I attempted to get it, trying to climb up him but finding myself pinned against him. If the maids were not talking before, which they most certainly were, they were now.

"You have not an ounce of patience in your entire body," Luka informed me, bouncing the bag on his finger just out of my reach.

"What did Kristin send you?" I demanded, plastered against him.

"Something that I asked for."

"What did you ask for?"

"Something that Kristin sent me."

I growled in irritation. Finally, he relented, likely sensing that he was pushing it. He lowered his arm, dangling the small bag in front of my face, his face urging me to take it but also looking slightly hesitant, like he was nervous about something.

My hand rose slowly, grabbing the bag from his fingers and inspecting it, suddenly a little slow to open it despite the fuss I'd caused. Whatever it was, it was important.

"Maybe I should," Luka began, and I nodded. So long as he showed me and didn't hide whatever it was then it would be fine. "Close your eyes."

"Why?" I asked, confused.

"Because it's easier that way," he informed me, barely sparing a glance as he took the bag back, pulling at its center to open it and pouring something into his palm before rather pointedly placing his other hand in front of my eyes, sighing. "You're impossible," he murmured.

It hit me what it was the moment that it hit his palm, and I froze. My face was warm, far too warm, and I was glad that he had covered my eyes, because I wasn't sure what I would do if he saw my expression, or how he would take it.

"I need your hand," he said, and I obediently provided it, my fingers twitching nervously. It had to be that, didn't it? And there I was, still in my nightgown. "You already know, don't you?" He asked, I could hear the slight smirk in his voice. Insistently, I shoved my hand further in his direction, bracing it against his chest. "Impossible," he reiterated, his voice filled with gentle humor.

"Do it before I change my mind," I replied.

"Do you think you will change your mind?" He teased, pressing his lips against my neck. His hand reaching for mine, peeling it from his chest and holding it up, the cool metal of a band sliding over it seconds later before my hand once again pressed against his chest.

I immediately tugged his other hand down, blinking at the gem pressed against his chest, my eyes wide. In my mind, all was silent. There was nothing else, just that stupid little gem and my shock. I think he must have felt me go stiff, because his hands were at my sides, caressing them gently as I stared at my hand.

"I had to ask Kristin," he informed me, "because if I asked the Laurents, you would know within the day exactly what I was doing. Of course, I had a wonderful idea for how I was going to do this, one that was actually quite elaborate— you'll have to apologize to the maids—but I should have assumed that you would have demanded it right away or found it beforehand." He made a sound of exasperation, informing me, "I have woken up before six every day this week to try to beat you to the mail. I didn't think to tell Kristin what it was, and by the time I did, he had already packed it away with your things." He added, "he's quite sorry for that."

Being articulate, I said only one thing. "It's a ring."

"I had to get one first, I told you that."

He did. Yet still, the idea knocked me off guard. I looked at it against his chest, taking it in. It was simple, a band without any engravings or additional crystals, just a small pinkish stone set amongst gold. Yet the very sight of it felt overwhelming, I could hardly look at anything else, just that. I'd have to take it off when I worked, of course, but...

"Have you changed your mind?" He asked cautiously.

My eyes snapped up to his, my fingers tensing in his shirt.

"Have you?" He repeated, attempting to hide his distress, his eyes giving him away.

"You haven't even asked me," I said, pointing out the elephant in the room. "You told me," I chided, "that I would have to wait."

I could have laughed at how startled that made him, Luka pulling back as the realization seemed to dawn on him. He had not formally asked, he had simply tried to get a rise out of me. Then, once he seemed to realize that, he frowned—actually, he scowled at me, looking anything but amused with my playfulness. "It was implied," he said with a glare, not amused by my teasing.

"But not said," I responded, as I tried to stand up. I wanted to walk around the kitchen and look at it, holding it up in all different matters of light, taking a good long gaze. Instead, I was held a bit tighter by a very irritated Luka, who likely felt the same way I had just minutes prior. He was nowhere near letting me go.

Instead, he leaned closer to me, scrutinizing me. "Do you wish to marry me?" He asked.

"No," I lied, grinning at him.

He leaned in closer, shaking his head at that answer. "Be serious."

"Never in a million years, Mister Kinsley," I teased, grinning far too widely, he only snorted at me. "That is no proposal now, is it Kinsley?" He would have to try harder, if he was so desperate.

Puzzled, but not unamused, Luka tugged me even closer, pulling my hips against his and gently holding me by the small of my waist, peering up at me from underneath his lashes. "Will you marry me, Wren? If given the chance, if asked with no bargain involved or peril around us—Would you marry me? Would you stay with me?"

I looked down at his nervous expression, perhaps he was starting to believe that I wouldn't. He looked shy, embarrassed to be caught wanting so desperately for something. He'd likely been waiting for the ring to arrive from the day we stood on the battlefield, watching the new king rise.

He tried to smile all the same, even if it was rife with nerves.

"No," I teased and my lips pressed against his nose before I pulled away, smiling at him like a madwoman. For most people, that would have been too much.

But most people were not Luka Kinsley. Most people did not know me like Luka Kinsley.

He studied me, taking in every inch of my being as if he was weighing the validity of my statement. He took in my expression, the crazed grin on my face, and the ring still on my finger—then he pulled me down, his lips only inches from mine. I couldn't help but look at them, wanting nothing more than to kiss them. But he didn't let me, not yet, instead he only watched my expression and informed me, "your throat would hurt horribly if you were a fae."

COMING SOON, LEGENDS OF HALDIA!

Return to Whynne and discover neighboring countries in August 2021!

ABOUT THE AUTHOR

Bethany Anne Lovejoy is a longtime reader of romance novels and occasionally writes a few herself. She specializes in fantasy romance and has a great interest in magic users and men with crooked smiles.

When she is not writing romance novels, she is a devoted dog mother, amateur seamstress, and succulent collector. Find exclusive bonus content and news about future releases on her website, Bethanyannelovejoy.com

www.ingramcontent.com/pod-product-compliance
Lightning Source LLC
LaVergne TN
LVHW091256150826
845673LV00006B/1435

9798452162902